**Books by Rita Mae Brown
with "Sister" Jane Arnold in the Outfoxed series**

Outfoxed
Hotspur
Full Cry
The Hunt Ball
The Hounds and the Fury
The Tell-Tale Horse

Books by Rita Mae Brown with Sneaky Pie Brown

Wish You Were Here
Rest in Pieces
Murder at Montecello
Pay Dirt
Murder, She Meowed
Murder on the Prowl
Cat on the Scent
Sneaky Pie's Cookbook for Mystery Lovers
Pawing Through the Past
Claws and Effects
Catch as Cat Can
The Tail of the Tip-Off
Whisker of Evil
Cat's Eyewitness
Sour Puss
Puss n' Cahoots
The Purrfect Murder

Books by Rita Mae Brown

The Hand That Cradles the Rock
Songs to a Handsome Woman
The Plain Brown Rapper
Rubyfruit Jungle
In Her Day
Six of One
Southern Discomfort
Sudden Death
High Hearts
Started from Scratch: A Different Kind of Writer's Manual
Bingo
Venus Envy
Dolley: A Novel of Dolley Madison in Love and War
Riding Shotgun
Rita Will: Memoir of a Literary Rabble-Rouser
Loose Lips
Alma Mater
The Sand Castle

HOUNDED
TO DEATH

HOUNDED TO DEATH

A NOVEL

RITA MAE BROWN

ILLUSTRATIONS BY LEE GILDEA, JR.

BALLANTINE BOOKS

NEW YORK

Hounded to Death is a work of fiction. Names, characters, places, and incidents
are the products of the author's imagination or are used fictitiously.
Any resemblance to actual events, locales, or persons, living
or dead, is entirely coincidental.

Copyright © 2008 by American Artists, Inc.
Illustrations copyright © 2008 by Lee Gildea, Jr.

Published in the United States by Ballantine Books, an imprint of
The Random House Publishing Group, a division of Random House, Inc., New York.

BALLANTINE and colophon are registered trademarks of Random House, Inc.

LIBRARY OF CONGRESS CATALOGING-IN-PUBLICATION DATA
Brown, Rita Mae.
Hounded to death: a novel / Rita Mae Brown.
p. cm.
ISBN 978-0-345-49026-1
1. Arnold, Jane (Fictitious character)—Fiction.   2. Fox hunting—Fiction.
3. Dog shows—Fiction.   4. Virginia—Fiction.   I. Title.
PS3552.R698H626 2008b   813'.54—dc22   2008026625

Printed in the United States of America on acid-free paper

www.ballantinebooks.com

2 4 6 8 9 7 5 3 1

First Edition

Dedicated to
Mr. Tommy Lee Jones, Huntsman
Casanova Hunt, Casanova, Virginia

Mr. Chris Ryan, MFH, Huntsman
Scarteen Hounds
Limerick, Ireland

Gentlemen, you asked for it

CAST OF CHARACTERS

THE HUMANS

Jane Arnold, Sister, is master of foxhounds of the Jefferson Hunt Club in central Virginia. She loves her hounds, her horses, and her house pets. Occasionally, she finds humans lovable, too. Strong, healthy, vibrant at seventy-three, she's proof of the benefits of the outdoor life.

Shaker Crown is the huntsman. He's acquired the discipline of holding his tongue and his temper—most times. He's wonderful with hounds. In his early forties, he's finding his way back to love with Lorraine Rasmussen.

Gray Lorillard, a now-retired high-powered accountant is in his late sixties, and is in love with Sister Jane.

Crawford Howard, a self-made man, moved to Virginia from Indiana. He's egotistical, ambitious, and thinks he knows more than he does about foxhunting. But he's also generous, intelligent, and fond of young people. His great disappointment is not being a father but he never speaks of this, especially to his wife, **Marty.**

Charlotte Norton is the young headmistress of Custis Hall, a prestigious prep school for young ladies.

Anne Harris, Tootie, is one of the brightest students Charlotte Norton has ever known. Taciturn, observant, yet capable of delivering a stinging barb, this senior shines with promise. She's beautiful, petite, African-American, and a strong rider. The fall will be her first year at Princeton. She'd rather stay at the kennels and work with hounds.

Valentina Smith is the class president. Blonde, tall, lean, and drop-dead gorgeous, the kid is a natural politician. She and Tootie clash at times, but they are friends. She loves foxhunting. Unlike Tootie, she can't wait to get to Princeton. Her ambitions need a wider scope.

Felicity Porter seems overshadowed by Tootie and Val ·but she is highly intelligent and has a sturdy self-regard. She's the kind of person who is quietly competent. She, too, is a good rider. She's in the last trimester of her pregnancy, will marry Howie Lindquist soon, and almost wishes she were going to Princeton also. Once the baby is born, she'll go to night school. Every bit as brilliant as Tootie and Val, her life is taking a dramatically different course.

Pamela Rene seems burdened by being African-American whereas for Tootie it's a given. Pamela can't stand Val and feels tremendously competitive with Tootie, whom she accuses of being an Oreo cookie. Her family substituted money for love, which makes Pamela poor. Underneath it all, she's basically a good person, but that can be hard to appreciate.

Betty Franklin is the long-serving honorary whipper-in at JHC. Her judgment, way with hounds, knowledge of territory, and ability to ride make her a standout. Many is the huntsman who would kill to have Betty Franklin whip in to him or her. She's in her mid-forties, a mother, happily married to Bobby, and a dear, dear friend to Sister.

Walter Lungrun, M.D., joint master of foxhounds, has held this position for over a year. He's learning all he can. He adores Sister, and the feeling is mutual. Their only complaint is there's so much work to do they rarely have time for a good talk. Walter is in his late thirties. He is the result of an affair that Raymond Arnold, Sr., Jane's husband, had with Walter's mother. Mr. Lungrun never knew—or pretended he didn't—and Sister didn't know until a year ago.

Hope Rogers is a highly respected equine veterinarian who takes care of Sister's horses.

Edward Bancroft, in his seventies, head of the Bancroft family, used to run a large corporation founded by his family in the mid-nineteenth century. His wife, **Tedi,** is one of Sister's oldest friends. Tedi rides splendid Thoroughbreds and is always impeccably turned out, as is her surviving daughter, **Sybil Fawkes,** who is in her second year as an honorary whipper-in. The Bancrofts are true givers in terms of money, time, and genuine caring.

Ben Sidell has been sheriff of the county for three years. Since he was hired from Ohio, he sometimes needs help in the labyrinthine ways of the South. He relies on Sister's knowledge and discretion.

Kasmir Barbhaiya is in his mid-forties, widowed, and a college classmate of High Vajay. He falls in love with Virginia while visiting High and Mandy. Eventually he will fall in love again guided by his deceased wife's spirit, but not in this book. He has made over a billion dollars in pharmaceuticals but would give it all up if he could bring his wife back. He keeps this to himself and is fantastically generous.

Judge Barry Baker is retired from the Virginia Supreme Court. He keeps his house in Richmond but rents a dependency at Skidby, a big estate. This delights Sister, as Barry and his late wife were friends of her and her late husband, Ray. He's charming and highly principled in his fashion.

Mo Schneider rubs everyone the wrong way. A string of ex-wives loathe him. Although a master, other foxhunters recoil from him. He's loaded and buys whatever he wants, but he can't buy a good reputation.

Francis Albert (Fonz) Riley bears his nickname with aplomb. Like the TV character, he was once rebellious, far more rebellious. Drink nearly killed him. Thanks to Barry Baker, he pulled himself together. He works for Mo and endures the man.

Grant Fuller expanded the family feed store into a large regional pet food business. He's warm, observant, and gregarious. Unlike Mo, most everyone likes Grant.

Jane Winegardner, MFH of Woodford Hunt in Lexington, Kentucky, is a real person. There doesn't seem to be anything she can't do unless it's to be ugly to horse, hound, or human. She's tight in the tack, too. Because Sister's name is Jane, I had to invent a nickname for this other Jane, so O.J. it is. If people start calling her that I hope she doesn't shoot me. Like Sister, Jane is a credit to our sport.

Dr. and Mrs. Mitchell Fisher bought Skidby, a huge estate in

Sister's western territory. Mitch and Lutrell are popular members of the club, although he can veer toward arrogance.

THE AMERICAN FOXHOUNDS

Sister and Shaker have carefully bred a balanced pack. The American foxhound blends English, French, and Irish blood, the first identifiable pack being brought here in 1650 by Robert de la Brooke of Maryland. Individual hounds had been shipped over earlier, but Brooke brought an entire pack. In 1785, General Lafayette sent his mentor and hero, George Washington, a pack of French hounds whose voices were said to sound like the bells of Moscow.

Whatever the strain, the American foxhound is highly intelligent and beautifully built, with strong sloping shoulders, powerful hips and thighs, and a nice tight foot. The whole aspect of the hound in motion is one of grace and power in the effortless covering of ground. The American hound is racier than the English hound and stands perhaps two feet at the shoulder, although size is not nearly as important as nose, drive, cry, and biddability. It is sensitive and extremely loving and has eyes that range from softest brown to gold to sky-blue. While one doesn't often see the sky-blue eye, there is a line that contains it. The hound lives to please its master and to chase foxes.

Cora is the strike hound, which means she often finds the scent first. She's the dominant female in the pack and is in her sixth season.

Asa is in his seventh season and is invaluable in teaching the younger hounds.

Diana is the anchor hound, and she's in her fourth season. All the other hounds trust her, and if they need direction she'll give it.

Dragon is her littermate. He possesses tremendous drive and a fabulous nose, but he's arrogant. He wants to be the strike hound. Cora hates him.

Dasher is also Diana and Dragon's littermate. He lacks his brother's brilliance, but he's steady and smart. A hound's name usually begins with the first letter of his mother's name, so the *D* hounds are out of Delia.

Giorgio is a young entry and just about the perfect example of what a male American foxhound should be. He is stolen from the Mid-America Hound Show and Sister is frantic, although she hides her emotions.

THE HORSES

Sister's horses are **Keepsake,** a Thoroughbred/quarter-horse cross (written TB/QH by horsemen), an intelligent gelding of eight years; **Lafayette,** a gray TB, eleven now, fabulously athletic and talented, who wants to go; **Rickyroo,** a seven-year-old TB gelding who shows great promise; **Aztec,** a six-year-old gelding TB, also very athletic, with great stamina and a good mind; and **Matador,** a gray TB, six years old, sixteen hands, a former steeplechaser.

Shaker's horses come from the steeplechase circuit, so all are TBs. **Showboat, HoJo, Gunpowder,** and **Kilowatt** can all jump the moon, as you might expect.

Betty's two horses are **Outlaw,** a tough QH who has seen it all and can do it all, and **Magellan,** a TB given to her by Sorrel

Buruss, a bigger and rangier horse than Betty was accustomed to riding, but she's now used to him.

Kilowatt is a superb jumper, bought for the huntsman by Kasmir Barbhaiya.

Nonni, tried and true, takes care of the sheriff.

THE FOXES

The reds can reach a height of sixteen inches and a length of forty-one inches, and they can weigh up to fifteen pounds. Obviously, since these are wild animals who do not willingly come forth to be measured and weighed, there's more variation than the standard just cited. **Target;** his spouse, **Charlene;** and his **Aunt Netty** and **Uncle Yancy** are the reds. They can be haughty. A red fox has a white tip on its luxurious brush, except for Aunt Netty, who has a wisp of a white tip for her brush is tatty.

The grays may reach fifteen inches in height and forty-four inches in length and may weigh up to fourteen pounds. The common wisdom is that grays are smaller than reds, but there are some big ones out there. Sometimes people call them slab-sided grays, because they can be reddish. They do not have a white tip on their tail but they may have a black one, as well as a black-tipped mane. Some grays are so dark as to be black.

The grays are **Comet, Inky,** and **Georgia.** Their dens are a bit more modest than those of the red foxes who like to announce their abodes with a prominent pile of dirt and bones outside. Perhaps not all grays are modest nor all reds full of themselves, but as a rule of thumb it's so.

THE BIRDS

Athena is a great horned owl. This type of owl can stand two feet and a half in height with a wingspread of four feet and can weigh up to five pounds.

Bitsy is a screech owl. She is eight and a half inches high with a twenty-inch wingspread. She weighs a whopping six ounces and she's reddish brown. Her considerable lungs make up for her small stature.

St. Just, a crow, is a foot and a half in height, his wingspread is a surprising three feet, and he weighs one pound.

THE HOUSE PETS

Raleigh is a Doberman who likes to be with Sister.

Rooster is a harrier, willed to Sister by an old lover, Peter Wheeler.

Golliwog, or Golly, is a large calico cat and would hate being included with the dogs as a pet. She is the Queen of All She Surveys.

SOME USEFUL TERMS

Away. A fox has *gone away* when he has left the covert. Hounds are *away* when they have left the covert on the line of the fox.

Brush. The fox's tail.

Burning scent. Scent so strong or hot that hounds pursue the line without hesitation.

Bye day. A day not regularly on the fixture card.

Cap. The fee nonmembers pay to hunt for that day's sport.

Carry a good head. When hounds run well together to a good scent, a scent spread wide enough for the whole pack to feel it.

Carry a line. When hounds follow the scent. This is also called *working a line.*

Cast. Hounds spread out in search of scent. They may cast themselves or be cast by the huntsman.

Charlie. A term for a fox. A fox may also be called *Reynard*.

Check. When hounds lose the scent and stop. The field must wait quietly while the hounds search for the scent.

Colors. A distinguishing color, usually worn on the collar but sometimes on the facings of a coat, that identifies a hunt. Colors can be awarded only by the master and can be worn only in the field.

Coop. A jump resembling a chicken coop.

Couple straps. Two-strap hound collars connected by a swivel link. Some members of staff will carry these on the right rear of the saddle. Since the days of the pharaohs in ancient Egypt, hounds have been brought to the meets coupled. Hounds are always spoken of and counted in couples. Today, hounds walk or are driven to the meets. Rarely, if ever, are they coupled, but a whipper-in still carries couple straps should a hound need assistance.

Covert. A patch of woods or bushes where a fox might hide. Pronounced *cover*.

Cry. How one hound tells another what is happening. The sound will differ according to the various stages of the chase. It's also called *giving tongue* and should occur when a hound is working a line.

Cub hunting. The informal hunting of young foxes in the late summer and early fall, before formal hunting. The main purpose is to enter young hounds into the pack. Until recently only the most knowledgeable members were invited to cub hunt, since they would not interfere with young hounds.

Dog fox. The male fox.

Dog hound. The male hound.

Double. A series of short sharp notes blown on the horn to alert all that a fox is afoot. The *gone away* series of notes is a form of doubling the horn.

Draft. To acquire hounds from another hunt is to accept a draft.

Draw. The plan by which a fox is hunted or searched for in a certain area, such as a covert.

Draw over the fox. Hounds go through a covert where the fox is but cannot pick up his scent. The only creature who understands how this is possible is the fox.

Drive. The desire to push the fox, to get up with the line. It's a very desirable trait in hounds, so long as they remain obedient.

Dually. A one-ton pickup truck with double wheels in back.

Dwell. To hunt without getting forward. A hound who dwells is a bit of a putterer.

Enter. Hounds are entered into the pack when they first hunt, usually during cubbing season.

Field. The group of people riding to hounds, exclusive of the master and hunt staff.

Field master. The person appointed by the master to control the field. Often it is the master him- or herself.

Fixture. A card sent to all dues-paying members, stating when and where the hounds will meet. A fixture card properly received is an invitation to hunt. This means the card would be mailed or handed to a member by the master.

Flea-bitten. A gray horse with spots or ticking which can be black or chestnut.

Gone away. The call on the horn when the fox leaves the covert.

Gone to ground. A fox who has ducked into his den or some other refuge has *gone to ground.*

Good night. The traditional farewell to the master after the hunt, regardless of the time of day.

Gyp. The female hound.

Hilltopper. A rider who follows the hunt but does not jump. Hilltoppers are also called the *second field*. The jumpers are called the *first flight*.

Hoick. The huntsman's cheer to the hounds. It is derived from the Latin *hic haec hoc,* which means *here.*

Hold hard. To stop immediately.

Huntsman. The person in charge of the hounds, in the field and in the kennel.

Kennelman. A hunt staff member who feeds the hounds and cleans the kennels. In wealthy hunts there may be a number of kennelmen. In hunts with a modest budget, the huntsman or even the master cleans the kennels and feeds the hounds.

Lark. To jump fences unnecessarily when hounds aren't running. Masters frown on this, since it is often an invitation to an accident.

Lieu in. Norman term for *go in.*

Lift. To take the hounds from a lost scent in the hopes of finding a better scent farther on.

Line. The scent trail of the fox.

Livery. The uniform worn by the professional members of the hunt staff. Usually it is scarlet, but blue, yellow, brown, and gray are also used. The recent dominance of scarlet has to do with people buying coats off the rack as opposed to having tailors cut them. (When anything is mass-produced, the choices usually dwindle, and such is the case with livery.)

Mask. The fox's head.

Meet. The site where the day's hunting begins.

MFH. The master of foxhounds; the individual in charge of the hunt: hiring, firing, landowner relations, opening territory (in large hunts this is the job of the hunt secretary), developing the pack of hounds, and determining the first cast of each meet. As in any leadership position, the master is also the lightning rod for criticism. The master may hunt the hounds, although this is usually done by a professional huntsman, who is also responsible for the hounds in the field and at the kennels. A long relationship between a master and a huntsman allows the hunt to develop and grow.

Nose. The scenting ability of a hound.

Override. To press hounds too closely.

Overrun. When hounds shoot past the line of a scent. Often the scent has been diverted or foiled by a clever fox.

Ratcatcher. Informal dress worn during cubbing season and bye days.

Stern. A hound's tail.

Stiff-necked fox. One who runs in a straight line.

Strike hounds. Those hounds who through keenness, nose, and often higher intelligence find the scent first and press it.

Tail hounds. Those hounds running at the rear of the pack. This is not necessarily because they aren't keen; they may be older hounds.

Tally-ho. The cheer when the fox is viewed. Derived from the Norman *ty a hillaut,* thus coming into the English language in 1066.

Tongue. To vocally pursue a fox.

View halloo (halloa). The cry given by a staff member who sees a fox. Staff may also say *tally-ho* or, should the fox turn back, *tally-back*. One reason a different cry may be used by staff, especially in territory where the huntsman can't see the staff, is that the field in their enthusiasm may cheer something other than a fox.

Vixen. The female fox.

Walk. Puppies are *walked out* in the summer and fall of their first year. It's part of their education and a delight for both puppies and staff.

Whippers-in. Also called whips, these are the staff members who assist the huntsman, who make sure the hounds "do right."

HOUNDED
TO DEATH

CHAPTER 1

Rose twilight lingered over Shaker Village in central Kentucky, which, this Saturday, May 24, was hosting the Mid-America Hound Show.

Jane Arnold, master of Jefferson Hunt Hounds in Virginia, drove alongside dry-laid stone walls, quietly relishing the village's three thousand well-tended acres of land. It was as if the spirits of the Shakers hovered everywhere. Sister Jane, as she was known, respected the sect's unswerving devotion to equality, peace, and love, qualities that suffused those past lives like the rose-lavender tinted twilight suffused the rolling pastures with ethereal beauty.

Pared-down functionalism, the essence of Shaker design, pure as fresh rainwater, prefigured later architectural and furniture development. Sister admired the care and intelligence the

Shakers used to build their houses while fortifying their spirits with song and hard work.

Much as she admired their clean straight lines, she herself felt more at home in a mix of eighteenth-century exuberance allied with modern comfort.

She laughed to herself that her nickname, Sister Jane, meant she'd fit right in if only she could slip back in time to work alongside the Shakers. However, she'd soon have run afoul of the sisters and brothers as they did not practice sex, which had eventually resulted in the extinction of the sect. No one had ever accused Sister of being celibate.

Shaker ideas and ideals lived after them. Perhaps most people hope to leave something behind, usually in the form of progeny. But some are able to also impart inventions, artistic achievements, or new ways of seeing the same old problems.

What Sister hoped to leave behind was a love of the environment, belief in the protection of American farmland, and respect for all living creatures. Foxhunting was one of the best ways to do that because a person could inhale the best values while having more fun than the legal limit.

It pained her that so many people thought that foxes were killed in the hunt. Countless times she'd patiently explained that hunting practices in the United States were different from those in England. Given that the Mid-America Hound Show would be made up of foxhunters showing their best hounds, she breathed in relief. She wouldn't need to have that conversation here.

Her new Subaru Forester followed the gray stone walls, rolling through a deep dip in the road, passing over a creek, and climbing a steep incline. She'd bought the SUV in hopes of saving a bit of money, seeing as her everyday vehicle was a big red gas-guzzling GMC half-ton truck. Like many Americans, she wanted to conserve fuel, but living out in the country made this a pipe dream.

Sister found pleasure in driving the handy little vehicle, which burned less gas, but she still had to use farm trucks for work. She couldn't envision how that would change without driving the cost of food up to the point where there'd be bread riots like those that helped jump-start the French and Russian revolutions.

At the top of the steep hill, a flat green pasture beckoned, now silvery in May evening haze. In the middle of this lushness, surrounded by large trees, rested a two-story Shaker house, perfect in its simplicity, and just beyond the house were horse trailers converted for hound use. Sister drove to the Jefferson Hunt trailer, proudly displaying the JHC logo, a fox mask with two brushes crossed underneath.

Before she could step out of the car, Shaker Crown, her huntsman, a rugged curly-haired man in his early forties, dashed over to open the door. His Christian name had nothing to do with the Shaker sect. It had been his great-uncle's name, bequeathed to him at birth.

"Boss, glad to see you."

She teased him. "You're glad to see me because I brought sandwiches and drinks."

Before the sentence was out of her mouth, he'd lifted the back hatch of the Forester to retrieve a large cooler.

Tootie, a senior at Custis Hall, a private girls' secondary school, slipped out of the trailer's side door. "Food?"

"You poor starved thing." Sister walked with Shaker as he plopped the cooler under the awning he'd set up off the side of the trailer.

Inside, a high covered fan ran to keep the six couple of hounds comfortable, a generator on the other side of the trailer providing the power. Kentucky could fool you in May, temperate one day and sweltering the next. Shaker and Sister put hound happiness before their own.

Tootie, full name Anne Harris, sat down in a director's chair and Sister handed each of them a sandwich.

"Are you tired? How can you be tired at seventeen?"

The young woman grinned. She was exceedingly beautiful. "Just hit a low plateau. After this"—she held up the sandwich—"I'll be right back up."

"Sure. You just can't keep up with an old lady in her seventies."

"You're not seventy, whatever." Shaker eagerly unwrapped his turkey sandwich. "Your mother lied on your birth certificate."

"That's a joyful thought." Sister could smell the tangy mustard on her roast beef and cheese sandwich. "Isn't this the loveliest setting for a hound show? Sure, nothing's as spectacular as the twin peaks of the Virginia Hound Show, or the Bryn Mawr Hound Show, but Shaker Village—well, to my mind it's the best location."

"That it is." Shaker had already devoured half his sandwich.

"Glad I brought two of everything," said Sister.

"I don't know why I'm so hungry."

"Sometimes I think it's cycles. Ever notice how your appetite and your sleep patterns change whenever the seasons change? At least mine does."

Tootie listened, as usual soaking everything up while remaining quiet.

"Yep, and I can't sleep during a full moon."

"Get up and howl, do you?" Sister smiled at her huntsman, whom she loved.

"I thought that was you." Tootie slipped that in.

"Well, so much for respect from the young." Sister laughed, which made Dragon, a hound, howl.

They all laughed.

"Does Woodford"—Tootie named the hosting hunt—"always have this show at Shaker Village?"

"No. Actually, they used to have it over at the Kentucky Horse Park, smack in the middle of Lexington, when Iroquois Hunt ran it for three years." Shaker named the other hunt outside of Lexington, Kentucky. "The Horse Park is a hotbed of activity. What a draw it's become for tourists. Anyway, I sure hope Woodford keeps it here even though its half an hour from Lexington."

Sister greatly admired Jane Winegardner, MFH of Woodford Hounds, whom she knew better than the two other joint masters, hard-hunting men. She always referred to Miss Winegardner as "O.J." for "the Other Jane."

A familiar voice sounded from behind the trailer. Hope Rogers, DVM, popped round and greeted them under the awning. "Party?"

"Sit down, honey." Sister pointed to a director's chair. "When did you get here?"

Hope, an equine vet specializing in lameness, most particularly navicular disease, kept a practice five miles from the Jefferson Hunt kennels. In her late thirties, she'd become a hot commodity in the equine world, being flown to Japan, Korea, the United Kingdom, Australia, New Zealand, Poland, and Austria to present her findings on degenerative diseases causing lameness. Her travels now comprised a great chunk of her practice, requiring her to take on a partner, Dan Clement, which was working out quite nicely.

"Last night. Had a lecture at the University of Kentucky. That facility knocks me out every time I go there."

"Better than Virginia Tech or the Marion DuPont Center?" Shaker named two outstanding Virginia equine facilities.

"As a Virginian, I can't answer that."

"Ah." Sister pointed to the cooler as Hope shook her head.

"Saving myself for the party at the kennels." She checked her watch. "There's a little time left but I want to wash up first. Wish I could stay for the show tomorrow, but I've got to get back. At least I'll see old friends at the party."

"O.J.'s been whirling around like the white tornado." Shaker laughed. "You know O.J., she checks and rechecks everything, a born organizer. She's over at Woodford kennels now."

"I'll catch up with her there." Hope reached into the cooler for a Mountain Dew. The caffeine hit would carry her through until she reached the party.

"Get to the back pastures of any farms?" Sister knew Hope had a wealth of contacts in the Thoroughbred world.

"No. I did get over to Bardstown to the Evan Williams distillery. You know I have a lot of Japanese clients." She paused a moment, then continued. "And I'm sure you know that Japanese buy brands. In bourbon, that means Maker's Mark, with the red wax covering the cork. 'Course it's not real wax anymore, but the Japanese can recognize Maker's Mark. I'm trying to educate some of my clients in the finer points of American whiskey, which is to say bourbon. So I bought two bottles of Evan Williams 1987 Single Barrel, number fifty-one. Not cheap. And then to sweeten the punch I drove down to Maker's Mark distillery and bought two bottles of Limited Edition Kentucky Straight Bourbon, the highest Maker's Mark, if that term applies."

"I don't think I've ever seen you drink bourbon." Sister carefully folded the aluminum foil wrapper of her now nonexistent sandwich.

"I'm learning." Hope smiled.

"Did you buy any for yourself?" Shaker asked.

"Actually, I did. One bottle of each for me, and I also bought a bottle of Wild Turkey Single Barrel, number ten, Rick number nine, Warehouse D. How's that for memory?"

"Drink enough bourbon and you won't have any memory left." Sister laughed.

"Don't fret. I won't. I've become so fascinated that each trip to Kentucky I visit a distillery. You know, I rather like the taste of these expensive bourbons. They're actually quite complex."

"And you're drinking a real drink," Sister stated, then paused to change the subject. "Romance?"

"I wish." Hope slumped in the chair for a moment. "My divorce will be final at the end of June. I have to live because I don't want Paul to get any more than he deserves. He's coming out ahead on this, the bastard." She stopped herself. "You know what Paul's real sin is? He's boring."

A small silence followed this, broken by Sister. "People say there is no such thing as a good divorce, but I don't know. If you can part without vats of hostility, maybe something can be salvaged." The talk of bourbon had brought up the word *vat*.

"We've been erratic about that." Hope sighed. "Let me go pull myself together. I'll root for JHC tomorrow while I drive east on Sixty-four." She stood up, then leaned over slightly. "Speaking of bourbon, I'll bet anyone here five dollars you won't see Gentleman Jack at the bar."

"Not taking that bet." Shaker laughed.

As Hope walked away, Tootie asked, "Why?"

"Gentleman Jack is a *Tennessee* bourbon, high end. Well, technically it's Tennessee Sour Mash but it's bourbon to the rest of us." Shaker, who had once had a problem with alcohol, was something of an expert. "Also, Jack Daniels Black, Label Number Seven, and George Dickel are Tennessee bourbons. Won't see them either."

"Shit," Sister whispered, then quickly said, "Sorry."

Shaker followed the direction of her eyes.

Striding toward them was a tall, whip-thin, hawk-nosed man.

"Master Arnold, looking divine as ever. America's own Artemis." Mo Schneider beamed, no doubt feeling he'd burnished his intellectual credentials by using the goddess of the hunt's Greek name.

Didn't work.

Sister responded coolly. "Evening, Mo. I thought you'd be at the party."

"On my way, on my way, and I do hope you'll be there to sully your reputation with me." His grin seemed like a sharp beak opening wide.

"Woodford puts on a good party," Sister replied.

Mo's eyes widened—as did those of most men of the hetero-sexual persuasion—when he spotted Tootie, with her café-au-lait skin and gold-flecked light-brown eyes.

Tootie extended her hand. A lady always extends her hand first, and at seventeen she certainly was a power-packed lady. "Pleased to meet you, Master."

"You come on down to Arkansas on one of your school vaca-tions and hunt with me."

"Thank you." Tootie smiled, which added to her consider-able allure.

Mo peered in at the hounds. "As always, you've got some lookers. Might I go in?"

Sister smiled at his double entendre, which was intentional. "Specialize in it." She rose, as did Shaker, to open the trailer door.

Sister stepped in, followed by Mo. "Four couple of young entry, two couple of hounds already hunting."

Mo surveyed the group: beautiful coats, shining eyes on everyone.

"Who's this? He's outstanding."

"Giorgio. American hound, obviously. Bywaters blood." Sis-ter cited a famous bloodline that had gone out of fashion in the 1970s but was making a comeback.

"You never waver from the Bywaters line."

"Works for me," Sister said pleasantly. "Plus it's a line devel-oped in northern Virginia for Virginia conditions."

He swept his eyes over the hounds. "Thanks for letting me see them."

They returned to the director's chairs.

"How many hounds did *you* bring?" Shaker inquired, as he

made a mental note to count Mo's hounds when he had the chance.

"Six couple. All entered." This meant they'd been hunted. *Unentered* designated a young hound who had not yet been out.

"Enough to keep you busy," Sister said.

"Shaker, didn't mean to ignore you," said Mo. "How have you been? Heard you decked a member." He turned to Sister. "Heard you decked him, too."

"We performed this service at different times." Sister smiled slyly. "He needed a lesson in Virginia manners."

"Bad. Needed the lesson bad." Shaker smiled also, at the memory of Crawford Howard, Midas rich, hitting the floor.

Mo laughed with false heartiness. "Sister, there are other ways to drop a man."

"Yes, Mo, I know them all," she replied lightly. "I went around the block before the block had sidewalks."

"Not you. You're a beautiful icon to us all." He cast his eyes again at Tootie, who wanted to squirm but didn't. "Well, on my way to the party. There's a horn-blowing contest. Going to try."

"Surely you'll toot your horn fine." Sister's voice was bland.

Shaker had to look away, because if he caught her eye he'd laugh.

Mo walked off, the slight missing him since he thought it was a compliment.

Once out of earshot, Shaker growled, "I hate that lying piece of shit."

"Tell me how you really feel." Sister reached over to touch his muscled forearm covered with light auburn hair.

"I'd kill him if I could." Shaker meant it.

"Why?" Tootie asked.

"He's cruel to hounds, horses, and women." Sister nodded, then turned to Tootie. "I guess because some men figure all three are obedient. They'll put up with it."

Sister stood up, then entered the hound trailer as Shaker patted his stomach. He'd already put up his generously sized tent next to the awning.

The hounds looked up as their master returned.

The trailer was spotless. Two levels connected by a ramp, with everything, even the trailer sides, covered in heavy rubber gave choices as to where to sleep. Although it was warm, Shaker had bedded the hounds down with straw that could easily be brushed off come morning. The night would cool down quickly, and if one of those famous Kentucky thunderstorms came up, the temperature could drop like a stone.

"Hello, Mother!" A happy chorus rang out.

Sister laid her hand on each glossy head, all six couple of them; hounds are always counted in twos, coupled. On reaching Diddy, she quietly reassured the youngster. "You're going to be a star tomorrow. You just reach out and show those judges your fluid movement."

Diddy blinked.

Sister, an animal person, knew that a soft voice, pitched low, calms an animal. Placing your hand on the head of a cat or dog also calms them. With horses, a hand on the head works, but if you press your fingers alongside and high on the horse's neck, moving from the poll down to the withers, that soothes them, too.

She left her hounds, quietly shutting the slatted door behind her.

No sooner had she left the trailer than a robust salt-and-pepper-haired man, arms swinging in easy rhythm, bore down on her.

He came right up, caught her in his arms, and gave her a big kiss. "You beauty!"

Sister hugged him back. "Where have you been?"

"Zurich."

Shaker stood to shake an outstretched hand once the newcomer had released Sister. "Been a long time."

"Too long, too long." Judge Barry Baker, retired from Virginia's Supreme Court, slapped Shaker on the back.

"This young lady will be attending your alma mater." Sister introduced Judge Baker to Tootie Harris.

Barry took Tootie's hand in both his own. "How I envy you. Some of the happiest days of my life were spent at Princeton."

Sister filled Tootie in. "Judge Baker was captain of the football team and the baseball team."

"But I liked foxhunting best, and when I could I'd slip away and hunt with Essex. In those days there was still country in New Jersey. Well, young lady, I wish you the best of luck. You have a grand teacher in Sister."

"Yes, sir."

"Her best friend at Custis Hall also got in. Unusual," Sister said.

"Princeton likes smart women, and Custis Hall specializes in them." He smiled again, his bleached-white teeth giving him a more youthful appearance than his seventy-four years.

"You just missed Mo Schneider," Sister remarked.

"Maybe someone will mix up a cyanide cocktail for him at the party. Do us all a world of good." His gray eyes glinted at Tootie. "If he so much as looks at you cross-eyed, you come straight to me, hear?"

"Yes, Judge."

"Are you showing hounds or spectating?" Shaker inquired.

"O.J. asked me to be ring steward. American ring." He threw up his hands in mock surrender. "Who doesn't want to be in demand?"

"You can show a hound. Drat." Sister snapped her fingers. "I was hoping we could go head-to-head."

He kissed her on the cheek. "We can, dear heart, we can. Head-to-head!"

After he left to go to the party, Tootie noted, "He's very distinguished-looking."

"That he is. He could have been governor, but he said he didn't have the stomach for electoral politics. He made the right choice."

"He really likes you. Not fake. Not like Mo."

Tootie, sensitive and observant, was right.

"Men always like Sister. Women, too. She gets along with both sexes." Shaker checked one of his tent poles.

"Are you sure you want to sleep out here?" Sister said.

"Boss, I do."

"You know you have a room next to mine."

"I'll use it to shower. I want to stay here with the hounds." He sucked in a breath. "Especially now I know Mo is here."

"Why?" Tootie was puzzled.

"He's been known to take a hound and then lie through his teeth, but we always know because two years later he'll arrive at a show with get that look just like the dog that went missing. He can hide the stolen hound so no one sees it in his kennels, but blood tells." Shaker crossed his arms over his chest. "Bloodlines are gold, you know. It's just like stealing gold."

"But you-all allow people to breed to our hounds and you go breed from other kennels." Tootie wasn't contradicting Shaker, just being curious.

"Tootie, we go to Middleburg or Deep Run, Casanova, Orange, Keswick, Farmington, or Colonial, and we do it properly, with permission. We know the people, and those hunts are within three hours' driving distance. Sometimes we'll drive to Maryland to Green Spring Valley for hounds. Not only do they have lines we want, the huntsmen take excellent care of their kennels. Mo doesn't take care of anything. He starves his hounds and then fattens up the pretty ones for the shows. He hunts his own hounds and can't hunt a hair of them. He's really a despicable human being." Sister felt that first chill of night air and shivered. "Although I did hear he hired a kennelman two years ago, so at least the starving and beating stopped. He once ran a horse to death, too."

"Why doesn't the Master of Foxhounds Association throw him out?" Tootie asked the right question.

"Because he's sneaky. They have to catch him at it. Somehow he gets word of surprise visits to his kennels or stables in time to spirit away the raggedy-looking hounds and horses. He's got so much money, who knows who he's paying to spy on the MFHA? If he is. Sooner or later, I swear, he'll get his," Sister answered.

"Ninety-nine percent of the people in this sport love animals, but there are a few who don't." Shaker shrugged. "Vicious
creeps."

"I say we send them to Congress where they'll be with their
brethren." Sister laughed.

Shaker laughed, too. "If I didn't know you better, I'd think
you don't believe in democracy."

"Don't." Sister inhaled. "All right, what's left to be done?"

"Nothing," Shaker replied.

"Let's party, then."

"Okay," Shaker said, "but I'm leaving early. I want to be
fresh tomorrow. And I want to feed hounds, walk them out at six-
thirty A.M., too. I'll unhitch the dually. I know once you get there
you won't be able to get away. Going to be a big day." Shaker felt
the buzz of competitiveness begin.

"You bet." Sister grinned.

Many competitors had already left for the party. Few people
were around or, if they were, they kept out of sight.

The three entered the house to freshen up before going to
the party.

Stepping back outside, Sister saw her hounds in full cry. She
dashed back into the house as Shaker and Tootie emerged from
the two bathrooms.

"Our hounds are out and scorching the wind."

"Holy shit!" Shaker tore out the door, Sister and Tootie behind him.

They reached the Subaru. Sister hopped in the driver's seat.
The back door of the trailer swung open like a slack jaw.

"Horn?" Sister asked, before cranking the motor.

"Goddammit." Shaker, upset, got back out, ran to the truck, and pulled his horn from the glove compartment.

Windows down, they listened to the hounds now turning toward the barn, perhaps half a mile from the house.

"Hope they don't go to Sixty-eight." Tootie mentioned the paved road leading to Shaker Village.

Sister gunned toward the barn as Shaker, hanging out the window, kept blowing the three long notes which asked hounds to return to him. With every rut in the road, he'd bob up, then drop down.

Hounds were already beyond the barn. Running flat out, they climbed the steep hill on the northern side of the barn.

The gate to that large pasture was shut.

Sister stopped. Shaker and Tootie got out.

"Locked. Goddammit to hell!" His face red, he threw his hands up in fury.

"We can lift it off the hinges." Tootie noticed the heavy chain.

Shaker lifted the gate up while Tootie steadied it. Because of the manner in which the chain held the gate to the fence post, there was enough room for Sister to squeeze the car through. Once on the other side of the gate, Shaker put it back on its hinges.

Back in the car, Sister drove to the top of the hill and parked, because it afforded them a commanding view. The pack was working beautifully together, the unentered hounds folded right in. Heartening as this was to behold, the three on the hill could only think of getting them back.

Shaker continued to blow. The horn, air clear today, could

be heard for three miles by human ears much as a train whistle can be heard for miles. Hounds can hear farther than that.

He blew and blew, then called, voice booming. "Come to me! Come to me!"

"Coyote." Sister cursed.

Tootie pressed her lips together; she knew what *coyote* meant.

Coyote scent is heavier than fox so it's easier for hounds to detect. Also, the coyote often runs in a blazing straight line, although he may make a big circle eventually to return to his den. Exciting though those runs may be, the larger predator lacks the skillful ruses, the engaging mental superiority of the fox. Hunting coyote, you want to stick in the saddle. Hunting the fox, you want to keep your senses razor sharp, since your quarry is smarter than you.

Often a coyote will run right out of the territory allowed to a hunt. This can create all manner of problems, of which a cranky landowner can be a big one.

Shaker kept blowing and one by one, hounds slowed, stopped, and listened.

Glitter, an unentered female, littermate to Giorgio, asked Diddy, *"Why are we stopping?"*

"Huntsman's calling us back."

"But," inquired Glenda, another littermate, *"we've been hearing those notes all along."*

Dragon, handsome and in his prime, a trifle blocky in the body, chuckled. *"Scent was so good we had to let 'er rip a little."*

"Look at that!" Shaker slapped his thigh as hounds trotted back to him.

"You know what my grandfather used to say." Sister held up a finger pointing to the sky, presumably where her grandfather was.

In unison, both Shaker and Tootie repeated his words. "Trust your hounds. If you don't trust your hounds, don't hunt them!"

Sister opened the hatch of the Forester as hounds neared.

Tootie counted heads. "Giorgio's missing."

"Blow again, Shaker. Case he got far ahead."

Shaker did as his master commanded, but they both knew the stunning unentered hound would not outstrip Dragon, a strike hound. Dragon would have turned on him like a snake. Cora, another strike hound and back in the kennel, would have bumped the younger hound, too. Cora and Dragon had to be used separately. They refused to cooperate with each other, so great was their pride in being first.

Diddy, first one to hop in the SUV, beamed. *"Invigorating!"*

Soon they were all in the green vehicle, Tootie happy with hounds since they had to flip the back seat down.

Tootie was one of those people who was most herself, most full of life, when with hounds. Her family, suburban people, just couldn't understand it.

Down at the gate, Tootie wiggled out of the back, and she and Shaker again lifted it off the hinges.

As Sister drove through she wondered if they should have stayed on the hill and blown longer. But she knew Giorgio, inexperienced though he was, would have returned. This country was much more open than her hunting country. At home, a hound might get separated, lost and scared or confused. Occasionally, a youngster would do that. But here, she could see for miles. A tri-color hound is easy to spot.

As Shaker and Tootie climbed back in the SUV, Sister, voice clipped, pronounced, "My hound has been stolen."

A silence followed. Then Shaker answered, "Yeah."

"You think . . . ?" Tootie's voice trailed off.

"Yes, I do," Shaker, angry, replied. "How can we prove it?"

"He created a distraction. Grabbed Giorgio and let the others out," said Sister.

"You think?" Tootie was appalled as the two in front nodded their affirmation.

"I will kill that bastard." Sister meant it, too.

CHAPTER 2

Woodford's brand-new kennels rested little more than a mile from the Shaker Village entrance. Starting at six in the evening, a yellow flashing light drew human contestants to the party. Tables lined the grassy area outside the kennels, a tent had been set up, and brands of famous Kentucky sipping whiskey lined the bar, as well as some single-cask specials. As Shaker had predicted, there wasn't a Tennessee bourbon in sight.

Sister allowed herself the pleasure of a wee draft of Blanton's Single Barrel No. 444, and what a pleasure it was. She needed to settle down. Externally she looked calm, but inside she seethed. Shaker stayed back with the hounds. There was little doubt in either of their minds that Mo had stolen Giorgio.

The issue was how to find the hound and, more, how to keep their tempers in check in the meantime. Tootie, sitting next to Sister on a hay bale, watched everything with both interest and suspicion.

"He's not here at the party," Tootie commented.

"Mo primps more than a woman." Sister brushed a paprika-colored ladybug off Tootie's shoulder. "You'll have luck since the ladybug chose you."

Smiling, Tootie replied, "Then we'll find Giorgio." She paused. "Maybe Mo didn't take him. Why would he be so obvious?"

"Arrogant. He figures he won't get caught. He's smart enough to hide Giorgio where we can't find him. Tomorrow, after the show, he'll pick him up on the way home. I'd bet my life on it."

"Shouldn't we tell O.J.?"

Sister shook her head. "She's on overload. There's nothing she can do since we can't prove it. We all know his reputation, but that's not proof. I'll tell her after the show. Plus, we don't want to tip off Mo. If we act as though nothing has happened we just might trip him up."

"How'd you get so smart?" Tootie admired Sister even as she teased her a bit.

"Foxes. They've taught me a lot."

"Like?"

"To expect the unexpected, for starters."

"I don't need to go to Princeton. I need to study foxes." Tootie dreaded leaving the place and the people she had grown to love, to say nothing of the hounds.

Sister leaned her shoulder on Tootie's. "Slip away and go over there and listen."

Sister indicated a large group of younger people—which is to say mid-teens to mid-thirties—clustered around Hope Rogers, who had inadvertently become the center of attention when she brought up the subject of West Nile virus, which can attack both horses and humans.

Tootie walked over to join them. Judge Baker and O.J., immersed in deep conversation, stood at the entrance to the kennels.

A plume of smoke curled up behind an exquisite Maserati. Mo Schneider loved to make an entrance. The machine ensured he'd attract attention. Next to him was his kennelman, Fonz Riley. For the past two years, whenever Mo had participated in a hound show, Fonz drove the rig; Mo drove whatever his latest purchase was. He changed cars like most men change socks. However, when Sister beheld the Maserati she thought he just might hang on to this car a bit longer. She caught herself wondering what a used one would cost. She couldn't imagine Mo putting Giorgio in the Maserati so she concluded that the hound couldn't be too far away.

Mo cut the motor, unfolding himself from behind the wheel without turning back to look at Fonz. He zipped straight for the bar, asked for a double vodka straight up, knocked it right back, and held out his glass for a refill. The bartender, a club member, poured another double, and Mo sauntered over to the crowd around Hope.

Fonz, another man who had battled the bottle, picked up a Co-Cola out of the huge cooler and joined other kennelmen.

By now, Hope was urging the young people around her to get involved with the Thoroughbred Retirement Foundation.

Mo listened for all of two minutes, then acidly interrupted, "Some of 'em aren't worth saving, Hope. That's what the knacker is for."

Knacker is an old horseman's word for the fellow who kills horses. It has been expanded to include the man who takes the horses to the slaughterhouse.

"It's true some are difficult, Mo, but it's worth trying to work with them," Hope responded, even-tempered.

"Bad horse costs as much to feed as a good horse." He enjoyed needling the good-looking woman.

"Mo, you can afford it," replied Carl Matacola, a member of Woodford.

Carl, at forty-one, was an associate professor at the University of Kentucky's College of Health Science. As director of athletic training, he also had a lot of experience in rehabilitation, making him very popular with Woodford's walking wounded.

The others laughed.

Ignoring them, Mo kept on. "Now that slaughtering horses is outlawed, what happens? People leave them to starve. I say kill them. It's more humane."

Those who knew Mo's reputation smirked when he said *humane.*

"Only if a horse is crazy—and some are, I agree," Hope maintained. "Otherwise, give the animal a chance. You'd be crazy too if you'd been stuffed with steroids, fed high-calorie grain, and stuck in a stall for twenty-three hours a day, only going outside to breeze a bit on the track and then be washed down."

"Oh, attacking the industry now, are you?" Mo stood up to his full height.

Since he was skinny he looked even taller than he was.

"Yes and no. Racing has to clean up after itself, or someone else will do it for us and then everyone loses."

"She's right about that," Jim Fitzgerald said, a stalwart of the Thoroughbred business, who'd walked up and heard the tail end of the discussion. "Anytime folks who aren't horse people stick their noses into it, everyone suffers, most especially the horses. Kind of like the vegetarians a few years ago who said you could feed your cats high protein and not feed them meat."

As a blank look covered a few faces, Hope said, "Cats are obligate carnivores; they have to eat meat, whereas hounds can live without it so long as they get the correct amount of protein—which, of course, depends on their activity level."

Mo drained his vodka. "I didn't come here for a lecture. When does the party start?"

Carl, handsome and well-mannered—unlike Mo—said, "We're enjoying ourselves. If you don't like the conversation, find another."

Secure in his wealth and little else, Mo sneered at the shorter man, without noticing how fit Carl was.

Before he could put his scorn into words, Hope moved toward Mo. "You obviously want to fuss at me, so why don't we go somewhere where you can? No point in spoiling other people's evening."

"Actually, Hope, I don't have a goddamned thing to say to you." Mo turned on his heel so fast that he tore up a little clump of grass and nearly knocked down Leslie Matacola, Carl's wife.

He bore down on O.J. and Barry, who viewed him with barely concealed distaste.

Carl, curious, asked, "How do you know Mo Schneider?"

Hope sighed. "Met him on the back stretch of a couple of racetracks. We didn't hit it off—which is an understatement."

"Pretty much the story of his life." Jim Fitzgerald couldn't help but laugh. "Ever notice how someone can be so smart in one department and woefully deficient in others?"

Hope laughed. "Makes me worry about myself."

Filled with Irish charm, Jim remarked, "Doctor, I think you're full up in every department."

Tootie rejoined Sister. "Hope kept her cool when Mo dissed her. He's really disgusting."

"That he is."

Much of being a master involves social duties. Sister was dog tired and ready to bite, although the Blanton's had somewhat improved her spirits. Still, she just wanted to go to her room at Shaker Village and go to bed.

Some masters, usually those who hunt hounds or whip in, can't be very social since their hound duties come first. Sister, being field master, naturally tended to the people. Now that she had a joint master, Dr. Walter Lungrun, they could share social obligations. The club was growing, and Sister had realized two years ago that she just couldn't go it alone as master. Walter, on call, couldn't come to this hound show, but he'd arranged his schedule so he could go to the Bryn Mawr Hound Show in Radnor, Pennsylvania, on the first Saturday in June, even though he wouldn't be taking hounds. Walter would miss the Virginia Hound Show but Sister would be there.

Friends passed and repassed as Sister, poised on the hay bale, indulged in her favorite topic, hounds and hunting. It was everyone else's main interest, too.

Encouraged by Sister, Tootie introduced herself to Leslie, who took her under her wing, introducing the young beauty to others. Tootie, senses alert, paid careful attention to everyone and everything in hopes of gleaning information.

Grant Fuller, florid, portly, and rich as Croesus, dropped down next to Sister. "Don't have the stamina I used to have."

She studied his Buddha belly and smiled. "You're doing just fine."

"That's eating, not partying." He smiled back. "How you doing?"

"Good. Yourself?"

"Busy. I shouldn't complain. Business is booming. Doesn't leave much time for other pursuits. When I was young, it was wine, women, and song. Now it's bourbon and steak."

The crackle of bugs on the scattered bug lights sounded like tiny punctuation marks to their conversation.

"I heard you've opened new processing plants."

This pleased him. "Expanded out of the Mid-America. Just opened a brand-new one in Kansas and am finishing one in southern Ohio. You know, making a great product isn't the hard part, the hard part is distribution."

"And?" She enjoyed learning about other people's businesses. Her late husband had taught her to appreciate a number of interests beyond her own favorite subjects: hounds, horses, and geology.

"Making inroads. In fact, I'm working on Augusta Co-op in your neck of the woods."

Augusta Co-op and Southern States were the two farm equipment and feed stores in Virginia, and neither one was part of a huge chain.

"Good for you." She paused. "You've worked hard and you hit the market at the right time. People are spending billions on their pets."

"Well, don't give me too much credit. I inherited the family business, one large feed store and two grain silos." He grinned. "Took us four generations to get that far. Yankees delayed our progress." He winked.

She laughed. "The song of the South. But hey, you could have stayed with that one big old feed store."

Grant puffed out his chest slightly. "Root, hog, or die." Then he burst out laughing. "I rooted a lot. But you know, if a person is going to be successful, whether it's Judge Baker, that pretty young vet"—he nodded in Hope's direction—"or you, you got to keep up with the times. Once I saw the handwriting on the wall for slaughterhouses, I sold them off and concentrated on dog and cat food."

"Most slaughterhouses comply with government rules and constant visits for inspection. However, the public perception is one of horror, so you were wise, really," Sister said.

"People want to eat meat, but they don't want to know how it gets to the table." He shrugged. "Ours is a nation where people put their heads in the sand. We should replace the eagle as our national symbol with an ostrich."

"True enough."

He lowered his voice. "Sister, I'll tell you something: chicken, beef, lamb, pork—all loaded. I mean, loaded with hormones. Like I said, I backed out of all that in the mid-nineties."

"But don't you still have to deal with the slaughterhouses?"

A thin sheen of sweat shone on his cheeks and forehead in the humid air, despite the coolness of evening coming on. "Might surprise you to know that, yes, I do use chicken byproducts and beef, but the real source of protein is chicken feathers."

"What?"

"We pick them up from the slaughterhouses by the trailer truckload, grind them, and pulp them. Boy, will that put a shine on a hound's coat. I'll toss a couple of bags in your trailer tomorrow. You pull out a hound that needs special care, someone a little light, and just see what happens in two weeks' time."

"Why, thank you, Grant. I'd be happy to try. What's the protein content?"

"I create three levels, based on activity, obviously. Let me give you three bags of the twenty-eight percent and three of the twenty-one. You just try it." He paused dramatically. "And I'll make you a promise. If you like the high-tech Hunter's Friend— the name was my wife's idea—I'll sell it to you for less per ton than anyone you do business with, even if I don't get the distribution deal with Augusta Co-op."

"That's very generous."

He put his hands behind him on the straw bale to lean back a little. "Not so generous. You're the queen of foxhunting. If you like my product—well, others will, too."

"You flatter me."

He shook his head. "No. Anyway, we're both Dixie brats. You've never made a fuss about your status, which is just as it should be. You know what my momma used to say?"

"I'm waiting."

"People who brag have to."

She let out a peal of laughter. "Hits the nail on the head."

"Take Mo Schneider. Can't believe they haven't run that braggart windbag out of Arkansas. If there's a state that should recognize hot air, it's that one." He enjoyed her company but knew he had to make the rounds. "Hate to leave you, but I need to do the shake-and-howdy."

Three loud blasts on the horn, notes signaling *Come to me,* sounded.

As Grant left, Sister wondered if Giorgio had heard Shaker blowing those notes when the hounds picked up scent. Sensitive, young, the beautiful boy would be so upset by not being able to reach Shaker. She wanted to cry because she knew how confused Giorgio must be. She prayed he wasn't chained. Chaining a dog infuriated her.

The horn-blowing contest, now starting, delighted every-one as the huntsmen, directed by the judges, began to perform various hound calls.

Sister noticed Mo, horn in his back pocket, back at the bar for another vodka. He ambled toward the lineup of men holding their horns; no lady huntsman was there to compete, although there are many these days.

Then Fonz brushed by his boss, jostled by another fellow, and Mo threw his vodka in Fonz's weather-beaten face.

Startled, Fonz stepped backward. Sister watched as the short, lean man carefully wiped the vodka off his face without tasting any of it. She thought it a cruel thing for Mo Schneider to do, throwing liquor at an ex-drunk, but she expected no better from him.

Later, that image of Fonz trying not to lick his lips would come back to her.

CHAPTER 3

Two rectangular rings set off with roped cordons marked the areas where the foxhounds, beagles, and bassets would be judged. Woodford had considered three rings but decided that if they ran the show like clockwork they could keep it intimate.

Quite a few fabulous hunts had driven to Harrodsburg, Kentucky, to be part of the show: Keswick, Longreen, and Beechgrove from Tennessee; Mooreland from Alabama; Midland from outside Columbus, Georgia; Why Worry Hounds from South Carolina; London Hunt from Ontario, Canada; Iroquois from nearby Lexington; Mission Valley and Coal Valley, both from Kansas; and Rosetree from York, Pennsylvania, all brought hounds.

O.J. checked her program, then her watch. One of her joint masters, Robbie Lyons, had been rushed to the hospital a scant two weeks ago for heart surgery, so he could only look on; the other master, Sam Adams, was working twice as hard to cover for him. As Woodford Hounds, founded in 1981, abounded with hardworking helpful people, the two healthy masters pulled it off—up to the start of the show, at least.

They'd wisely put the rings under the old trees. Across the narrow farm road on the house side they'd thrown up a large tent where food would be served later. The layout utilized the best features of the site and kept the action close together. Occasionally at hound shows the different rings are set so far apart that a spectator will have to huff and puff, running to catch the action.

Masters, huntsmen, and onlookers eagerly awaited the start of the first class: Single Dog Unentered (*dog hound* means a male hound). Part of the excitement involved the judges. Chris Ryan, MFH, huntsman of the famous Scarteen pack in Ireland, had been flown over. He would be scrutinizing the English and Cross-bred hounds. Tommy Lee Jones, huntsman of Casanova Hunt, the idol of many a young and not-so-young huntsman, would judge the American and Penn-Marydel hounds. Stanley D. Petter, Jr., would judge beagles and bassets. His grasp of conformation was so refined he was often consulted by devotees of the sport.

Woodford Hounds certainly assembled extraordinary judges, which naturally brought in the top competitors. People want their hounds to be seen by the best eyes. Just watching how a class is pinned is instructive. No one likes to be dismissed early from a class, but if one can take it in stride, there's much to gain from the experience.

Hope stopped by the trailer. "Good luck, you-all. I've got to head back, but give me a full report when you get home."

Sister thanked her, wishing her a safe trip. From Shaker Village to Hope's clinic was a seven-and-a-half-hour drive.

Sister handed Grady, an unentered dog hound, Giorgio's littermate, to Tootie. He had his mother's gorgeous head and powerful shoulders. His front legs from the knee downward turned in slightly, a conformation flaw. Small though it was, in this type of competition it would probably keep him from the ribbons. This fall would be his first season, and Sister, Shaker, and their whippers-in had high hopes for the *G* litter. Hounds are typically named according to the first letter of their mother's name. Giorgio was out of a gyp named Greta, drafted from Middleburg, and she'd been bred to Dasher, a solid hound full of good old Virginia blood, which is to say, Bywaters. The other great Virginia bloodline, Skinker, filled the kennels of Orange County Hunt, Casanova, and others.

Many of the spectators knew at least a bit of this, but their main focus was on the present crop of hounds and judges. The ladies particularly liked watching the judges. Tommy Lee Jones, silver-haired, kind, and good-natured, could turn a girl's head. Chris Ryan, wiry, rugged, bursting with energy and with that charm only the Irish possess, also dazzled. Stanley Petter, turnout crisp, treated ladies with respect, so he, too, was always in demand. In fact, some women never got around to looking at the hounds.

Each ring had a steward, a person responsible for unfastening the cordon so hounds and handlers could enter and exit. The steward, ascertaining the judges' results, would deliver them to the official ringside if that was necessary. A good steward is critical to a well-run hound show, for if a problem does occur in the ring—say, a dogfight—it is the steward's responsibility to attend to it, not the judges. As a judge, Barry Baker had the quiet authority and experience necessary for a good steward. Today he would need it.

Tootie, in a white kennel coat starched to perfection, a black hunt cap, ribbons up since she wasn't staff, made both Sister and Shaker grin. Apart from appreciating proper turnout, they both loved getting young people involved with hounds.

O.J., joining Sister Jane, remarked, "I'm so glad to see you're letting a junior handle the hound."

"She could go in the junior class but she's good, O.J., and I don't see any reason for her not to go up against the adults. We know"—Sister Jane nodded toward Shaker on her other side—"that Grady toes in. He's not going to get pinned. You find that toe-in a lot with the old Bywaters blood."

"It was the fashion in the late forties and fifties," O.J. commented. " 'Course we weren't on the ground there," she joked.

"They thought it would give the hound better purchase; I doubt if they were right," Sister replied. "Maybe you weren't on the ground then, but you know I was. Glad of it, too. More country people. People in general were more realistic."

Keswick Hunt had three hounds in the class, shown by the huntsman, Tony Gammell, and his wife, Whitney. Claudia Lynn, wife of Andy Lynn, one of the Keswick masters, showed the third hound. Charlotte Tieken, the other Keswick master, was chained to her desk, working. No show for her this time.

Far from being pushy or crassly competitive, all three Keswick people beamed at Tootie when she came into the ring. "You look the very part," Tony said, his lovely Irish lilt lightening Tootie's stride.

Longreen Foxhounds near Germantown, Tennessee, the other hunt with hounds in the ring, were also cordial to Jefferson Hunt, though the camaraderie didn't come close to Jefferson's relationship with Keswick, another Tennessee hunt. Everyone liked seeing a young person in the ring.

Tommy Lee asked them to walk around, then reverse. He studied each hound. Chris Ryan, the Irish judge, though not judging the American hounds, keenly watched the proceedings, as did the two hundred spectators.

Tootie lost her nervousness, partly because Grady, ham that he was, loved being the center of attention. Sister was right. Grady received no ribbon because of his toeing in. While not pronounced, it was at variance with the clean, straight limbs of Keswick Kiely, who took first, followed by his littermate, Kaiser, who snagged the red ribbon.

Tommy Jones placed his hand on Tootie's shoulder as she waited to go out of the ring. "You're doing a good job, and that's a lovely hound. Just toes in a tad."

"Thank you, Mr. Jones." She smiled broadly because she hadn't thought so august a huntsman would even notice her.

Of course he would. He didn't think he was august, which was part of his appeal.

The morning turned sultry. Still, the classes ran like clock-work. People shifted between the foxhound ring and the beagle and basset ring, depending on who was showing and being shown.

Tootie and Shaker showed hounds in the couples classes, which Tootie loved. Couples classes almost always had hounds who were closely matched littermates. Watching the pairs move together on and off lead was a special treat.

Sister went in the ring for Class 5, showing Dragon and Dasher, racy tricolor American hounds. The boys were on. They snared a second, which pleased both hounds and humans.

Mo Schneider hadn't received one ribbon for his hounds. He showed them with his whipper-in, Fonz Riley. The two men wore kennel coats and derbies, the proper headgear for show-ing English hounds. Mo had English, Crossbred, American, and Penn-Marydel, thinking to cover all the bases. Didn't work. Fonz handled the hounds much better than the master, but Mo's ego was in a gaseous state, ever expanding. The humidity and the lack of ribbons began to tell on him. Judge Baker, wearing a tan sport coat and tie in the ring as steward, clearly felt the humidity, as did everyone else. Those starched kennel coats felt like sweat suits. That's hound shows. No point in bitching and moaning.

The lunch break arrived in the nick of time. Ice-cold drinks helped restore bodies and spirits. Mary Pierson, a Woodford mem-ber, guided folks toward the tent. The food, perfect for a now-sweltering day, also helped.

Grant Fuller, already tired from walking back and forth from trailer to ring, headed toward the drinks.

Mo Schneider pushed his way toward O.J. to sit next to her. Given that he wasn't invited, she bore him with good grace. O.J.'s table had been organized before with the idea of giving the judges a respite.

Sister Jane just winked at O.J. when Mo took her place. She repaired to the next table to sit with Shaker and Tootie where the diminutive Woodford member Louise Kelly, black-eyed, black-haired, entertained everyone with her stories.

"You don't know one end of a hound from another." Mo's voice rose as he berated Chris Ryan.

Face reddening, Chris simply replied, "There's always another day for your hound."

"Don't give me that bullshit," Mo screeched, now pointing his finger at Tommy Lee. "It's the old boys' club. Always is."

O.J. spoke sternly. "Mo, this has been a wonderful show, and more is to come. Don't spoil it."

"You shut up. You're part of the old boys' club, too."

This frosted Sister Jane, who had ample reason to loathe Mo. She stood up. "Mo, you quite forget yourself."

His retort was, "I'd rather forget you."

She doubled her fist, moving toward him. Shaker knocked over his chair getting up to restrain his master. Sister rarely lost her temper but when she did, watch out.

Tommy Lee Jones, Judge Baker at table three, and Tony Gammell all stood. From behind Mo came Carl Matacola. All the men were strong, with Tommy Lee being the most formidable.

Judge Baker caused Mo to turn from Sister. "We don't speak to ladies this way. You're excused."

"I'm what?" His eyes bugged out of his head.

"Get out." Judge Baker simplified his request.

"Best you go," Tony reiterated. "You've insulted two masters, two lovely ladies."

Whitney, Tony's wife, looked on, proud of her husband's demeanor but worried that he would take a shot at the now frothing

Mo. It wouldn't do for Tony to break his hand, with so much work to be done this summer.

James Keogh, a strapping six-foot-four-inch Irishman and Woodford whipper-in, who'd been outside the tent, hurried in, ready to help drag Mo out. He wanted to make sure that Robbie Lyons didn't try to do it because his chest was still full of stitches from the heart surgery.

Mo took a swing at Judge Baker, who ducked.

Carl grabbed the swinging arm as Tommy Lee grabbed the other one. The two men pushed Mo's arms up against his back, which was painful, and then they literally picked him up and threw him out of the tent.

Shaker let loose of Sister Jane. "Boss, I know you've got a mean right cross, but you stay here."

Mo charged back into the tent. Carl stopped him, bending low and hitting him with a solid block below the knees. As Mo crumpled, Shaker grabbed hold of his coat collar and began dragging him back toward the trailers, the other men following as Mo flailed and cursed with abandon.

The ladies watched, quite impressed.

"Testosterone poisoning," Louise said laconically.

"Actually, I suspect he's deficient," Sister Jane added, which made everyone laugh louder.

Back at the trailers, the men surrounded Mo. Outnumbered and realizing vaguely he shouldn't have crossed a former Virginia supreme court justice while he was showing hounds, he calmed down. Crossing two of the most respected men in fox-hunting, Tommy Lee Jones and Chris Ryan, evidenced galloping stupidity, too.

When the men left him, Fonz started loading up the trailer.

"What the hell are you doing?" Mo shouted at him.

"We're going home, aren't we?"

"No, we goddam well are not. I came to show my hounds, and I will."

He did, too, actually winning a ribbon for single bitch entered.

Sister Jane thought Mo's hound rather nice. She also fell in love with Keswick Tally and Keswick Rustic as well as a lovely Crossbred, Why Worry Fairy.

Jefferson Hunt gathered four more ribbons and ended the day hot, tired, but happy, although plagued with worry over Giorgio.

Judge Baker walked back, his coat now off, his tie loosened, his shirtsleeves rolled up. Accompanying him was Jim Fitzgerald, the two in animated conversation.

Sister liked him. "Jim, I never got a chance to catch up with you."

"That kind of day. Didn't lack for drama."

Judge Baker shrugged. "I couldn't believe that Mo would still show his hounds. I had a mind to turn him away, but when I asked Chris Ryan he winked at me so I let the bastard in."

"Thoroughly disagreeable man." Jim nodded. "I was bringing up more ice from the trucks so I missed most of the championship fight."

"It's a foolish man who goes up against Tommy Lee Jones." Shaker laughed. "Foolish man to cross Sister, too."

Jim Fitzgerald spoke to Tootie, who was standing quietly next to Sister Jane. "Young lady, you've a gift with hounds."

"Thank you, sir."

"Where do you get these juniors?" Jim asked Sister.

"I'm on the board of Custis Hall. I recruit them. I have quite a few who hunt with me and four seniors who are outstanding. Tootie is one. The other three are back in Virginia madly finishing up term papers."

"Come back to Sister when you've finished college," Jim advised her.

"I've finished college." Judge Baker looked at Sister. "I could come, too."

"Any time, you handsome devil." Sister and her late husband had known Barry and his recently deceased wife for close to forty years.

"You'll see more of me come hunt season. You know, Mitch and Lutrell Fisher bought Skidby. Has a lovely dependency and I've rented it, so I'll hunt one day a week with Deep Run and one with you. Hunt every day if I could." Judge Baker meant it.

Skidby, a large landholding on the western edge of Sister Jane's hunt territory, was famous locally for its caverns. Immediately after the War Between the States, when the Yankees rode through, Confederate officers hid in the caves. No one knew if they'd be shot or imprisoned.

"You're still keeping the house in Richmond, aren't you?"

"Yes. I've half a mind to give it to my son and daughter-in-law. Too big to keep. But I'm not quite there yet."

"I can understand," Sister said. "I didn't know you knew Mitch and Lutrell."

"Lutrell and I are both on the board of the Richmond Ballet. She's the one with the big bucks; well, you know that. Mitch might be a doctor, but he's in research, so he doesn't make all that much."

"He hunts with me. She doesn't. She's a bit fearful. Actually, thank you for reminding me that they've finally moved into Skidby. I'll call on them."

"You'll find a warm reception." He kissed her on the cheek. "You might even find me."

After more pleasantries, chatting with other masters and huntsmen, Sister finally pulled O.J. aside and filled her in on Giorgio's disappearance.

"Why didn't you tell me sooner?" O.J.'s eyes widened and she raised her hands, palms up.

"Overload. There's nothing you could have done. Then, too, I didn't want to tip him off. I can't prove Mo stole my hound, but let's just say I figure the chances of his *not* stealing Giorgio are about the same as the sun rising in the west."

O.J. scanned the grounds; many trailers were pulling out. "Well, his trailer's not here."

"Damn." Sister paused. "I know Giorgio wasn't with his hounds. Tootie snuck back and checked a couple of times. Where could he have hidden a hound so someone wouldn't find it? My beautiful boy would have howled his displeasure, but he's so sweet he would be easy to muzzle. Couldn't howl then."

The late-afternoon sun showed up the lighter highlights in O.J.'s dark hair. "Someone who works for Shaker Village certainly would have found him if Mo had hidden him around here." She gazed at Sister, lost in thought for a bit, and then grabbed her arm. "Come on! There *is* a place, just outside the Village."

Once in O.J.'s truck, Sister pulled out her cell phone to call

Shaker and Tootie, who were readying the trailer to leave. That accomplished, she paid attention as O.J. turned right toward Harrodsburg on Route 68. O.J. then turned right on the next paved road. Large homes, freshly painted new barns, and expensive fencing signaled that money flowed to Mercer County.

"New money."

"Better than no money." O.J. turned right on a sharp turn, onto a narrow road. "Jim Fitzgerald was thinking about buying an old training track back here. This land has been let go, but it wouldn't take too much to rehab it. Anyway, the track is no secret, and Mo has come to the Mid-America Hound Show enough times to know of it." She now turned left, where a battered sign hung precariously on chains that swayed in the light breeze.

The track, guardrail still intact, lay just ahead. Mo's trailer was parked alongside it.

"That bastard!" Sister cursed.

"A lot of outbuildings. Good place to hide anything." Seeing the trailer, O.J. felt sure this was the place.

The moment Woodford's master had parked, Sister opened the door to sprint toward the trailer. She stepped up on the running boards between the wheel wells. "Not a thing! Not even his hounds!"

O.J. did not respond. Transfixed, she stood like a statue looking at the faded white guardrail.

"Are you all right?" Sister asked, then cast her eyes in the direction of O.J.'s unrelenting stare. "Jesus H. Christ!"

Sister put a hand on the guardrail and swung herself over as O.J., snapping out of it, did likewise. The two fit women ran across the infield to the other side of the track.

The ground underfoot, still good, gave their steps a spring. They stopped.

"Dead as a doornail," Sister pronounced.

Mo Schneider lay facedown in the track. Stripped to the waist, feet bare, head turned to the side, he stared at nothing—or perhaps at eternity.

O.J., mind clear, pointed to his back. "What do you make of that?"

Sister knelt down, careful not to touch the corpse. "Rat shot."

Rat shot is what foxhunters call bird shot. It is generally loaded into a .22 pistol and used only in extremis. If hounds rush toward a superhighway, scent burning, the whipper-in has to turn them. He or she might fire once in the air if there is time. The next shot is aimed directly at hindquarters. Better to pick out rat shot in the kennels than pick up crushed hounds on the road.

Now kneeling next to Sister, O.J. peered closely. "He's peppered with it." She pulled a handkerchief from the pocket of her linen skirt and used it to touch his wrist. "No pulse. Just in case. He's cooling but a long way from being cold."

"How long do you think he's been dead?"

"Warm day." O.J. stood up. "Not more than a hour, hour and a half."

"ATV tracks." Sister noticed tire tracks from an all-terrain vehicle alongside Mo's footprints.

"Kids sneak down here all the time."

"Fresh."

O.J. knelt down again to check the tracks. "You're right, and some of them have run over Mo's footprints."

"Mo ran around this track more than once." Sister shook

her head. "No hounds. No Fonz. No Maserati. No shoes. Why would he run barefoot?"

"You think this is some kind of ritual killing?"

"I don't know, but it *is* bizarre." A glint of humor returned. "Should we roll him over and drive a stake through his heart?"

Sister sent Shaker and Tootie home with hounds once she and O.J. discovered Mo's body. The authorities arrived; questioning went on. It made sense to spend the night and leave for Virginia in the morning. O.J. kindly invited Sister home with her. She also volunteered to call the various animal rescue groups.

The Mid-America Hound Show provided more drama than Woodford could have ever imagined. O.J. prayed there wouldn't be more to come.

CHAPTER 4

Tico Caracalla's work boots were already soaked with heavy dew at four-thirty in the morning. Keeneland, quiet and beautiful in any season, felt like it was all his at this hour. The back shed rows, his responsibility, were empty this time of year. Nonetheless, being a stickler for order and cleanliness, he inspected every stall. No matter how hungry he had been when he first came into the United States, Tico refused to work for sloppy outfits. When he finally worked his way up to Keeneland, he knew he'd found his true place. He'd inspect latches, check bucket fasteners, kneel down to make sure no pave-safe blocking was becoming dislodged. It never was, but he couldn't be too careful when it came to the horses and their safety.

The last stall in the shed row was closed up. He hurried down the line, because this was not the way he'd left that stall yesterday—or any of the others. He opened the stall door and nearly passed out. Fresh buckets of water had been placed on the stall floor, along with a huge pile of kibble. Sleepy-headed hounds started to rise. He stepped inside quickly and closed the door behind him. As a horseman he'd spent much of his life around dogs of one sort or another and he knew these animals meant no harm. His biggest shock arrived when a few hounds moved away from the human they'd been cuddling. Fonz Riley, bound and gagged, looked up.

"*Dei!*" Tico bent down and pulled the gag out of the small middle-aged man's mouth.

"Thank God," Fonz gasped.

"One minute." Tico slipped his pocket knife out of his pocket and cut the ropes around Fonz's wrists and ankles.

Fonz rubbed the circulation back into his limbs as Tico called security. Wisely, Tico asked no questions. He hadn't worked twenty years in the shed rows for nothing. Security called the Lexington police. Both arrived at the same time.

"Could I have something to drink?" Fonz asked.

"*Sí.*" Tico left, returning five minutes later with a cup of hot coffee and a Co-Cola in case Fonz wanted something cold. Tico kept a well-stocked cooler in the back of his truck, plus he'd just made himself a thermos of coffee.

As Fonz gratefully swigged both liquids, he began to revive.

Harry Bickle, the officer from the city, had seen plenty but nothing like this. "Your name?"

"Francis Albert Riley. Fonz. I don't know how I got here. I'd loaded the hounds, I was facing the trailer, and I felt a pain in my head. That's all I remember."

Bickle stepped closer to see if his pupils were the same size or possibly dilated. His nose informed him Fonz wasn't drunk.

"Could I go to the bathroom? I only need to step outside."

Fonz's request horrified Tico. He didn't want anyone urinating publicly, even though no one else was there. What if somebody drove by at that exact moment? "I'll take you," Tito volunteered.

Harry Bickle waited, as did the twenty-two-year-old night guard, who was moonlighting while studying at Transylvania College in Lexington, Kentucky. The kid had heard enough cracks about Dracula to last him a lifetime. Fortunately for him, the good education he was receiving would last a lifetime, too.

Fonz came back, ushered into the stall by Tico.

"These hounds sure are calm. No one's bolted for the door." Bickle didn't know much about foxhounds.

"No, sir. They're a good pack of hounds with a bad master. I try to make up for it." He rubbed the back of his head where he'd been hit, feeling the tender knot.

"Who's that?"

"Mo Schneider. Has a big place in Arkansas. Big money, small sense."

"That's not a nice way to talk about your boss." Bickle felt a cold wet nose touch his hand.

"No one likes him. I stay on because of the hounds. He'd mistreat them or kill them if I didn't protect them."

"Where's your boss now?"

"I don't know."

"Where's your vehicle?" Bickle continued.

"I don't know."

"Do you have any identification?"

Fonz reached into his hind pocket, extracting a well-worn wallet, western tooled.

Tico watched, taking in every detail as Bickle read the license, looked at the license photo, and then glanced back at Fonz as he returned the wallet.

"Would you like a ride to the hospital to have your head checked over?" Bickle offered. "Sometimes a blow to the head can fool you, more damage than you realize."

"No, sir. I can't leave the hounds. I need to find Mo. I need the trailer."

"What did the trailer look like?" Bickle was putting two and two together, although he hadn't been on duty when Mo Schneider was discovered.

"Four-horse Featherlite, two years old. The front half of the trailer is modified for the hounds."

Featherlite was a good brand of horse trailer.

"I think we have your trailer. It's impounded."

"What?"

"We have your boss, too. Trailer's registered in his name." Bickle took a long deep breath. "He's been murdered."

"About time," Fonz blurted out.

"What kind of crack is that?" Bickle asked.

"If you knew him, you'd understand."

"Come with me. I need you to identify the body, and I'd like to ask a few more questions."

"Officer, I can't leave the hounds."

Tico stepped in. "They need to be with him, Señor. Perhaps they don't listen to me and escape. Much harm could be done."

Bickle, in a pickle, thought a moment, then Fonz figured a way out.

"If you let me use your phone, I think I can find help." When Fonz explained his plan, Officer Bickle handed over his cell.

Fonz called O.J. He'd memorized the number on the drive up from Arkansas just in case there was a problem. That way he wouldn't have to pull over, hunt the number, and call.

"Hello," came O.J.'s sunny reply, at what was now six in the morning.

"Master Winegardner, it's Fonz."

"Fonz, where are you?" She didn't want to tell him about Mo.

"Keeneland, last shed row, with Mo's hounds. I got hit over the head. There's a policeman here who wants to ask questions, but I can't leave the hounds."

"Fonz, put the man on the phone."

"Officer Bickle here."

"Officer Bickle, this is Jane Winegardner, Master of Woodford Hounds. Will you allow me to pick up the hounds and take them to our kennels until you get things cleared away with Fonz? He's a good man, if my testimony is any help. Anyone who could work with Mo Schneider and last for two years is a saint."

"Well, ma'am, I guess that's all right."

"You have to wait until I get there, Officer, because I'll need Fonz to help me load. The hounds don't know me. I can be there in forty-five minutes."

"All right." Officer Bickle clicked off his phone. "Tell you what, you all wait here. You, too." The last was said directly to Jude, the Transylvania student. "I'll bring back breakfast for everyone. Your friend is bringing her trailer. She must be a good friend." He spoke to Fonz.

"She's a master of foxhounds, sir. I don't know her all that well, but all masters worth their salt will help hounds."

Officer Bickle drove off to the nearest fast food place, beginning to realize he'd stepped into a whole new world.

When he returned, the four men ate outside the stall so as not to tempt hounds overmuch. By the time they'd drained the last drop of coffee, the rumble of a big trailer could be heard.

O.J. drove the rig while Carl and Leslie Matacola followed by car. Mary Pierson, who'd fallen asleep in the truck cab, sat up when O.J. stopped. Sister Jane followed in her Subaru.

Opening the door, O.J. walked right up to Officer Bickle as Carl headed for Fonz. She held out her hand. "I'm Jane Winegardner. Thank you so much for thinking of the hounds."

He liked the tall lady right on sight, so he smiled. "Well, ma'am, I couldn't very well put them in jail." He then stared at Carl. "Don't I know you?"

"No, sir, but you might have seen me around. I'm director of athletic training at UK."

"I *have* seen you, on TV. And you're a hound person, too?"

"Yes, sir."

"Officer Bickle, allow me to send you an invitation to our opening hunt. It will be Thanksgiving weekend at Shakertown. I'll stay in touch. You'll enjoy it, especially the Blessing of the Hounds." O.J. always rewarded people who helped the hounds or the club. An invitation to Opening Hunt was very special. She then turned to Fonz. "You heard about Mo?"

"The officer told me. Master, will you call Blake, our stable manager, and ask him to feed hounds and pick us up at home? I hope I'll get back tonight."

"I will," O.J. answered.

Mary, one step ahead, was drawing a map to the kennels.

"Officer Bickle, if it's all right with you, we'll follow you to the station, and when you're done with Fonz, we'll take him to his hounds," Carl suggested.

"They've impounded the trailer. I don't know how to carry them home." Fonz used the country southern expression.

"Can you release the truck and trailer?" O.J. inquired.

"Not right away, ma'am. We have to go over it for evidence."

"Fonz, don't worry. We'll get you to Arkansas, safe and sound."

"Master, I hate to put you to this trouble."

"Hounds first, Fonz." She laid her hand gently on his shoulder, for she could see he'd been hard used. "We both know that."

"Yes, ma'am. Well, let's load them up."

Mary opened the door to the Woodford trailer as Fonz opened the door to the stall. Fonz stood on the trailer ramp and hounds came right to him before he even opened his mouth. Officer Bickle hadn't seen that kind of obedience before by that many dogs. (To him they were *dogs* because he hadn't yet learned the nomenclature.)

Not wishing to spoil O.J.'s work with the officer, Sister tried to be patient. But ever since O.J. had filled her in on the discovery of Fonz, along with Mo's hounds, she'd had a feeling. . . . She was dying to open the stall door because she felt Giorgio was there.

Knowing hounds, she also had to be patient as they emerged from the stall. These hounds didn't know her. She didn't want to spook them.

In the middle of the pack, Giorgio smelled his master. He knew she was there before she knew he was there.

Standing up on his hind legs he let out a yelp of happiness. *"Mom!"*

"Giorgio!" Sister held out her arms as the stunning hound bounded over to her.

"He is a beauty," O.J. admitted.

"Officer Bickle, this is my hound. He'd been stolen."

"I missed you." Giorgio, again on his hind legs, put his paws on Sister's shoulders.

Fonz blinked. "Where did *he* come from?"

"Good question. How did he get in your pack?" Sister's voice was hard.

"I don't know."

"Bullshit," Sister blurted out.

O.J. astutely intervened. "Officer, this hound belongs to Mrs. Jane Arnold. We think Mo stole him."

"I swear I didn't know," Fonz protested.

Sister, this time, bit her tongue.

"Officer, she needs to get her hound back to Virginia, if you have no objection."

"Well—uh, I think that will be okay."

"O.J., let me help you here," said Sister. "There's going to be a lot to do."

"I've got Carl, Leslie, and Mary. You'd best get out before traffic picks up."

Giorgio offered his opinion. *"Yes!"*

Sister hugged him again and followed O.J.'s advice. Giorgio hopped in the back but before Sister reached the impressive entrance to Keeneland he'd crawled into the passenger seat, chatting the whole time.

"Master, the little lemon-spotted gyp, that's Tillie. She's hocky, but she'll go where the others go," Fonz told O.J.

"What's hocky?" Officer Bickle was becoming quite intrigued, plus he really wanted to see Jane Winegardner again.

"Shy," Carl answered.

After hounds had been loaded, Officer Bickle took Fonz to the morgue. Much as Fonz loathed Mo Schneider, seeing him on a slab came as a nasty jolt. When the attendant rolled him over to show the rat shot peppering his back and legs with round bumps, Fonz gasped.

"Ever see anything like that? Bird shot?" Officer Bickle pointed to the bumps.

"Not on a human."

"Me neither. Do you have any idea who would do something like this?"

"Someone who knew Mo pretty good. Someone who paid him back for his cruelty. We could start with his three ex-wives."

Two hours later, which was actually good time, Fonz was released and Carl drove him out to the Woodford kennels.

The visiting hounds in adjoining yards had enjoyed chats with the Woodford hounds. Again, they loaded right up. O.J. and Mary, along with Fonz, all squeezed into the cab for the long drive home.

By the time O.J., finally home, called Sister, the older woman and Giorgio had just passed Hinton, West Virginia, situated on a high mountain plateau about two and a half hours from home.

"Do you think Fonz has any idea who killed Mo?" Sister asked, after O.J. filled her in.

"He rattled off a list of eight or nine people. Those were just the front-runners."

A long silence followed. "O.J., maybe we're better off not knowing. Maybe the trail will grow cold. We don't need to know."

"Well, I don't know if I agree. Murder is murder."

"Some people deserve it." Sister thought there were some people walking around who do nothing but cause pain.

"Then what happens to the rule of law?"

"What rule of law? For Christ's sake, whoever has the most money gets away with just about anything. And we're thinking about individual crimes. What about great big crimes like the rape of resources, the pollution of water, or sending young men and women soldiers to their deaths? I'm old. Listen to me. You wrap crimes in the flag or a dollar bill, and suddenly everyone looks the other way."

"Hadn't thought about it like that." O.J., very moral, hadn't.

"You wouldn't. You're a straight shooter."

"So are you."

"Yes and no. I'm a cynical straight shooter. I expect authority to be corrupt. I expect most corporations to hide skeletons. And I expect regular folks to stick their heads in the sand until the sand becomes poisoned. We always wait until it's a ten-squared crisis before we move our sorry asses."

"Good point. But what if Mo's murder isn't isolated?" O.J. worried.

"How can that—"

"What I mean is, What if there's a serial killer out there, popping off foxhunters they don't like?"

"You think they'd start elsewhere." Sister hadn't considered such a possibility.

"It could happen."

"Give me your list."

A long pause followed. "Not until you give me yours."

They both laughed; then Sister Jane said, "Ever think about how many people you would have killed if you could have gotten away with it?"

"No, but I am now."

"Odd. I mean every one of us is capable of killing, whether in self-defense—which is perfectly justified—revenge, or blind rage, yet few of us ever do kill."

"You're making me realize my real point." O.J. sighed. "It's one of the reasons I cherish our friendship. Somehow you always lead me back to the scent. Here's what I really meant to say. Except in self-defense, we *don't* kill, and we've all been tremendously provoked. If that restraint has eroded, what's possible?"

"Good point. I don't know the answer. But I'm betting Mo is a one-off."

"I hope so." O.J. changed the subject. "How's Giorgio?"

"Being the navigator. He's still sitting straight up, hasn't taken his eyes off the road."

"Too bad he can't talk."

"He does in his own way."

"I'm so happy!" Giorgio said.

Sister didn't walk into her house until four that afternoon. Golly, Raleigh, and Rooster—calico cat, Doberman, and harrier, respectively—greeted her rapturously. Only when she walked into the den, her favorite room, did she remember it was Memorial Day.

Sister looked at the silver-framed photo of herself, her husband, and her son, age fourteen, his age when he died, all spiffed up to ride in the family class at the Jefferson Hunt Horse Show.

What would it be like to have her RayRay, who would be forty-seven now, sitting in the den with her, most likely with a good wife, grandchildren coming and going, and laughter filling the house?

She'd never know, but that was life. You take what the good Lord gives you.

She fought back her tears, petted Golly, and said, "What next?"

CHAPTER 5

Tuesday at Roughneck Farm brought an avalanche of chores, phone calls, and interruptions.

Sister and Shaker cleaned the kennels with the big power washer early, since they both wanted to get the jump on the day. The spray felt good on their faces because at 8 A.M. the thermometer read 73 degrees Fahrenheit. Going to be a hot one. Sister walked back through the special runs for hounds needing a little extra care: Often, during the hunt season, roughly from Labor Day to St. Patrick's Day in central Virginia, some hounds, certain bloodlines especially, would run the fat right off themselves by New Year's. Putting the weight back on was easier said than done. Other hounds, usually the girls, stayed weedy.

First she checked Giorgio, none the worse for wear. Next she opened the chain-link gate and sat with Aurora, a hound from Archie's litter. Now fourteen, she was flatfooted and a touch deaf. Her nose was keen, her eyes less bright. Her hunting days were long over. Many a master or huntsman would have put Aurora down, but Sister just couldn't do that. A hound or horse who had served her well lived out his or her last years in comfort and love.

"Aurora, you look chipper today."

Wise brown eyes looked into her own. *"You, too, Master."*

Her pockets filled with dried liver tidbits left over from the Kentucky show, Sister sat on an old stool next to the hound's commodious sleeping box, complete with large canvas-covered cushion.

She handed a treat to Aurora, who took it daintily with her worn teeth. "Do you ever think about the old days?"

Crunching, then swallowing, the sweet hound replied, *"I dream a lot. I dream I'm young and I'm flying in front of the pack."*

Sister gave Aurora more tidbits, petting the hound's head. "It goes by so fast, so fast. Sometimes, Aurora, it scares me. I don't *feel* old but I *am* old."

"Well, I feel old, but life is still good." Aurora took another liver bit, relishing the taste as it exploded in her mouth.

Sister heard the door into the hall open. Shaker, in his wellies, walked up to the gate. "Two happy girls."

"Memories."

"That was a golden litter, that *A* litter. Every single hound was spectacular." He smiled as he watched the old hound eat her liver treats. "Remember the time I wanted to wheel the pack to the right, toward Mudfence Farm, and Aurora sat down and just howled?" He slapped his thigh. "I got a little hot and spoke harshly to her. She stood up but she howled again. Then she turned her whole body in the opposite direction, and by God there was the biggest red in the state of Virginia just popping out of a tangle. Taught me a lesson."

"Which was?" Sister smiled broadly.

"Trust your hounds."

"Now that's a fact. If you can't trust them, don't hunt them. That's why I'm suspicious when I see a boatload of whippers-in at other hunts. It's one thing if you're training people; other than that, less is more."

"Some masters get bulldozed by rich members. Not you."

Grateful to serve under a strong master, Shaker was refer-ring to the practice whereby wealthy members pay up and a mas-ter allows them to be whippers-in, a glamorous position. However, it's a very tough position and requires good riding, hound sense, and fox sense, as well as a great sense of direction. As rich people often possess just one of those qualities, they are generally affixed to the true whipper-in like an enema bag.

In truth, very few people possess all four virtues in marked degree, but if one is to whip in, best to have at least three in good working order.

"I know Thursday is usually errand day, but I'm heading down to the feed store in town and I'll swing by Hope Rogers's, too. Espilac."

Espilac was used as a milk replacer or enhancement. Violet, a draft to Jefferson Hunt, was due any day now. Best to be prepared, should she be low in milk. Sister also needed to pick up oxytocin. If the gyp had difficulty birthing her puppies, this drug would help her expel them. One always prayed for an easy time of it for the mother, but anything could happen.

"Violet does look ready to pop." Shaker knew Sister had been thinking about Violet, the only hound close to term.

"Always get excited when the puppies arrive."

"What saint's day is it?" Shaker was always amused by Sister's vast knowledge of saint's days.

"I guess the most important is Augustine of Canterbury, who evangelized the Anglo-Saxons in the sixth century A.D. He died in 604."

"Think he succeeded?" Shaker grinned.

"Maybe, in Kent." She laughed. "He built the first cathedral in Canterbury. You going religious on me?"

"No." He smiled. "Just wondering if there was a saint to help with whelping."

"Let's propose a saint for the deliverance of canine births. I'm sure the pope will be supportive," she called over her shoulder, as she left the kennels.

She crossed the rich green grass on her way to the stable. All the horses were turned out, on vacation after the end of hunt season. As she walked into the center aisle, a low swish overhead made her duck, then look up.

Bitsy, the screech owl, a juicy earthworm in her beak, thought herself very funny flying right over Sister's head. No sooner did she land in her nest in the rafters than little sounds filled the barn. Bitsy had hatched four owlets, growing bigger every day. The thought of five screech owls made Sister wonder if she ought to stop by the sporting goods store to buy earplugs.

She went back outside. Having two vehicles provoked her to a rare moment of indecision. Which one to take? Life was easier when her choice was only the red GMC half-ton.

She no sooner cranked up the Forester than Raleigh and Rooster shot out of the house, the dog door now in service.

"All right." She got out and opened the hatch.

Two very happy dogs jumped in, ready for adventure.

First call was the feed store, a red and white Purina checkerboard painted on the brick side wall. Sister left the windows open for the dogs. A good twenty minutes later, she emerged with a shopping cart filled with items she hadn't intended to buy: cat and dog toys, including a rubber chicken that made her laugh when she looked at it; more treats; a new brand of dog kibble, which she thought she'd try with the foxes whom she fed regularly. Big square handkerchiefs were on sale, so she bought one in every color, ten hankies at $2.95 apiece. When the heat rose up, she'd roll ice cubes in a work handkerchief and tie it around her neck. Worked a treat.

"*I smell dog bones.*" Rooster's ears pricked up.

"Don't make a mess." Sister handed each dog a treat in the shape of a bone.

"*She understood.*" Rooster was incredulous.

"*Situational,*" the Doberman answered.

Within ten minutes they reached Central Virginia Equine Clinic, a large Morton pre-fab building. In the operating room, Hope had installed a large, circular, flat, rotating operating table, which was on a hydraulic lift. She also had water therapy pools, treadmills, even an enormous MRI. Whatever the latest advance in technology, Hope purchased it.

All these major purchases had been in the last three years. Hope's international reputation had filled her coffers, and so had an aunt in Iowa, who died leaving everything to her. No one had even met the aunt, but all were grateful. While it is never proper to celebrate a death, all that money was a blessing.

Bottles of animal supplements, as well as Espilac, were in the front office, as so many of her clients would pick up things for pets when dropping by. Hope made a bit of money on these items.

Hope herself, petite, fooled people, particularly men, who didn't believe such a small person could handle large animals. That she could. The eight stalls for patients today contained only one horse. Troubles could hit a horse at any time, but spring problems started with people, those who were not horsemen, who turned their horses out in verdant pastures. Some horses would overeat and founder, an inflammation within the laminae of the foot. The worst of those days had passed, so the clinic's patient list had dropped off, although Hope could depend on the odd injury, now and then, or the birth of a late foal.

Sister walked into the reception room. Dan Clement, Hope's partner, stood behind Lisa, the office manager, peering at the computer screen.

"Sister, how are you?" Dan smiled.

"Fine. Stopped by for some Espilac and oxytocin, which I hope I don't need."

"Sure thing." Before the words were out of his mouth, Lisa sped to the supply room.

Hope sailed in through the front door, carrying two large bags. "Sister Jane. Just picked up lunch. Like some?"

"Oh, thank you, no. How are you?"

Hope seemed a little frazzled. "I'm three weeks from my divorce being final, and when I got home Sunday that bastard, Paul, called and said he wanted two hundred and fifty thousand dollars. He thought it over and felt he was entitled to more of my money. Entitled! He never lifted a finger to build this practice. He never even mowed the lawn."

"I'm sorry."

"I just want to kill him." Hope dropped the bags on the office desk.

"Don't do that." Dan tried to lighten the conversation. "That will cost more than two hundred and fifty thousand dollars, plus we need you here."

"He's right," Sister agreed. "We do need you."

"You-all make me feel better." Hope calmed down.

"Get up early some morning and go on hound walk with us," Sister suggested. "You'd be surprised at how it starts off the day: perfectly."

"Thanks. I will." Hope appreciated Sister's concern.

Dan's beeper went off. He walked outside as he dialed back on his cell.

"Hope, when are you going to come hunt with me?" Sister teased. "Think of how happy that will make your clients."

"When I have more time," the diminutive vet replied. "But I will come to hound walk. I promise." She pulled sandwiches out of the bag. A couple of bourbon labels were stuck to her plastic sandwich wrappers. "Recovered?"

Sister knew Hope referred to the Kentucky show, finding Mo and then Giorgio. They'd had a phone conversation the day before, when Sister got home.

"Pretty much."

"I still can't believe it."

Sister shrugged. "The question is, Why did someone wait so long to kill him?"

"Should have been strangled in the cradle," Hope half joked.

"If you think about it, Mo Schneider makes a good case for free abortion on demand."

Both women laughed, then Hope said, "Any more news on that point?"

"No. And I heard from O.J. Fonz still has no memory of who attacked him or how he ended up in that shed at Keeneland."

"How's Giorgio?"

"Good. He liked driving back with me." Sister pointed to the labels. "Where's the bourbon?"

Hope's eyebrows lifted. "Be nice if I had all these brands. I've started lately to study them." She pointed to an Evan Williams label. "Simple. Old-fashioned. Then there are bottles like Woodford Reserve. No labels. The name is on the glass."

"I like that." Sister picked up a cream-colored label. "Not much information."

"No."

"You know who loves bourbon and I suspect is well versed in it, since he's the type to learn all about something? Grant Fuller."

Hope stiffened slightly. "We've talked." She looked up as Dan came back in.

He replied to the unasked question. "Lab results in on Caroline Silverman's mare. Negative."

"Good." Hope smiled.

"You need to eat lunch and I need to push on. Good to see you-all."

"Fair enough. Take care."

Sister left, bag in hand, and drove back home.

The rest of her day passed in chores. She reminded Walter Lungrun, her joint master, to get a burn on the jump-building parties before the heat really became oppressive and the chiggers came out.

Chiggers could make a woman question the wisdom of the Almighty.

She wanted to clean the house because Gray Lorillard, her boyfriend, would be back Wednesday from visiting his aunt. She knew she'd not get to it tomorrow morning. Now or never.

Back in the house, the phone rang: Felicity Porter.

"Felicity, how are you?"

"I'm fine," the Custis Hall senior said. "Mom and Dad refuse to come to my graduation. You'll be there, won't you?"

"Of course I will."

Sister wanted to slap Felicity's parents. The girl was pregnant and would marry when she turned eighteen, next month. The Porters, having envisioned a brilliant career for their daughter as an investment banker or stockbroker, had turned their backs on her. She planned to get a job, go to night school if possible, and raise her child. The baby's father, Howie Lindquist, quarterback on the Miller School football team, loved Felicity and seemed to be a responsible young man.

"You'll be my only friend."

"You have many friends, Felicity."

"My only older friend."

This made Sister laugh. "Well, honey, I'm a trustee. You know I'll be there, but if you want other older friends why don't you ask Walter Lungrun and Betty and Bobby Franklin? They'll stand by you. I know it's terribly upsetting, honey, your parents not coming, but you'll pull through. I believe in you."

"Thank you." A pause followed. "Pamela's mother and father are coming. Pamela says her mother is going to make a last-ditch effort to get her to drop Ol' Miss and go to the University of Pennsylvania. With her father's money and her grades they'll let her in even though it's after the deadline. She was accepted there but turned them down."

"You-all got accepted at so many colleges."

"We really are the best class to graduate from Custis Hall."

"No, mine was." Sister teased her. "Class of Fifty-three. We're the ones who gave the school the gorgeous silver tea service. See if the class of 2008 can top that."

"We can try." Felicity enjoyed the challenge. "The kitty is now at $1002."

At the beginning of last year's hunt season, Val, Tootie, and Felicity agreed to pay a dollar to the kitty each time one of them swore. The bulk of that sum had been paid by Val. The goal was to throw themselves a huge graduation party.

"Val apparently has not yet learned the virtue of restraint."

"Good for us." Felicity paused. "Thank you, Sister. You helped Howie and me find a place to live, you got me a job, you—well, I promise you I will be worth it."

"Honey, all I did was open doors. You had to walk through them."

"I promise you I will support myself and I will support Jefferson Hunt. I swear it."

"I believe you will."

After Sister hung up she finished the cleaning, surprised at how fast she did it. Usually it dragged on because she didn't want to do it. But talking to Felicity picked up her energy.

Fortunate in the young people who hunted with her, she couldn't understand people who complained about the young. It seemed to her that young people were like old people, good and bad in every bunch. She was surrounded by good ones.

By nine in the evening, she had showered and was headed for bed when Golly, moving at warp speed, nearly knocked her down, heading for the closet.

"The end is coming!" The long-haired calico declared.

Sister couldn't feel changes in atmospheric pressure as early as the cats, dogs, hounds, and horses, but there had to be a storm brewing. Golly always headed straight for the folded cashmere sweaters, burying herself underneath them at the first hint of a boomer.

Sister opened the bedroom windows. The air felt oppressively still. The sun had set but a glimmer of gray colored the west, and she could still see the tops of the Blue Ridge Mountains directly behind her. In the north sky she also saw enormous boiling black clouds.

"Uh-oh." She threw on her slippers and robe, ran downstairs, pushed opened the mudroom door, hurried outside, and closed the windows of the Forester.

She hadn't even gotten a foot out of the car when the first roll of thunder gave fair warning. What was odd was that it didn't stop. The rolling thunder lasted for a full seven minutes. Lightning, still behind the Blue Ridge, was heading southwest. Within minutes it would be over the mountain, and then it would take fifteen minutes, tops, to reach the farm.

She grabbed the phone in the kitchen just as another flash, a sheet of light, made everything stand out in sharp relief.

"Shaker."

"I'm on my way."

She hung up. She and Shaker were telepathic. She had called to tell him to get to the kennel, because often a storm can provoke a particularly sensitive hound into labor and Violet was sensitive. If the mother panicked she might roll on her puppies.

"Oh, boy, this is going to be a whopper," she told Raleigh and Rooster.

Neither dog was afraid of thunderstorms. Sister wondered if fear is inbred somehow, just as some phobias seem to run in families. Then again, they could be teaching one another the phobia.

A crash overhead rattled the glassware. This was followed by a bolt of lightning, which blasted Hangman's Ridge, three miles distant from the house and eight hundred feet higher.

Here was a thunderstorm of biblical intensity. Two minutes after the strike on Hangman's Ridge the rain started. Water lashed at windowpanes. Coupled with the thunder, the sound made Sister jump a few times.

Worried, she hurried back upstairs from the kitchen, the

old winding wooden steps reverberating underfoot. Once in her bedroom she walked into her closet, spying a fluffy tail hanging out from under the cashmere sweaters.

"It's all right, Golly. It's all right."

"*I'm going to die,*" Golly cried.

"*I wish.*" Rooster taunted her, as he followed on Sister's heels.

Under any other circumstances, Golly would have attacked Rooster.

Sister patted the top of the cashmere sweaters. "You're safe in here. You just sit tight."

"*I don't want to die,*" Golly shook.

By eleven-fifteen the storm was continuing, but with slower intervals between thunderclaps. Sister pulled on overalls, a slicker, and her green wellies and was in the kennels within minutes. "She all right?"

"Four so far."

"You go, girl." Sister smiled down at the lovely hound. "Shaker, I'm going to check the pastures. They all have run-in sheds, but half the time the horses don't use them in a storm. I don't get it."

She grabbed the large flashlight from the kennel office and walked to the first pasture. Aztec, Lafayette, and Matador were fine and, no, they weren't standing in the run-in shed.

She climbed the fence between pastures and walked toward Shaker's horses. Gunpowder hung his head.

She walked faster but didn't run. Animals, especially ones as sensitive as horses, pick up human emotion. If you're scared, they're scared.

"Gunpowder." She stopped before him.

Blood was everywhere. She ran the flashlight over his body until she found a deep wound in his upper inner thigh near his sheath. There was no way to determine the direction of the wound. The rain still came down, and even with the flashlight it was hard to see. She took hold of his halter, gently walking him toward the barn, lifted the kiwi latch on the gate, and got him into the wash stall.

Oh, God, she thought to herself. *Don't let him have a perforated intestine. Please.*

She began to wash him with warm water. A spurt of blood rewarded her. She now had a better look at the site. A two-inch hole where the upper leg meets the underside of the animal gushed like Old Faithful.

Gunpowder wobbled.

She ran for the cell in the tack room and dialed Hope's emergency number at the clinic. No answer. She called the home number.

"Hello," came a sleepy voice.

"Hope? Sister. Can you get here?"

"Be there as fast as I can."

She ran back in the wash stall, took a half roll of vet wrap and squished it to make it smaller, wrapped a thin old towel around it, and plugged the hole with her left hand while holding not too hard, above it with her right, to slow the bleeding. If he dropped, she'd never get him in the trailer. It was obvious he needed to go to the clinic, but first she needed the vet here. In a crisis, Hope could stretch out a plastic tarp, knock him out, and operate. But dropping a horse in a barn or pasture can lead to other injuries. That's why Hope's padded operating table was sheer genius.

She waited for what seemed forever, praying she could stanch the flow, all the while talking to Gunpowder.

Bitsy left her owlets to watch, and for once the tiny little thing had the sense to keep her beak shut.

Headlights shone through the rain. Thank God.

Hope appeared in the barn twenty minutes after Sister's call. She must have driven like a madwoman to get there so fast. She removed Sister's bandages, a second set.

"Good work, you stopped the flow," Hope said briskly; then, all business, she performed a brief exam. Blood had covered the washroom floor, filled the drains, and splashed all over Sister and Hope.

"Let's load him. No time to lose. He's in shock."

The two of them carefully walked the wobbly big gray out of the wash stall and down the aisle. Sister ran out; the trailer was parked near the barn. She dropped the back walkway. They got him up. She didn't tie him for fear he would drop during the ride. No need for his head to be yanked up.

Driving as fast as they could in the rain, they arrived at the clinic in twenty minutes.

One on each side of Gunpowder, the women walked him into the operating room. The outside garage door had allowed Sister to back right up to it.

Sister marveled at Hope's efficiency and skill. It's one thing to see the vet at your farm for routine checks or small problems; it's another to see her in a full-blown crisis.

Hope hit Gunpowder with a shot of anesthetic. The big guy went to his knees, both women steadying him so he would go down with the wound side exposed. In a short time he was completely sedated. They stretched him out carefully.

Hope pressed the hydraulic lift, and the operating table came up to waist level. She put on her coat and mouth cover, pointing to Sister to do the same. When she probed and cleaned the wound, a bit more blood came out, but thankfully the major artery there hadn't been severed.

Reaching in while Sister held the small snake light, Hope irrigated the wound again, checked to see if she'd missed any dirt, and sewed the wound closed.

The major problem now was that Gunpowder was in shock. Hope quickly began to replace fluids intravenously. "Want a career as a vet tech?"

"Be fascinating. You need steady nerves."

Hope removed her surgical gloves and Sister did the same; then she removed her mask and turned to the older woman. "He's going to be out for a couple of hours. I'll sleep in here. When he starts to rouse I can get him into a stall. 'Course, Dan or Lisa might be here by then."

"How are his chances?"

"Good. I expect there will be swelling, and if there's too much I'll take out the stitches and insert a drain tube. I'd like to try to get him through without doing that. I've got to keep the IV bag on him for"—she swept her gaze back to the recumbent animal—"well, at least three days and maybe more. And he'll be on a program of antibiotics for a full two weeks. After that, we'll see. The last thing we want, Sister, is for this to turn into a full-blown infection. The wound itself is deep enough."

"Missed his intestines, thank God."

"Yes. And whatever he got into didn't shred a lot of muscle. It's a very deep puncture wound but no ligaments are torn; you know how bad that gets." She paused. "He has to heal from the inside out, but I'd be surprised if it affects his movement at all. When I probed I didn't find anything that set off alarm bells." She exhaled. "I need a cigarette."

"I didn't know you smoked." Sister had removed all her paraphernalia, washing up after Hope finished.

"When no one's looking." Hope walked over to check Gunpowder one more time. "You ever smoke?"

"At college and in my twenties; then I gave it up. Every now and then, though, I miss it. Tobacco may be bad for your health, but it's good for your nerves." Sister followed Hope out of the operating room and into the small lounge. "Need me to help you roll in a cot?"

"No, I can do it. God, listen to that rain. It's coming down hard again. We haven't had a storm this fierce in years. I just hope the roof on the house holds up. Soon time to put on new shingles." Hope dropped wearily into the deep cushioned sofa. "Ah." Irritated that she forgot the cigarettes, she got up, walked to the front desk, opened a drawer, and pulled out a pack of Nat Shermans. Then she rejoined Sister.

Sister was surprised at the brand. "I used to smoke those. I'd have them sent down from New York."

"If you're going to fill your lungs with smoke, you ought to do it from really good weeds." Hope lit up, closed her eyes, and inhaled. "Filthy night."

Sister leaned back, enjoying the fragrance of her old brand. "Thank you."

"Sister." Hope smiled. "That's my job." Another long drag followed. "Actually, I like the tough cases. I like having to think fast. It doesn't allow you time to worry about yourself."

"True."

"I've been thinking too much about myself lately, and I resent it, you know? I mean, I resent my divorce because in a funny way it has made me self-centered. Maybe we're all self-centered to a degree, but I didn't think I was all that awful about it."

"I don't think you are." Sister crossed her arms across her chest, slid down a bit in the sofa, and stretched out her legs. "Oppression does that to people. It's a kind of reverse narcissism."

Hope was not one to think in social terms. "What do you mean?"

"I mean if you see the world through a preconceived belief—that women are mistreated or blacks and gay people are second-class citizens, take your pick—then in a bizarre way you've become self-centered. Divorce, in its way, is a form of institutional oppression and misery. It's more than understandable, but if I think about the times I've been held back because I'm a woman, I'm not thinking about the Middle East, I'm not thinking about the true function of the Federal Reserve. So the folks in power—and we all know who they are—remain unchallenged."

Hope drew on the Nat Sherman, then turned to Sister. "You have an original mind."

Sister laughed. "No, Hope, I have a different *kind* of mind. You're a scientist."

"Now that you mention it, what *is* the function of the Federal Reserve?"

"To stabilize banking. It has no business tampering with the economy. Its function most assuredly is not to stimulate the economy but, people being human, those reservists, for lack of a better term, cave to political pressure. Anyway, that's how I see it." She closed her eyes for a moment, then opened them. "You know, I have to get back to the farm because Violet is whelping and I left Shaker alone. Hey, you sit here, you did a lot more work than I did. Let me roll the cot into the operating room. Where is it?"

"Closet." Hope didn't protest this time.

It took Sister a few minutes to roll the little bed out and set it up, then she knelt down to stroke Gunpowder's head and kissed him on the nose.

When she came back, Hope had fallen asleep. Sister took the cigarette out of her fingers in the nick of time. "Hope."

"Huh?" Hope sat bolt upright. "I've never done that!" She viewed the stub in Sister's fingers.

"How Jack Cassidy died." Sister named a talented actor from the past. "Fell asleep with a cigarette and burned to death."

Hope shuddered. "Awful way to go, but then there aren't many good ones. Speaking of dying, the first thing I did when I left Paul was to change my will. If I die before the divorce is final he doesn't get one red cent."

Sister patted her on the back. "You're too young to think of dying."

They walked into the operating room, the double doors swinging to close behind them.

"At least Mo Schneider's exit was spectacular. His last minutes had to be filled with exhaustion, pain, and fear," Sister replied.

"Wonder if I could run Paul to death?" Hope kicked off her boots.

"Mo was proof that money can't buy happiness. Remind Paul. Maybe he'll lower his new set of demands."

"Fat chance," Hope growled. She stretched out. "How did Mo make his fortune?"

"Recycling. You know when you pull on a fake fleece coat or a Polar Tec blanket? That's Mo."

"I'll be. He was smart."

"About some things. Fundamentally, he was a cruel man, but my experience has taught me that apart from those who are born bad—and believe me, some are—most people who are cruel learned it early."

"Mother's milk that curdled." Hope folded her hands over her chest.

"Something like that."

"Are you sure you don't want to go to the house and sleep?" Hope offered. "You've got to be more tired than I am."

"I got just wet enough out there with Gunpowder in the paddock that the discomfort will keep me awake. I can make it back to the kennel. Shall I cut the lights on the way out?"

"Yes, thank you. With the lightning we don't need them." As Sister flicked the switch and opened the door to the operating room, Hope called out, "You're tough as nails, Sister. You know that?"

"So I've been told. Good night."

" 'Night." And Hope was asleep before Sister climbed back in the dually.

The storm, seemingly tethered over the pastures, meadows, and eastern slopes of the Blue Ridge, had intensified again. Sister drove out slowly. It was four in the morning. At least no one would be on the road so she could go as slowly as she needed.

As she pulled out of the long driveway, she thought she saw a car parked on the macadam behind the large veterinary sign. She was too tired to look more closely, figuring someone had ditched the vehicle or the storm had scared them so bad they decided to sleep until it was over.

She peered over the steering wheel. A flash of lightning, lavender in its heat, knocked her back against the seat. Her eyes burned.

"Shit," she muttered, then laughed. If her mother were alive and had been riding shotgun, a correction to Sister's vocabulary would surely have followed.

Squinting, driving thirty miles an hour and even slower on the curves as water rushed across the low spots, Sister finally made it home to Roughneck Farm.

She got out, closed the door, and headed for the kennels. Might as well stay wet for a while as the rain, despite her efforts to keep dry, had found its way behind the collar of the Barbour coat and she was still clammy from her first dose of rain.

Shaker woke when she entered, even though she was quiet.

"Five. One was born dead."

Sister came in, knelt down, and stroked Violet's head. "It's hard work, girl. I know from personal experience." She looked closely at the young mother. "Still a little swollen. Might be another."

She gathered up the bloody towels and Shaker started to stand.

"Boss, what happened to you?" He noticed the bloodstains.

"Tell you in a minute." She threw the bloody towels in the big hamper in the washroom, where an industrial-strength washer and dryer made life a lot easier. She returned with an armful of fresh towels and gave Shaker the report on Gunpowder, his horse.

"You should have gotten me."

"Violet needed you. Hope and I were fine. I *am* bone weary, though. I'm going up to take a nap."

As she walked through the still-driving rain she hoped the basement hadn't flooded. She thought of Hope asleep near Gunpowder and knew that Dan would find her in the morning.

He did.

CHAPTER 6

Betty Franklin made a bracing pot of coffee and waited for the aroma to waft up the back stairway into Sister's bedroom. She'd stopped by the kennels for hound walk to find Shaker asleep. He woke up, when hounds welcomed Betty, and told her about the night's drama.

In the off season, Sister, Shaker, Betty, and Sybil Fawkes, when she could make it, walked out the pack and worked with young entry five mornings each week. Did hounds a world of good—and the people, too.

The walks covered a mile out and a mile back. As the summer temperatures rose, takeoff time moved ever backward. Right now it was nine in the morning. By July they'd go out at seven-thirty.

Betty and Sister, about twenty years apart in age, were as

close as second skin. They shared many similar interests, but it was the hound work that drew them together, as it does most people who feed, clean, walk hounds, birth, and bury them. The actual hunting teaches each human to depend on the other, but hound work teaches them one great lesson: love—of hounds and of the people who love them. Betty whipped out the heavy old Number 5 iron skillet and pulled four eggs out of the fridge. She heard footsteps upstairs.

By the time Sister walked into the kitchen, the crackle of frying eggs had made her realize she was famished.

"What would I do without you?"

"Be miserable." Betty flipped the eggs over. Sister liked them over easy. "Sit down, table's set. All you have to do is lift your fork. Muffins will be out of the toaster in a minute."

Golly, thinking she was unobtrusive, sat on a chair, her head resting on the big farm table, white whiskers sweeping forward.

"Here we go." Betty placed the eggs in front of Sister, followed with a large mug of coffee as the toaster rang.

"Aren't you having any?"

"One egg and an English muffin. Ate cereal for breakfast, but I am hungry. Golly, how about some crunchy bits?"

"Yes, please." Golly perked right up.

The two dogs on the floor hoped for treats. Betty poured the grease from the frying pan over their kibble. Grease, corn oil, or bacon drippings will all put a shine on a carnivore's coat.

"You spoil my cat."

"Like you don't?" Betty placed a dainty china bowl in the shape of a fish before the delighted cat and sat down opposite Sister.

"What with everything going on, I forgot to tell you," said Sister. "The Great Biddy called me yesterday morning."

Great Biddy was Sister's term for her mother-in-law, still alive, still healthy, and still imperious. The two women had disliked each other from day one and had little to say now.

"What did she want?"

"I'm not at all sure. Usually she launches right in, but yesterday she only mentioned that Ray and RayRay's grave sites look especially beautiful in late spring."

"Maybe she's softening at last," Betty said cheerily.

"She's getting damned close to one hundred. If it doesn't happen now it never will." Sister laughed. "She also said she'd been watching a television show; I don't know the name; never watch TV except for sports. Well, anyway, the series has a kid on it from Richmond. So she said, 'New York is for people who can't make it in Richmond.' I had to laugh."

Betty folded her hands together. "Are you sure you want to go to the Virginia Hound Show?"

"Sure, why not?" Sister was surprised.

"After what happened at the Mid-America? Aren't you a little worried?"

"Betty, I'm surprised at you. Mo Schneider getting his just rewards has nothing to do with hound shows."

Shifting in her seat, partly because Golly, claws out, reached up to pat her thigh, Betty responded, "You're right. I've been watching too many Netflix lately. But Fonz was roughly treated, too. Preys on my mind."

"If all you knew of America was from films and TV, you'd

conclude we're a nation of sex fiends and serial killers." She thought a moment. "Sometimes in the same individual."

"Maybe Bobby and I need to take a break from watching movies."

"Golly, leave Betty alone." Sister put her fork down. "I wish Hope or Dan would call. Maybe Hope's still asleep."

"They'll call."

"Betty's food is better than mine," Golly sassed.

"She will."

"Forgot to tell you. I don't know where my brains have gone. Anyway, when we were at the Mid-America Hound Show, Barry Baker was the steward."

"How is the good judge?" Betty found him a lively soul.

"Handsome as ever. The news is . . . are you ready? . . . He rented a hunt box at Skidby!"

"No!"

"Says he'll divide his time between Deep Run Hunt and us."

"I'm surprised he's stayed a widower so long."

"Mmm, only two years." Sister felt the caffeine start to kick in. "They were well matched. He won't lack for female companionship—too handsome—but that doesn't mean he'll connect. Know what I mean?"

"I do. Think of all the men we dated before we married."

"Honey, I think of all the men I dated *after* I married."

The two exploded, laughing.

Betty shook her head. "You were a bad girl."

"What do you mean *were?*"

"Oh?" Betty raised her eyebrows.

"Nah. I've been virtuous. Boring, really. To change the subject, I called the Fishers. Now that they've moved in, I bet I can add Skidby as a fixture. Barry will work it from his end."

"Fab!" Betty pretended she was one of the *Absolutely Fabulous* actresses from British TV, her favorite show.

"Sure is."

The phone rang. Sister jumped up.

"Hello," came a deep voice on the other end.

"Barry Baker!"

"I'm moving things into Skidby for a few days, and I was hoping I could take you to dinner."

"I'll go you one better. Why don't you come here, you pick the day, and I'll cook you a meal?"

"That's an offer I can't refuse. Would Thursday work? Say I get there around four and you can show me hounds? Heard you found a new horse late in the season."

"Yes, Matador. Word gets around fast."

"Good horse. I saw him run. Thursday?"

"Thursday it is." She hung up the phone, saying to Betty, "Speak of the devil."

"Ever notice how that happens? You think of someone and they call or you get a letter?"

"Is." Sister sat back down. " 'Course, these days you'd get an e-mail."

"Felicity called me and asked if Bobby and I would come to her graduation. Sweet kid. Can't believe her parents are being such buttheads. She also asked us to print her wedding invitations, a pitifully small number."

The Franklins owned a large printing company.

"Me neither. People can be so incredibly selfish."

The phone rang again.

"Bet it's Hope with a report on Gunpowder," Betty chirped.

Sister picked up the phone, heard Dan's voice, and winked at Betty while holding one thumb up. "Dan, how's my boy."

"Going to be fine." His voice sounded strangled.

"I can barely hear you. We have a bad connection."

"Sister, I called to tell you that Hope was found dead this morning. Ben Sidell just left. He's treating it as a suspicious death, but I think the verdict will be suicide."

"What?" Sister steadied herself with her hand on the kitchen counter.

"She shot herself in the mouth." Dan broke down, then pulled himself together. "You know she was despondent over the divorce but, Sister, I can't believe it. Found her in the operating room with Gunpowder."

"It can't be true, Dan. I left her after she operated on Gunpowder and she was tired; angry, too, at Paul's last-minute holdup. But depressed, suicidal? No!"

"I don't know what to say." Dan felt crushed by the weight of the event. The sight of her had been unnerving.

"She didn't kill herself, Dan."

That sentence stopped Betty in her tracks.

"I want to believe that." He stopped. "What a mess, Sister, what a terrible mess. I'm a vet. I'm used to blood and tissue, but still—"

"What can I do for you? If you need help with horses, you know Shaker and I are good hands with a horse. We'll do anything you need for as long as you need it."

"I know. I know."

Sister's voice lowered. "Dan, steel yourself. We don't know what will slither out of the investigation, but I *know* Hope did not take her own life. I don't care how it looks."

Dan fought back tears. "I'll let you know what her family decides."

"Would you like me to call Peggy Augustus? She and Hope were working on a big fund-raiser at Saratoga. They'd become very close."

Peggy Augustus bred fabulous Thoroughbreds and was well known in horse circles.

"She was the second person I called after Hope's parents. You're the third. Couldn't notify people until Ben left." He paused. "If it *is* suicide, I don't know why. I don't understand it, but I can't sit in judgment of another person's life."

"None of us can, Dan. That's up to God."

After hanging up the phone, Sister told Betty exactly what Dan had told her.

"No. Oh, no!" Betty's eyes filled with tears as she reached for Sister.

The two women hugged each other.

"Betty, there is no way in hot hell that Hope killed herself. In my bones I know she didn't do it; she would never do it."

"I expect Ben made straight for Paul. He'd be my prime subject." Betty wiped her eyes.

Betty was right. Ben was on his way.

"We've got to start the telephone tree." Sister rubbed her temples. "The membership needs this information presented in a responsible manner. A lot of our people were her people, you know."

"I'll call Peggy and tell her we'll fill in where we can on the fund-raiser." Betty reached for the phone.

"While you do that, I'm going to find Shaker. Tell Peggy if she wants to change the date of the meeting or whatever, we'll help with whatever she needs."

"This will hit her hard. Peggy's the brains behind the outfit, but Hope could go out there and say all the medical stuff. God, this is awful. It's just awful."

Sister gave Betty a kiss on the cheek, then hurried out to find Shaker on the back run of the kennels.

Shocked, he pushed back his baseball cap. "Why would anyone kill Hope Rogers?"

Sister touched his hand. "Strange. There's a squadron of people who wanted Mo Schneider dead, but who would want to kill Hope? By God, I intend to find out!"

CHAPTER 7

Fifteen couple of hounds marched down the muddy farm road, water standing in the deep ruts. No matter what yesterday's shocking news, hounds must go out. As heat came up earlier, hounds walked out earlier.

Trinity and Tinsel, second-year hounds, enjoyed splashing.

Giorgio had told everyone how Mo opened the trailer door and snatched him. No one wanted to hear it again, so he walked along quietly. The other *G*s babbled a bit.

Asa, an older hound, who after cubbing would be retired to lounge on the sofa this year, grumbled, *"Damn kids."*

Diana and her littermate, Dasher, laughed.

Hounds loved their walks. As summer progressed, Sister, Shaker, and Betty might even go along on bicycles. This only worked if youngsters weren't coupled to older hounds, since a confused youngster could drag the older hound right into the bicycle. Drawings of couple straps appear on Egyptian tombs thousands of years old. Humans learned early that yoking a younger hound to an older hound often shortened the learning time. The pharaohs or their minions had long ago figured this out, too. Foxhunters tend not to "improve" what works. If it was effective in 2000 B.C. or earlier, it would be effective now.

Today no one was coupled, a reward for how quickly the young entry were coming along.

Since everyone settled down, the humans could chat.

"What did Gray say?" Betty asked Sister, who had called her boyfriend to give him the horrible news.

"Shock. Dismay."

"Seems to be everyone's response."

"One great thing is there are so many wonderful vets in the area," Shaker said. "They'll step in and help Dan. But that poor guy will have nightmares for a long, long time."

Betty wore her wellies, now muddy up to the tops. "I didn't see it and *I'll* have nightmares."

"You don't suppose Hope ran afoul of one of the bigwigs, do you?" Shaker further explained his thoughts. "Her rescue work might have uncovered abuse or cheating with drugs. Big money in the Thoroughbred world can sometimes lead to big sins."

"Long shot. After all, she was taking horses off their hands that weren't winning and weren't suitable for breeding. Wouldn't matter if an owner was rich or not so rich; she was doing everyone a favor. Hell, she'd hook up her rig and go to Charleston, Mountaineer Track, Pimlico. She'd even haul all the way up to Saratoga and back. 'Course, if she threatened to expose someone, an abuser, you might be right. As for drugs, she wasn't on the racetracks, so it's doubtful she had knowledge of that." Sister's voice rose and Dragon turned to look at her. "Sorry, Dragon, you-all are fine."

"Always want to be first, don't you, boy?" Shaker liked Dragon, but his hardheaded ways tested the huntsman's patience.

Diana and Dasher, his littermates, good as gold, just proved the axiom that breeding is Nature's roulette.

"I do." Dragon puffed out his broad chest.

"Idiot," Asa remarked.

They walked toward Hangman's Ridge, which loomed over Roughneck Farm. The ridge had earned its gloomy name in 1702 when the first criminal, Lawrence Pollard, was dispatched to the Hereafter from that very spot. There were precious few people this far west—the Wild West back then—it had been quite dangerous, so Pollard must have had it coming.

The early settlers struggled to create a lawful society. Up until the early nineteenth century, seventeen others followed Lawrence Pollard to the grave. At sixteen hundred feet above sea level, the swinging bodies would have been seen for miles around. Their ghosts haunted the ridge.

"When people commit suicide, usually they leave a note either to blame someone or excuse someone. Dan made no mention of a note. I keep turning it over in my mind; maybe I'll find something. And you know she'd never fire a gun with a traumatized horse in the recovery room." Sister paused to jump over a big puddle. "Made it," she announced with pride, then continued, "Look, she didn't commit suicide. I don't care if her prints *are* all over that gun. How hard is it to shoot somebody, wipe down the gun and put it in the victim's hand?"

"Easy," Shaker said. "When Ben studies the wound and the splatter pattern—gross but important—he'll have a better idea of whether she killed herself or not."

"Even if it looks like she did, what if her killer were, say, a police officer? He'd know how to fake it." Sister's T-shirt was already soaked with sweat.

"That's stretching it," Betty responded.

"I know." Sister sighed. "She was so special, always ready to help out. I can't give it up. Actually, I just started."

"That's what scares me," Shaker replied.

"Oh, come on, I'm not that bad, am I?"

"I refuse to answer on the grounds that it may incriminate me." Tinsel was drifting out. He whistled low and she moved back.

"If it were Paul, we'll all be relieved." Betty was sweating, too.

"Guess we'll find out soon enough." Shaker noticed Georgia, a gray fox, pop out of her den as they walked along the orchard.

"Saucy wench." Sister smiled as Georgia watched the hounds walk along.

When Diana turned to look Georgia's way, the young vixen slipped back into her den.

"Haven't had as many litters of cubs as usual this spring." Shaker kept up with the foxes, as did Sister. "It will be a hard winter, I expect. They know about the weather and the food supply long before we do."

"Amazing. If only I knew what a fox knows," Betty said admiringly.

"*We'd have to chase you then,*" Dasher teased.

The hounds, overhearing the humans, had learned about

Hope's demise. As she was the equine vet, not theirs, they weren't close to her but they knew who she was. She'd visited the farm many times on call and sometimes just dropped by. No one had an opinion on her death, since they hadn't been in her presence for months. As well as fear, the hounds could smell serious illness in a human. On Hope's last visit, no one had picked up on either of these.

By the time Gray arrived at the farm at six, Sister's chores were done. The light had softened; long thin wisps of clouds streaked through the sky.

He found her in the kitchen and gave her a big hug and a kiss. "I'm glad to see you."

"How are you?"

"Frazzled." He opened the fridge and pulled out a bottle of tonic water. "Want one?"

"No." She watched as he poured tonic over two ice cubes, then filled a jigger half full with scotch.

He drank the scotch neat, chasing it with the tonic. "That will help."

"It must have been quite a day." She smiled as she checked the chicken in the oven.

"For starters, the news about Hope Rogers is deeply disquieting. I can't get her off my mind. Next, my aunt about ran me crazy. Sam and I"—Sam was his younger brother, a recovering alcoholic—"spent Sunday with her. My sister, of course, was too grand to make the trip. But the old girl bitched and moaned the entire time. Sam and I puttied windows, fixed floors, cleaned behind the stove and refrigerator. Christ, she wore me out. Then I got home at three to find the pipe under the kitchen sink had broken. I needed a paddle to cross the kitchen floor."

"Oh, no! Did it ruin that beautiful hardwood?"

"Funny. The pipe must have burst not more than ten minutes before I walked through the door. Now that I've mopped it up, the floor is cleaner than it has been for a long time. I'll never convince Sam to remove his boots on the porch before he comes in." The two brothers lived together in a clapboard house, federal style, built at the time of the Revolution.

"Still want to go into reconstruction?"

Gray, a former partner in a prestigious accounting firm in Washington, D.C., had retired but did consulting work. He needed a full-time job, although not for the money. The first year of retirement had proved pleasant enough, then massive boredom had set in.

"I do."

"Who fixed the pipe?"

"I did. I have extra pipe, all types and diameters, out in the shed from when I ran water to all the outbuildings. So I threaded a pipe and popped her in."

"I hate threading pipe. That's why PVC is so good. Give me sturdy, heavy plastic any day."

"PVC's fine for some purposes, but this was the hot water line. I used copper."

"Fancy."

"Only the best for a Lorillard." He grinned. "That's why I'm besotted with you."

. . .

After dinner, Gray had the opportunity to demonstrate his besottedness; then they opened the bedroom windows. The night air had turned deliciously cool.

Odd thing about death, Sister thought, it reaffirms life and sex begets life. Even if the human can't reproduce, the body tries. One falls out, one comes in. Nature's logic.

"Sixty-nine looms ever closer." Gray put his hands behind his head on the pillow.

"Are you preparing me so I won't forget? I already have your present."

He turned toward her. "No. Only that the next one is seventy. It sounds so old."

"It *is* old."

"You're seventy-three, and you look maybe early fifties."

"Liar."

"It's true. But I'm not you, honey. I'm starting to feel creaky."

"Gray, if I'd been switched on the back of my legs by my ancient aunt, then spent time on my hands and knees fixing a broken pipe, bending over to mop up the floor, I'd feel creaky, too."

"You're right. It's all attitude. Anyway, if I want to really feel rotten, I'll focus on myself. I never have seen a happy narcissist."

"That's a thought." She turned on her side as he flopped back, hands behind his head again. "Just think, Gray, how much life we've lived and how much we still hope to live. Hope Rogers didn't even make it to forty."

"That puts it in perspective."

"I wonder if this has anything to do with the club? Her murder. I'm viewing it as murder."

"Janie, no way."

"Well, I can't find a thread, but as master my first thought is always the club. So many of our people were her clients—well, their horses were. You know what I mean." She rubbed his close-cut hair. "And my second thought is I want revenge. She was a good woman."

CHAPTER 8

The light played off Barry Baker's platinum signet ring. Of all the men Sister knew, Barry and her late husband, Ray, were the only ones who wore platinum, a subtle metal. They noted who thought it was steel or silver and who recognized the expensive metal for what it was. Both men also understood the difference between a sport watch and a watch one wore to work. Neither man would have been caught dead wearing a sport watch to the office, which marked a man as socially off-key regardless of his achievements in other areas.

While not quite as ready to make judgments based on inanimate objects, Sister recognized the wisdom in Barry and Ray's observations.

Barry swept his hand toward the kennels. "I remember

when you two built the first section. Such practical yet pleasing architecture." He gazed at the long rows of arches connecting the runs and sighed. "Couldn't afford it today."

"I know. The bricks would cost plenty, but the labor cost would be ruinous. You know, Barry, the American worker has pretty well priced himself out of global competition."

"True enough. But as long as taxes keep going up, so will wages. It's an ugly spiral." He smiled broadly. "And I don't give a damn."

She laughed. "You used to."

"Oh, I used to believe a lot of things."

As they walked under the arches, a cool breeze swept through, which was most welcome.

"Asa's still going strong but Aurora's slowing down," Sister said.

"Your *A* line has been outstanding."

"What a memory you have."

"I always remember good hounds, fast horses, and beautiful women. I remember the fast women, too." The twinkle in his eye made him look twenty years younger at that moment.

"Some things never change." Sister strode toward the boys' yard. "Asa, come visit."

Asa raised his head where he'd been snoozing under a sweet gum tree. He roused, shook himself, and ambled over, tail wagging.

Once inside the boys' yard, Barry knelt down to speak to the hound. "Asa, you look just the same. I'd never know you were an old man."

Most people can be taught the basics of hounds' language, but some are born with hound sense, that special ability to reach an animal. Barry had hound sense.

"I remember you, too. When you visited, you rode a good-looking bay mare, light bay with dapples on her hindquarters."

Other hounds came over, Sister introducing each to Barry.

Walking back toward the house, Raleigh and Rooster in tow, Sister asked, "What will become of Mo Schneider's hounds?"

"Funny you bring that up. I spoke to Fonz this morning." He put his arm around Sister's shoulders. He was the same height. "He asked O.J. to take some. You know, Mo bred a few good hounds, even though he couldn't hunt them. Anyway, he has some good ones left. Obviously, O.J. has only so much room in her kennels. One of the things I was going to ask you was whether you wanted four couple. Bywaters blood, if you go back to the sixth generation."

"Yes, I'd be most appreciative. You know how I feel about the Bywaters blood."

"I do." He opened the door to the mudroom.

"Any leads on who tied up Fonz?" she asked.

Barry just said, "No. Nothing."

Raleigh and Rooster waited for the humans to go in before they did. Golly hopped out the cat door into the mudroom and then hopped back into the kitchen.

"What was that all about?" Rooster wondered.

Raleigh smirked. *"Showing how agile she is."*

A voice came from the other side of the cat door. *"Don't get smart, Raleigh."*

Raleigh, wisely, kept his peace.

The wonderful aroma of roast lamb filled the kitchen. Sister ate early, which was fine with Barry. They enjoyed the meal and caught up on old friends.

Barry, not a drinker, sipped unsweetened tea. "Sister, that beautiful young girl: Tootie. Was that her name? She has a gift with hounds."

Sister brightened. "She wants to work here for the summer. Her parents prefer a more 'suitable' job. Tootie has so many gifts. I pray when she's finished with Princeton, and maybe even graduate school, that she returns to me. Whatever her profession, I just hope she can do it here. She has the makings of a master. I have to hand this hunt over to someone else someday. She could do it. Might could hunt hounds, too, if she studied with Shaker. Then the club could save one salary." She smiled. "Tell you what, Shaker is worth every penny. The understudy would be good for him and the club."

"Melvin Poe's hunting in his eighties."

"Melvin Poe is one of a kind."

Barry laughed. "What kind?"

"The best. But remember he has a fabulous wife, and that raises up any man."

Barry smiled, remembering his own wife. "I always thought I'd die first. Men do."

"Fate."

"You never realize how much you've come to depend on someone until they're gone. Oh, I knew I depended on Noddy to keep the social calendar, write the thank-yous—well, I wrote some—and manage all the details of life, down to how much starch I liked in my collars. What I didn't realize is how much I relied on her judgment concerning people and her political insights. The first year after she passed I walked into walls. I still do sometimes."

"I know the feeling. Thank God I took an interest in our investments and didn't turn the checkbook over to Ray. So many widows struggle with money. But I found out how much Ray did in other areas, down to figuring out seed mixtures for the pastures, when timber was properly dried, how to know when to hold and when to fold when it came to stocks. Ray could figure out most anything."

"Man possessed an uncanny sense of the market."

"Do you think everyone is born with some gift? His success with stocks, that was his biggest gift."

"No. Oh, when I was young and idealistic, I thought everyone had something special. But parking my rear end on the bench all those years, I saw the tail end of the human race. Talk about a bad gene pool. The only gift some cretins possess is that of making everyone around them unhappy."

"I go back and forth."

"Sister, trust me, there are billions of people on earth who add nothing to anyone's life, and certainly not to the other creatures of the earth. We've overbred and inbred ourselves. When you look at the people and the nations breeding the most, it makes my blood run cold." He suddenly smiled. "See why I never ran for public office?"

"I do."

She served apple cobbler for dessert and made hot tea for herself. Barry stuck to his iced tea. They laughed over old times and dished about who was still kicking around. Then Sister returned to a subject they'd discussed earlier. "I think Hope was killed."

"So you said."

"It troubles me. Someone is literally getting away with murder."

"Don't jump to conclusions, number one. And number two, people get away with murder every day. Trust me on that."

Before he could continue, she poked him with her forefinger. "You sound just like Ray."

"He kept you level."

"Oh, please."

"He did. I think men balance women and women direct men but, hey, I'm an old sexist. But *don't* jump to conclusions. Obviously, I didn't know Hope as well as you or Shaker knew her. But since I'm a member of the Thoroughbred Retirement Foundation, I did talk to her now and again, and she seemed perfectly fine. Honey, people sometimes lead secret lives."

"Like what? I can't imagine Hope having a secret that big. I know just about everyone that Hope knew in central Virginia anyway. Never a whiff of anything off-key. What kind of secret could she have had that we wouldn't have known or suspected?"

"Sexual perversion. Remember—oh, it must be ten years ago—when they found that Member of Parliament in London who had asphyxiated himself while masturbating? He put a plastic bag over his head to heighten the sensation and I guess it must have been pretty much of a blowout, because he didn't get the bag off in time. People do strange things."

"Somehow I can't feature Hope Rogers as one who skates near asphyxiation while masturbating," she replied dryly.

"You know what I'm driving at. Don't be contrary." He was an old friend and spoke directly. "She might have had some condition of which no one was aware, some medical problem, or she could have been on medication for, say, mild depression and the medication went haywire. Stranger things have happened."

"Yes, I agree there, but I can't find a thread that leads me to Hope's death."

"Did she ever have lawsuits brought against her for malpractice?"

"No. Well, not that I heard of, and I think I'd know."

"Ever cross another vet? Or maybe she was engaged in a research project with commercial application. You know, like an injection to halt the progress of navicular."

He named a degenerative disease in a horse's hoof, often with multiple causes. The navicular bone rests on the back of the coffin joint. Oddly enough, for the condition is still poorly understood, the lameness almost always occurs in the front feet. Whoever solves the problems with navicular deserves the Nobel Prize.

"She'd be given samples of products. She'd give us some, but I don't think she was ever involved in a research project gone sour. She would have told us. Hope was usually forthcoming. She'd developed an interest in bourbon, partly because of her Japanese clients. This was a new thing—well, new to me. But I can't see where that would lead to peculiarity or perversion." She paused. "I'm going to miss her terribly."

"The divorce?"

"That's where everyone headed, and I know Sheriff Sidell

questioned her not-yet-ex-husband first. But no charges have been pressed."

Barry put down his fork. "That's not to say they won't be in the future if Ben Sidell finds more evidence against the husband."

"Paul does seem to be the most likely possibility."

"It could be something from her past that set her off. Perhaps she had a child out of wedlock when she was a teenager. The child finds her. As I said, strange things provoke people to commit strange deeds. In time, it will come out. It almost always does."

"I remember something my mother used to say: 'Everything matters but nothing makes sense.' "

"Your mother was a pistol. Chip off the old block." He smiled at her.

"Isn't it lovely to spend time with someone who knew people you knew, such as your parents, who have gone on? Much as I love Tootie and my juniors, there's a wealth of relationships in my life that I can't share."

"But you do."

"How?"

"By being you." He reached over to squeeze her hand, then dropped it. "Did I ever tell you that I first met Fonz in the courtroom?" He paused. "He's a Southside Virginia boy. Came up before me years ago on charges of being drunk and disorderly. He pleaded guilty. I liked him. I threw him in the can for a weekend and made him go to AA afterward. He dried out, stayed dry, and came to my office two years after the incident to thank me. Anyway, we've kept track of each other over the years. I was the one who actually recommended him to Mo Schneider. I figured Fonz could handle him."

"Such a shit Mo was." She reached in and took a dollar out of her pocket.

"What's that for?"

"The girls' kitty." She explained the kitty, then returned to Fonz. "At any rate, Mo did pay him well and Fonz made Mo look good with the hounds. Let me amend that: as good as Mo could possibly look." She stopped herself, turning to gaze directly at Barry. "You don't think Fonz killed Mo, do you?"

"And tied himself up?"

"Now, Barry, you're smarter than that. He could have had an accomplice who hit him over the head and then tied him up."

"There is that but, no, Fonz isn't a killer."

"Aren't we all?"

He thought about this a long time, long enough for Sister to refill the tall frosted tea glass. "Under the right circumstances, I think ninety-nine percent of us will kill. But there really are people who will not kill, regardless of provocation. Think of the Quakers."

"Or the Shakers."

"Right."

"What will become of Fonz, I wonder?"

"He'll find a good job with a hunt club if he's willing to move. I'll recommend him again if he asks. By the way, if you want those four couple of hounds, I can arrange for him to bring them to the Virginia Hound Show."

"Perfect. And Barry, I'll pay him for all this."

"Anyone who knows you knows that. I'll call him before I go back to Richmond."

"Thank you for securing those hounds for me," said Sister. "If you say they're good, they're good."

"Sweet flattery." He sighed. "As I age, I'm much better at recognizing flattery. When I was young, filled with typical male conceit, I believed it. Now I'm afraid I'm turning into an old bore."

"You're never boring. People truly want to know what you think, like Ray with the market. Some people are uncanny, and your legal experience plus all the backroom stuff from the Democratic Party in the good old days? There's a lot of gold there." She tapped her temple.

He smiled. "Yes, I suppose, but more and more I know I must leave this earth. I'm in rude good health, it's not that, but I *am* in my middle seventies. I can't live forever, nor do I wish to do so. But on the other hand, I so love life. I hate knowing I'm on the home stretch."

"I think of that, too. So I run harder. If I'm going, I'm going out a winner."

He laughed. "Hell, you came in a winner."

"Flattery will get you everywhere."

"My intent." He blushed.

"Speaking of Hope, do you really think most people have dark secrets or silly secrets?"

"I do."

"I do, too. Mine are more silly than dark, but secrets they will remain."

"Me, too. One of mine did come to light, though, when one of my old fraternity brothers unearthed a photo of when my pledge class was hazed and I was painted blue like a Pict, naked to boot."

"What's so bad about that?"

"My dick was so hard you could have done chin-ups on it." He laughed uproariously.

"One of those fraternity brothers must have looked good."

"Well, I was drunk; I don't remember any of those brothers looking that good. Nonetheless, imagine if that photo had been available on the Internet when I was in my glory?"

"Imagine the Internet when we were both in our glory."

"Now there is a scary thought."

The evening glowed, richer and warmer, until the two of them landed in Sister's bed.

She awoke the next morning, made them both breakfast, and kissed him goodbye. He'd be discreet. He knew she was seeing someone. She knew the pull of old friends was powerful and sometimes sexual. Sister felt no guilt, but she truly didn't want Gray to find out.

She now had her own new secret.

CHAPTER 9

Putting a gun to the roof of one's mouth and pulling the trigger creates an extremely unpleasant sight for anyone coming into contact with the corpse.

When Sheriff Ben Sidell viewed Hope Rogers at the coroner's, he was surprised at how recognizable she was. Often people intending to kill themselves get a little shaky at the last moment. But Hope must have had a steady hand. She aimed straight up and slightly back. Neither of her eyes popped out, her teeth stayed intact, but the back of her head was shattered.

Ben had questioned Hope's husband. Paul had said he'd spent the night with his new girlfriend. Granted, she might be lying for him, but Ben thought not.

Over time in law enforcement he'd learned to read people.

He could be fooled, anyone can, but he was fooled far less than most other people.

Friday, May 30, he stopped by the kennels on his way back from Roger's Corner, a crossroads sporting a convenience store and little else. Someone had cut the lock on the outdoor ice dispenser and stolen half the ice. As crimes go, this one smacked of someone wanting to party who lacked sufficient funds. The culprit had tried to break into the store but the alarm had sounded.

Like Hansel and Gretel, a trail of beer cans would have led the way. Pity those children didn't drink beer because birds wouldn't eat the cans as they'd eaten the bread crumbs.

Sooner or later, Ben would find who did it, although the ice would be long gone. Meanwhile, he had more pressing matters to attend to, such as finding Sister Jane.

"Shaker, how are you?" Ben walked to the girls' yard, which Shaker was picking clean.

"Fine. Yourself?"

"Good. Is the master about?"

"She's over at Skidby, and then she's going to stop at Tatten-hall Station to see how Kasmir is coming along."

"I'll catch up with her there." He noticed six youngsters in the side yard. "Is that the second *T* litter? Can't believe how they've grown."

"Thimble, Tattoo"—Shaker pointed to a fellow with a sickle tail, a conformation flaw but it was a long way from the hound's nose—"Tootsie, Trooper, Taz, and Twist."

"Coming on, are they?"

"We'll see. Boss and I will hunt them here on the farm midcubbing. We'll go from there. The *G* litter will hunt from the get-go."

"That's a beautiful litter of hounds, the *G*s."

"Sure is. Boss told me this morning we'll be taking four couple of hounds from Mo Schneider's pack."

"Isn't that the man who was found on a track outside of Lexington, Kentucky?"

"Yes."

"A most unusual death."

"He deserved it." Shaker smiled.

"You know, I'd be out of work if people didn't rob, bludgeon, cut up, and kill one another. The Schneider case is one I'd like to have." He paused. "Not that I wish such a death on anyone here."

"There's one or two we could say goodbye to without tears." Shaker smiled again.

"And the rat shot. There's a message in that rat shot."

"Closer to home, do you think Hope Rogers's death was by her own hand?"

"Yes, I do, but that's why I stopped by. Sister called me about it yesterday, and she's far from convinced. If anyone can approach Hope's death from a different angle, it will be our master."

"Part fox, the boss." Shaker leaned on his rake.

"What do you think, Shaker?"

"I can't see any reason why Hope would take her own life, and I've known her for years." He shrugged. "But maybe I didn't know her as well as I thought."

"We could say that about any one of us." Ben shaded his eyes. "Good to see you."

"Same here. Hey, are you going to ride first flight next season?"

"Well. . . ."

"Come on, Ben. You're the sheriff. You need to go first flight."

"Better start back with my lessons." His farewell smile was rueful.

After leaving the kennels, Ben drove toward Paradise. Then at Chapel Cross he hooked left on the secondary road, heading west along hunt club fixtures until he came to Skidby, an eight-hundred-acre estate bordering Little Dalby, and stopped at the old Skidby sign, a faded blue unicorn on a white background.

If Sister could add this to the existing fixtures in the western part of her territory, she'd have a block totaling about eleven thousand acres, a great triumph for any master.

He sat by the sign, waiting. No need to intrude on her chatting up Mitch and Lutrell. Apart from the occasional squawk on the two-way radio, the quiet afforded him time to think.

Twenty minutes later, on her way out, Sister saw him1 sitting there and stopped.

Ben hopped out of the car and walked over to the driver's window. "I can't get used to seeing you in the Forester."

"It's a good little machine. I'm glad I finally pulled the money out of my purse to buy it. I didn't even suffer buyer's remorse." She smiled. "What are you doing out here?"

"Waiting for you."

"Problem?"

"No, I need your wisdom."

"Oh, honey, my wisdom is in short supply." She smiled. "I'm waiting."

"Do you think Hope Rogers killed herself?"

"No."

"Why?"

"First of all, she was angry, not depressed. She would have killed Paul before killing herself. Second, she loved her work. She really had no compelling reason."

"I viewed her body. The splatter report is consistent with someone shooting herself."

"That still doesn't mean she did it. If someone with medical or police knowledge killed her, he would know exactly how to make it look like a suicide."

"There was no struggle. No alcohol or drugs in her system."

"Yes, but we had that terrible storm. She might not have heard someone come in. The power was out, too, remember. The generator cut on in the operating room but she cut it off afterward. No lights. Black as the devil's eyebrows. If her killer had a pin light, he or she could have quickly rolled her over before she was fully awake and done the deed. I haven't one skinny fact to support my theory, but if nothing else I want to clear Hope's name, so to speak. To die by one's own hand is a terrible thing."

"Maybe she had reasons of which we are unaware."

"That's what Barry Baker suggested yesterday."

"Shrewd judge, Baker." Ben knew of the judge's reputation.

"He is, and so are you."

She smiled at him and Ben, although only in his thirties,

could see the allure that drove men to make fools of themselves over Sister Jane.

"Barry said we all carry secrets, usually about money or sexual perversions or even some desire to take revenge on someone who has humiliated us. He was more eloquent than I am about this, and he said, How can any of us be sure that Hope didn't have a heavy secret she couldn't shoulder anymore?"

"Sister, all we have is a death that is consistent with suicide."

"But Ben, I thought killing oneself with a gun was the male way out. Women take poison."

"Times are changing. Feminism has had all kinds of effects, and women being more aggressive in all directions is one. Granted, fewer women pull the trigger than men but more do than in the past."

"Do they tend to be younger? I mean, if a woman my age were going to commit suicide, would she not be more likely to poison herself or take an overdose?"

"Yes." He put his hands on the windowsill. "Paul looks to be in the clear."

"Figured that."

"Did you suspect him?" Ben crossed his arms over his chest but dropped them down again. His shoulders started aching; he couldn't find a comfortable position.

"No. The man's a complete wimp. That's why she finally divorced him." Sister blinked. "That doesn't sound right, does it? Am I saying a real man would kill his wife?"

"No. I don't take it that way."

"It's easier to live with a man you respect but don't love than to live with a man you love but don't respect. Speaking of love, how are you doing with Margaret DuCharme?"

Margaret DuCharme was a highly successful sports physician. Pro football teams recommended her to players who had shredded knees and shoulders. She never lacked for patients.

"Love's a big word. I think I'm on second base. She spends as much time with me as she can. We laugh all the time together."

"You're good for Margaret. I've known her since she was born. She's the reserved type. The poor kid has been a go-between since she arrived. Her father and uncle, while I like them both, have perfected immaturity. I believe one will die before talking to the other, and I expect the surviving brother will not attend the funeral."

"Families."

"Heaven or hell. But I'm delighted that things are going well with Margaret. She's a good woman as well as a pretty one."

"Shaker told me, to change the subject, that you're on your way to Tattenhall Station."

"I am. Come with me."

"Meet you there. Before we go, will you do me one big favor? Will you find out if, over the years, there have been crimes at hound shows? Maybe covered up by the old boys' network?"

"I can try, but I'm not part of that network."

Twenty minutes later, they pulled into the parking lot of the old C&O train station.

"When did he paint this?" Ben got out of the squad car.

Sister joined him. "The community painted it two years ago,

but you know Kasmir, everything has to be sparkling. He's building up on the rise; the view is commanding. This really is the perfect location for him. The Vajays' farm is across the road. Did you know he's put in an offer on Faith's farm?"

The Vajays, from northern India, were good friends of Kasmir Barbhaiya, also from India.

"When did he do that?"

"Last week."

Ben rubbed his chin as they walked behind the station, heading up the rise to the building site. "What's he going to do with it?"

"Entice his relatives to live here. If that fails, he wants to put a farm manager there. And he's determined to refurbish the station. If his relatives don't come, the manager can live here."

"And if the manager lives at Faith's?"

Sister stepped over an upturned rock. "He says he'll know when he knows." She stopped a moment. "Here's the best part. You have to let him show you where he wants to put a ha-ha."

"What the hell is a ha-ha?"

"A stout fence on one side of a ditch."

"Good God." Ben's eyes grew large.

"They jump them all the time in the grass country of England and in Ireland. Well, I expect we'll be jumping them here, too. Never too late to learn."

"Anyone ever tell you you have ice water in your veins?" They had reached the top of the rise where the building site was already cleared. Kasmir was directing three men in work clothes.

"Not in so many words." She waved at the personable Kasmir. "I brought company."

. . .

Two hours later an overinformed but highly entertained Sister and Ben arrived back at their vehicles.

"Best thing to happen to this hunt club in years, that man." Sister beamed.

"I think he has more money than Crawford Howard." Ben named an ex-member and Sister's current nemesis, after a nasty run-in over the treatment of one of Sister's hounds.

"There are different kinds of best things. Money's always good, but people who give with their hearts are even better. Most of our members are those kind of people. Givers."

"Forgot to ask while on the subject of giving. Skidby?"

The biggest grin crossed her face. "Yes."

When Sister reached home, a huge floral display had been left in the mudroom. Fortunately, Golly hadn't gone in. She had a habit of tasting flowers. If they weren't what she liked she simply pulled them out.

Sister checked the water, then placed the flowers on the coffee table in the den.

She tucked the card into her jeans pocket.

It read:

> To whom thy secret thou dost tell,
> to him thy freedom thou dost sell.
> —BENJAMIN FRANKLIN

She knew Barry had sent them. She thought it funny that he was counseling her to keep last night secret. But then he might well have a lover in Richmond, so he had his own reason to keep their pleasurable evening private.

CHAPTER 10

On Sunday, June 1, the day of the Virginia Hound Show, over one thousand foxhounds appeared at Westmoreland Mansion in northern Virginia, escorted by a phalanx of humans. Huntsmen, masters, kennelmen, moonlighting show-ring handlers—all devoted themselves to these extraordinary canines.

People flocked from different parts of the United States, Canada, and the United Kingdom, although *united* was a misnomer. All the animosities held somewhat in check since the eighteenth century had opened once again. Would hounds and hunting be valued in Ireland? Surely the Irish wouldn't shoot themselves in the foot as the English had under the sway of Labour. After betraying their followers on so many other issues, they threw them the bone of a ban on hunting. As for Scotland, foxhunting was banned in theory, but the Scots had long displayed a healthy disregard for rules, as the Romans found out two thousand years ago. Despite all this turmoil, hound people crossed the Atlantic just as Americans crossed to visit the European shows, regardless of political differences.

A few French citizens came. Once upon a time the various duchies of France each bred hounds, which they hunted with pride. Kings kept huge kennels. But France paid dearly in World War I, when thousands of lives had been lost, hound as well as human. The canine hunting population never quite recovered from that first gruesome bugle call of the twentieth century. Still, away from Paris there remained people who cherished a beautiful hound.

Germany, too, lost thousands of hounds and horses. Europe, like Chronos, devoured its children in the twentieth century, both the bipeds and the quadripeds.

Perhaps a few people with a view toward history—and what are bloodlines but history?—still considered what happened to the long-standing traditions of hunting Over There.

Sister often thought of it. If she saw a bluetick hound, she wondered if it carried Blue Gascon blood; could the blood be traced back to Lafayette's gift of a pack to his hero and hers, George Washington? And those sleek ring-necked Orange County hounds, did they carry a hint of redbone or was the blood really from the Talbot tan packs of Olde England?

Overwhelmed by all the incredible animals to study, she felt dizzy as she stood under the shade at the American hound ring.

As a long-serving master, she spent hours that morning saying hello, catching up, all the while wearing her kennel coat, washing hounds, wiping down leads, and telling Tootie to just go out and do her best.

Shaker, too, kept busy. This time they had Valentina and Betty along. Finally finished with her term paper, Val had eagerly hopped into the Forester. She would also be showing hounds.

Tootie showed Giorgio. Dog hound classes always preceded female hound classes, and Giorgio came in second, to Jefferson Hunt's great joy. Fred Duncan, former huntsman at Warrenton and now head kennelman at Middleburg, strode over to Sister, long legs covering the distance in the blink of an eye. He leaned his shoulder on hers—he was a bit taller—and whispered in her ear, "I'm seventy-three. You know, seen a lot."

She nodded. "We share that."

"And I'm telling you"—his voice was low, quite distinctive— "that young'un is a natural. A real natural."

"I know."

"Doris agrees." He nodded at his wife, dressed in a cool linen shirt and blouse. "She said, Let's pray this kid goes into hunt service."

"I don't know, Fred. Her father is hell-bent on her being the next Condoleezza Rice. She goes to Princeton mid-August for orientation, but I have her until then."

"The blonde girl is good, too, but this pint-sized kid"—he smiled broadly—"must be part hound herself."

"Thanks, Fred. You know I prize my juniors." She thought a moment as hounds were taken off lead in the ring. "Actually, I prize all my members." He raised his eyebrows. "I said I prized them, not that I like all of them."

"There's an honest opinion." He put his arm around her

waist and gave her a squeeze. "Glad you got your hound back. That is one man I won't miss."

"Me neither. I rest a little easier at this show knowing Mo's not here. However, just in case there's another creep lurking around, someone will be near the Jefferson trailer at all times."

"Good thinking." He noticed Doris waving and added, voice low, "My bride needs me." Married fifty-two years, Fred and Doris remained wild for each other.

As the lovely man walked away, Sister wondered what it would be like to still have Ray.

If life is a necklace, each year a pearl, Sister figured she wore an invisible double strand of nine millimeter pearls. Her years were her wealth.

The heat rose and clouds began to pile up in the west. If they could get through this show before a thunderstorm, it would be a miracle. She looked around at the people fanning themselves and watched the judges, all of them outstanding people. These people, these hounds, this event was the string on which those pearls were set.

What would she have become had she not been a master? A profession shapes you over the years until you transform into someone perhaps deeper or perhaps more shallow than you were when you started.

Whatever their individual faults, she recognized that all these people crowding the four rings shared a passion for hounds and, most likely, hunting.

A life without passion isn't worth living. A terribly sophisticated urban person might look scornfully at this gathering, but she hoped not. Or if that person did, Sister at least hoped he or she had a passion. A human being without an emotional force divorced from money and material goods is a sorry soul indeed.

These thoughts flitted through her head as the judges made their selections and the crowd at the American ring applauded. As it turned out, Grant Fuller was handling the winning hound. He smiled broadly. Spectators knew hounds at this show. If they disagreed with the judges they withheld their applause. Sometimes the roar for the second pick would shake the leaves on the trees. Judges couldn't help but notice.

"Master." Tootie slipped next to her.

"Oh." Sister put her hand on Tootie's shoulder. "Lost in reverie there."

"Val and I don't show until the gyps. Would you mind if we walked along the tents?"

"Go ahead. Be careful your credit card doesn't burn a hole in your pocket."

"I'm pretty disciplined, but"—Tootie smiled shyly— "sometimes a girl can't help it." She'd picked up that phrase from Betty. "Val and I are looking for something for Felicity's baby. 'Course, we don't know the sex yet, but maybe we can find a stuffed toy fox or something."

"Bet you can. Go on, honey."

As hounds exited the ring, Sister walked back to the trailer. It was half a mile away, but she wanted to sit quietly with Shaker and Betty for a spell. Much as she adored seeing old friends, the frenzy wore her out. Physical activity rarely tired her as much as people.

All along the way she stopped folks or was stopped by them. News about hounds, horses, members. Quite a few people remarked on Mo Schneider's murder.

O.J. and Woodford brought a few hounds. In the moments between classes, O.J., who stayed in constant touch with Sister, again confirmed that nothing new had turned up regarding Mo's murder, other than that it appeared to be the work of a single person.

It took her a half hour to get back to the trailer parked under giant trees. Shaker had put up the big awning and was sitting in its shade.

Betty Franklin set out a table. If anyone trotted over for a chat, there'd be drinks, sandwiches, and treats. Her setup complete, Betty fanned herself with a big palm frond fan, the kind that used to be passed out in church before air-conditioning.

Sister laughed as she strode toward them. "Have you had that fan since childhood?"

"Don't start with me. I'm sweating bullets. The air is stagnant and it's working on my mood." Betty tossed her hair, perfectly frosted for the occasion.

"Well, you look cool enough. You, too, Shaker." She filled them in on the classes she'd watched. "Pretty much going as you would expect. The big hunts are pulling in most ribbons. But every now and then a smaller hunt wins a blue."

"Damn hard to go up against a hunt that can breed seventy puppies or more a year." Shaker leaned back in his chair.

"Yeah, but thank God for those hunts. They really carry the ball for the rest of us. If we put twenty puppies on the ground, that's a hell of a lot for us. We have to be so incredibly careful in our breeding." Sister flopped into a master's director's chair.

The chair, a gift from Betty, sure felt good.

"Tired?" Betty inquired.

"Yes, I'm tired, and my feet hurt."

"Funny, we can ride hard for four hours in sleet or snow, but it's a different kind of tired. I've seen a lot of people I want to see and a few I could pass on." Betty fanned herself more vigorously. "This weather is going to break before the pack class. I guarantee it."

The pack class, last class of the day, involves different hunts walking their hounds as a pack and following directions from the judges as to where to stop, turn, etc. Always the highlight of the show, it not only illustrates pack discipline but shows a lot about the various huntsmen and masters. Some behave graciously if they lose, maybe because one hound hooked left instead of right. Others, petulant, would fit right into sixth grade.

"You told me it's the Feast of the Visitation," said Betty. "Any other saints celebrating today?"

"Feast of Saint Peter's supposed daughter, Petronilla."

"Saint Peter had a daughter?" Betty, never a religious student, raised her fan slightly.

"Well, no. Or let's say the paternity is in doubt. The story goes that Petronilla was an early Roman martyr. Her remains are in the catacomb of the Domitilla family. She fasted and died after three days."

"Fad diet?" Shaker teased.

"Could be. Nothing is new under the sun. Well, a Count Flaccus wanted to marry her, against her wishes. With a name like that, I'd have my doubts, too." Sister laughed. "So she starved herself. Her emblem is a set of keys, just like Saint Peter's. Did she borrow them, or was Petronilla light-fingered?"

Out of the corner of her eye, Sister saw a familiar elegant figure approaching, accompanied by a smaller, less confident man.

"Hello, Master." Barry Baker reached Sister, bent over, and kissed her hand, then repeated the gesture for Betty.

Shaker stood and the men shook hands. "Good to see you."

Fonz and Shaker exchanged a nod.

"Come on. Let's get those hounds," said Barry.

Sister and Shaker followed; Betty stayed behind to keep an eye on things.

They reached Mo's fancy trailer, with its comfortable living quarters for people as well as hounds.

"How'd you get the trailer back so fast, Fonz?" Knowing the glacial rate at which official business can be transacted, Sister was astounded.

"Judge Baker talked to the Lexington people," said Fonz.

The corner of Barry's mouth turned up slightly. "I told them they'd know where to find it."

If Barry Baker asked a favor, he usually got it.

Fonz opened the back door, and the hounds walked out as he called their names one by one. "This is Moxie; she's got Mission Valley blood, but at the fifth generation it's Bywaters. This is Tillie; she's shy."

A thunder rumble interrupted his introduction.

"Fonz, let's walk these hounds back quickly, and once we're in the trailer we can worry about introductions." Shaker knew how fast storms rolled in.

"Splendid idea." Barry walked to the other side of the opened door.

Once the four couple of hounds stood outside the trailer, Barry closed the door and Fonz, walking at the head of the small pack with Shaker, quietly led them a quarter mile through a parking lot up to the shaded Jefferson Hunt trailer.

Sister fell in behind the pack with Barry. "Thank you for the beautiful flowers."

"You're worth a greenhouse." He beamed. "And I knew you'd like the quote from Ben Franklin."

She noticed that hounds accepted Barry. No queer looks at him.

Tootie and Val, back with Betty, stood up to help.

"Think we've got it, girls," Shaker called to them.

Fonz opened the door, called each hound by name. Shaker had jumped into the trailer and closed a divider so the new hounds wouldn't mix with the JHC pack. No point in having a fight, especially when the atmospheric pressure was changing, which can cause tempers to fray. The girls each brought two big buckets of water, and within minutes all hounds were settled, although black noses were thrust under the divider, which did not entirely touch the floor.

A grumble echoed.

"Dragon." Shaker's voice, clipped, meant business.

"That litter is quite exceptional, isn't it?" Barry asked. "*D*s."

"Hunting fools." Sister smiled, ever ready to discuss a hound. "They show well, but I don't think we'll win any ribbons. They're a bit long-backed."

"Depends on the class." Barry was encouraging. "And I don't mind a long-backed hound. Again, what's the territory like? Oh, well, I ought to shut up. I'm not judging. No pun intended."

Sister said to Fonz, "I'm sure you're sorry to say goodbye to these hounds."

Fonz shrugged, holding back his emotion. "They're good hounds. I will miss them but they're going to the right person."

"Thank you." Sister took his hand in hers. "I'm glad you've recovered from your ordeal."

"Wish I could remember. I felt a thump on my head and next woke up at Keeneland."

A terrific crack of thunder made everyone jump.

"Here." Fonz thrust hound paperwork, in a smudged envelope, into Sister's hands.

"We're literally going to run, because I need to catch up with Mason Lampton." Barry mentioned the former president of the MFHA, a man bursting with conviviality and fearless on a horse.

As the two men ran across the lawn, Sister watched them just make it to the winding path up past the tents when one monster drop fell. Betty and the girls were already packing up the food and quickly putting it in the back of the Forester. Shaker hopped into the trailer with the JHC hounds. Sister slid in the back to stay with Mo's hounds. Another splat hit the roof, then another and another. Betty and the girls ducked into the SUV and no sooner had Betty closed the driver's door than rain fell, beating like thousands of snare drums.

Sister shouted through the divider, trying to make herself heard above the din and the fan. "Good Lord, if this keeps up we'd better build an ark."

"They okay?" Shaker called.

"Doing quite well for being in a strange trailer with a strange woman in the middle of a terrifying thunderstorm."

Ten minutes passed but the rain kept coming. If anything, it intensified. Then the wind rose.

Shaker called out again. "I'm soaked."

"Me, too."

The trailer had long narrow openings near the roof to facilitate air flow. In winter, Shaker would slide heavy clear plastic panels in to close them up.

"Wish I'd turned off the generator," he remarked.

"No time." She shivered. "Temperature's dropping."

"I know. The soil up here is really good, but there's no way those rings can drain fast enough. Hounds will be wading."

Sister laughed. "We'll find out who is afraid of water. Actually, it's hardest on the high desert hounds. They don't see these conditions, and they're used to running on sand or rock. Boy, you've got to have the nose for that territory."

"Got to see it one day."

"We will. The trick is getting the rest of the club to go. A joint meet would be fun with Red Rock in Reno." She waited a moment. "That assumes we survive this storm."

A loud crack and pink lightning rocked the trailer. A small gyp jumped on Sister, nearly knocking her down. Since she was already wet and becoming bedraggled, Sister sat down on a ramp as she hugged hounds close to her.

"You all right?"

"Yeah. You?"

"Yeah. Pink. That strike was pink!"

"Read somewhere that lightning can hit four miles from the storm. Sky might be clear over your head, but *whammo!*"

"Bet it hurts like hell." Shaker shivered.

"Jeez, is this ever going to let up?"

"Has to eventually. I envy Betty and the girls in the Forester."

"We'll get them for this." He laughed.

"Did you bring extra clothes?" Sister asked.

"A shirt. The kennel coats are in the tack room. At least they'll be dry. You bring anything extra?"

"Sweater. Damn, I hate this. The pack class, if the show can resume, won't even go off until after sundown."

She was right about that, for the storm raged on, bringing tree limbs down.

The Virginia Foxhound Club, sponsor of the Virginia Hound Show, had dealt with many an emergency in the past. Once the storm blew farther east, they rapidly assessed the damage and cleared debris from the rings. Why the electric lines didn't come down onto the mansion was a miracle. Even so, it took another hour for the show to continue.

The bitches worked ankle deep in water but being foxhounds—which is to say, naturally cheerful and intelligent creatures—they showed to advantage.

Val showed Diana in single bitch entered, and she swept the ring. Shoes wet, Val strode out, beaming.

Sister and Shaker commended her. "Good work."

Tommy Lee Jones, showing an elegant young bitch, came in second. He came up to Val, Sister, Shaker, and Tootie on the sidelines. "What a wonderful hound. And you did a very good job showing her."

"Thank you, Mr. Jones." Val blushed.

Tommy Lee then focused on Tootie, holding a pair of *G* girls to go in for the pairs class. "You ready?"

"I am."

"I'll see you in the ring then." He smiled again.

As he walked away, Val whispered to the little group, "He's so nice. I beat his hound, and he's so nice."

Sister nodded. "Val, that's one of the best hound men that's ever been born. He loves a good hound. He's actually happy that Diana is a great one. Tommy Lee doesn't have to win. He knows if hounds are fine, we all win."

"Not everyone is like that." Shaker's mouth turned up on one side as Grant Fuller entered the ring with his pair. "Didn't mean Grant. He's okay." Then he laughed. "Selling dog food but, hey, the stuff is good."

Tootie, now in the ring against Grant, Tommy Lee, and other exceptional huntsmen and handlers, thought she had no chance of getting pinned, but Glitter and Gorgeous, although toeing in the tiniest bit, were marvelously well made. The slope of their shoulders allowed them to reach out fully yet effortlessly. Their hindquarters, powerful but not chunky, added to the fluidity of their movement. They weren't as broad in the chest as Sister liked, but truly they were glamour girls.

Tommy Lee smiled as he showed his girls.

Grant followed him, huffing a little as he trotted with hounds.

"Good class," Judge Barry Baker, now up with Sister and Shaker, observed.

"Yep," came the terse reply from both adults.

As it turned out, Tootie, Glitter, and Gorgeous took third, Grant came in second, and Tommy Lee won the class—or, more specifically, the perfectly matched littermates from Casanova kennels took the blue.

The mercury never did come back up. Sister was glad of her light sweater, but her legs started to ache with the cold.

Twilight graced the rich green grounds. Fireflies emerged to attend the show. Finally, the pack class went off, despite the fact that some of the last entrants would be working in the dark.

All competing packs were to work the same course, now dotted with water. Led by huntsmen and accompanied by whippers-in, the hounds went through on cue. They checked, waited, and then moved on, often working in a figure eight. At one spot, near a huge old holly tree, the pack reversed. Their pace changed, finishing up with a lively run, the humans doing their best to keep up.

Watching a pack class was always the highlight for Sister. She enjoyed seeing if hounds were tuned in to their huntsmen. Then, too, different huntsmen liked whippers-in at different positions.

Potomac, so far, had been thrilling. Not a false move on the part of the two-legged or four-legged group.

"Sister, if I work really hard, maybe someday you'll let Shaker, Betty, and me go in the pack class," said Tootie.

"We'll see. Best graduate from Princeton first." She put one arm around Tootie's shoulders, then flung her other arm around Val on her left.

Sister loved her girls.

Betty sighed. "If I have to go out there with you, Tootie, I'll need to run to get in shape."

"You walk hounds five days a week." Sister was incredulous.

"If I'm going to show myself on foot before all these people, I want to look like a goddess." Betty teased.

Val, ever the politician, murmured, "You already are."

Betty, not one to be sidetracked, giggled. "Which one, Hecuba?"

"Oh, Betty." Sister dropped her arm from Tootie and Val's shoulders to reach over and give Betty a pinch.

Judge Barry Baker, standing near the judges for the hound pack, watched the action with rapt gaze.

"One hundred percent attention," Shaker commented, on Barry and the working pack.

Bits of brightness from firefly abdomens punctuated the light. Lanterns and flashlights pulled together were held by the stewards of all the rings. The last pack to show would have a rough go. There weren't enough flashlights to cover the large area.

The judges waited. The incoming pack wasn't in sight.

Finally, a steward, Sherry Buttrick, an ex-MFH, hopped in a golf cart to see if she couldn't push up the master and hounds.

Stalls could be rented for the show, and Stone Mountain, the hunt in question, had leased one, unlike Jefferson Hunt, which used their trailer.

Sherry, tiny, efficient, and good at herding people along, cut the motor. No master or whippers-in appeared. The other hunts who had rented stable space had already packed up their hounds.

"Anyone home?" Sherry called, as she entered the stable. The lights were off. That was strange, she thought. She hit the switch by the entrance door. "Yoo-hoo!"

Dammit. She knew for sure she was facing some sort of problem.

She reached the stall. Hounds, groomed and sleek, looked at her.

"Anyone home?"

"Nope." A tricolor dog hound replied.

Sherry walked the length of the stable, checking every single stall: nothing amiss. She thought she'd better check the restroom in the next building and ran over, ducking under the dripping eaves.

Stopping at the door marked MEN she rapped. Nothing. Tentatively, she opened the door and checked: nothing.

Not a person given to fancy or wild flights of imagination, Sherry felt a creeping unease. She ran back to the stable.

Carefully opening the door, she spoke kindly to the hounds. As the pack moved about, she noticed a wallet on the floor. Without thinking, she picked it up.

It was Grant Fuller's, filled with cash and credit cards. However, Grant had been helping Hillsboro Hounds, not Stone Mountain.

She flipped open the mobile phone and called the judge. "We've got a problem."

After explaining the dilemma, she clicked off the phone. It was then that she cursed herself because she realized she'd put her fingerprints all over the well-worn leather. There wasn't a doubt in Sherry Buttrick's mind that this could be a problem.

Within a few minutes a bedraggled Stone Mountain whipper-in ran to the stall.

"What's going on?" Sherry demanded.

"Edwards had an angina attack," Miriam, his whipper-in, informed her. "Did we miss the pack class?"

"Yes."

"Damn."

"Where's Grant Fuller?" Sherry asked.

"I don't know. He's got nothing to do with us."

Edwards, with the help of his wife, a nurse, who was the other whipper-in, managed to get through his angina attack.

Grant Fuller, however, had vanished into thin air—or, in this case, thick, moist air.

CHAPTER 11

To be foxhunters, humans, hounds, and horses need to be physically tough, possess stamina, and exhibit a healthy sense of humor. The horses seem to have the best senses of humor, knowing exactly when to discomfit their rider to achieve maximum humiliation.

Gunpowder, old but still fit and strong, was healing rapidly. The swelling was down and he was bored shitless standing in a stall, so bored he kicked the walls, despite his injury, and was all the more furious when he couldn't chew on the stall doors or windows; they had iron bars. He tried one chomp, which put an end to that.

Since no one rushed to baby him, he thought screaming might help. It did.

Dan Clement called Sister, informing her that Gunpowder

was recovering enough to be ugly. He'd still need to finish his antibiotic cycle, but please could she carry him home?

Although tired from Sunday's events at the hound show, Sister pulled the rig out but then thought better of taking off alone. She might need Shaker just in case Gunpowder decided not to be grateful for her efforts to save him.

Shaker cut off the power hose, changed from his wellies to his trusty old mulehide Justin boots, and hopped in next to the boss.

The big diesel engine of the dually rumbled as they pulled out of the circular drive at the stable.

"I still can't believe a deluge worthy of Noah about washed us away up at Morven and here not a drop." Sister shifted up.

"Central Virginia has its own weather system."

"Well"—Sister was fascinated by weather—"Virginia truly is the buffer between north and south. Our swath here in the country is the true boundary between two different weather cycles, soil differences, crop possibilities. Lakes of air jam up next to the mountains, then slide off, hit Hangman's Ridge, creep over, and slide down to us before heading east. I mean, we could have a weather report just for us."

"It *is* strange," said Shaker. "Twenty miles south of here they can grow Bermuda grass and it will winter through. We can't. Twenty miles north and they can plant certain kinds of alfalfa and orchard grass that would burn to a crisp here in the summer."

"We've been pretty lucky with the alfalfa and orchard grass. I study those seed catalogs."

"I don't have the patience for it. Hounds use up all my patience." He settled back in the comfortable seat. "Nothing more about Grant Fuller?"

"Nope. Barry called this morning. The sheriff's department hasn't found him; his car sits in the parking lot. No crime has been committed." She breathed deeply. "They say." She downshifted for the sharp curve ahead. "Very weird. Two bizarre occurrences at hound shows."

"I'm glad we're not going to Bryn Mawr's show—just in case." Shaker sighed.

"You know, I am, too." Sister pulled around behind the stables and cut the motor. "Shaker, it's going to be strange without Hope."

Dan Clement walked out from the stables. Sister had called before leaving.

"Dan, how are you doing?" She hugged him.

"I feel like I'm sleepwalking." He hugged her in return. "Lisa's been great. Our clients have, too. Every equine vet in central Virginia has called to help with the workload, and Reynolds Cowles"—he named a prominent equine vet—"gave me the name of a young vet just out of Auburn who might be worth hiring." His eyes moistened. "People have just been wonderful." He grabbed Shaker's extended hand, and the two men hugged briefly. "Well, come on. He's ready to go and I'm ready to see the last of those hindquarters."

The second Gunpowder heard Sister and Shaker's voices, he started complaining. *"You're here. At last you're here. I want to blow this joint!"*

Dan had already put on the Thoroughbred's halter. He walked in the stall with the cotton lead rope, easier on the hands, snapped the hook into the ring—and Gunpowder tried to pull him out of the stall.

Quick as a cat, Shaker grabbed the dangling end of the lead rope. "Where are your manners?"

"I want to go home." Gunpowder dropped his head, pushed Shaker, and then reached over to nuzzle Sister.

As he walked toward the trailer, Sister bent her knees to look at the wound. "Amazing."

Dan said, "He's an amazing horse. Do you know his bloodlines?"

"I do. Ultimately they trace back to Domino, a stallion at the turn of the last century. It's staying blood. Now I'm not saying that all you need is Domino in the pedigree, but if you do your homework you can find who carried it, over the last century plus. If you keep weaving together the traits that impart stamina, soundness, and—hopefully—brains, you'll get a great horse."

"A science"—Dan paused—"and an art. He's being a lamb now." Then he laughed. "Glad I don't have to throw a leg over him."

Inside the trailer, windows open, Shaker tied a slip knot by the hay bag. "He's a great ride, Dan. Bold. Not a chicken bone in his body."

"That's the truth," Gunpowder said, with a mouth full of his favorite hay.

That was another thing, he was going to complain about the food at the clinic when he got a chance.

"Shaker, I'll be right back," Sister said. "Let me pay the bill."

"I'll bill you," Dan said.

"One less thing for you to do."

She walked into the front office, and as Lisa printed out the bill she noticed two cartons, opened, behind Lisa. She could see bottles inside.

"Are those for Hope's Japanese clients?"

Lisa nodded. "Had them all wrapped up, and Ben Sidell unwrapped everything. I'll put it all back together. They went through her house, and—I have to give them credit—they didn't make a mess. They put everything back. The only thing was, and I have no idea how they managed it, they spilled some ink from her big printer, the inkjet, you know. Well, it's not really ink, it's powder. But that was the only thing I had to clean up."

"Ben is very meticulous, but he's sensitive, too."

"And good-looking." Lisa, unmarried, was almost purring.

"That, too." Sister examined the bill, sighed, and wrote a check for sixty-three hundred dollars.

"It's a big bill, I know."

"He's worth it, and he had the best of care. Do I owe you anything for his damage to the stall?"

"He left hoof marks on the wall but those boards in there are thick." She laughed. "He's a pistol."

"Hey, do you mind if I look at the bourbon?"

"No. Hope was making quite a study of it."

"Yes, she gave us a little lesson out in Kentucky, and now I want to study it myself." Sister flipped up the divider and peered into the baskets, pulling out the limited edition of Maker's Mark. She noticed a smudge of red on the label but paid it no mind. "She certainly took good care of her patients, human and equine."

"She did."

"Lisa, I know all this has been hard on you. Let me know if you need anything."

Lisa cast her large eyes upward. "Thank you. I will." She paused, sucked in a deep breath. "I will never *ever* believe she took her own life."

"I won't either."

Once back at the farm, Sister and Shaker turned out Gunpowder. He'd had limited turnout at the clinic. Dan said he'd be stiff perhaps for six weeks but better off outside. Confinement brought

out the worst in him. Of course, Dan didn't know that it wasn't nervousness that kept Gunpowder from eating. He didn't care for the hay mix.

The gray stood in the field with his friends and, like any man of a certain age, began to declaim about his condition. *"The food was awful. They ran a tube up my leg after the first day. Then they finally took it out. The damned tube hurt more than the injury."*

HoJo, hanging over the fence—for he was in the adjoining pasture with another group of horses—commiserated. *"Must have been horrible. You like to eat."*

"Are you mocking your elders?" Gunpowder cocked his head.

Matador, Aztec, and Lafayette walked up, too.

"No. You have a good appetite." Aztec was glad to see Gunpowder home, even if the gray could be a pain sometimes.

"And I saw Hope's killer." He'd saved this tidbit. Everyone was gathered around.

"Who was it?" HoJo was bug-eyed with curiosity.

"I don't know. I only saw his back, and I'm pretty sure it was a man. I was coming out of the anesthesia so I probably missed a lot."

"But you could smell him. You'd recognize his scent," Matador remarked, also excited.

"I could smell oilskin and a funny food smell. He wore an Australian rain hat and long Outback coat. That was it, pungent oilskin."

"Did you tell the sheriff?" Keepsake asked.

Gunpowder snorted. *"As if it would do any good. They're all blistering idiots. Don't understand one thing we tell them."*

"Shaker and Sister aren't blistering idiots." Lafayette took slight offense.

Gunpowder stretched out his hind legs; it was a little stiff back there. *"No, they're functionally illiterate."*

Much as the horses did love the two humans, they couldn't help laughing.

Sister and Shaker, walking back to the kennels, heard the neighing.

"Glad to be home." Shaker smiled.

Not until cubbing season would Sister realize when she saw the smudge on the label that she'd drawn over her fox and hadn't even known he was there.

CHAPTER 12

June 7, Saturday, gleamed like a new penny. A light breeze on the soccer field accentuated the glorious sunshine of Commencement Day, and the mercury cooperated by hanging right at 70 degrees.

Sister sat on the dais with the other Custis Hall board members, including Crawford Howard. Naturally, they were civil to one another on this special occasion, despite their differences.

She wore her robes, the long hood signifying her discipline, which had been geology back when she taught at Mary Baldwin. The soft cap crowned her silver hair and she tried dutifully to listen to the drone of the various speakers, not one of whom possessed an original thought.

Charlotte Norton, the headmistress, was mercifully brief. She kept to the point, congratulating the graduates. The one good speech of the day came from Felicity, who had edged out Valentina by half a point in her grade average to become valedictorian. As her pregnancy had begun to show, she was grateful for the robe.

Felicity ended her seven-minute speech with, "No graduating class knows what the future will bring. We may live in peace or be at war. We will see medical breakthroughs yet suffer new lethal pestilence. We may learn to renew the earth's resources or kill one another for dwindling water and food. We don't know; we can't know. What we can do is remember what we learned here: Face life with courage, conviction, and compassion.

"Congratulations, Class of 2008! We'll always be Custis Hall girls, which means we'll always come through."

The large crowd of graduates, underclassmen, parents, and friends awarded her a standing ovation.

Sister thought Felicity's parents missed a fine valedictory. Their pigheadedness meant they'd miss more than that. However, Betty and Bobby Franklin, Tedi and Edward Bancroft, Sybil Fawkes, Shaker and Lorraine, Ronnie Haslip, Xavier, and his wife had all come to support a young person they all liked.

Her most enthusiastic supporter, apart from the Jefferson Hunt crowd, was Howie Lindquist. Felicity would be eighteen in three weeks and he would marry her then.

The graduates crossed the dais, where Charlotte handed each girl her diploma and said a few words. Off the young women walked, flipping their tassels to the other side of their mortar boards. Many cried.

Val winked at Sister, who winked back.

Pamela Rene actually cried, which surprised everyone, but she trooped off in style as her ever-glamorous mother watched and seemed actually to enjoy the moment.

Tootie received a huge cheer when she received her diploma, and as she walked by the board members she said to Sister, "Thank you."

The large quad filled with people after the outdoor ceremony. Under yellow and white striped tents, food, drinks, and gossip were in ample supply.

Marty Howard, who had slipped away from her husband, came up to Sister. "How are the hounds?"

"Oh, Marty, how good to see you! I miss you." Sister bent down to kiss her on the cheek. "Hounds are fine. How about yours?"

A long significant pause followed. "They're healthy."

"I see. Well, Marty, Dumfriesshire hounds are both handsome and willful. They'll only hunt for a strong huntsman. And remember, they're an English hound. They lack the nose of the American hound."

"I know." A sigh followed. "I'm working on Crawford. For one thing, he has to give up the idea that he can hunt them. For another, he needs to come back to the club."

"It'll take time. What can I do to sweeten the punch?"

"You've done as much as you can at this point. He dimly recognizes that you decked him for a good reason. He abused one of your hounds."

"The situation was tense. I might have satisfied myself with harsh language but—well"—Sister threw up her hands—"I did apologize for hitting him."

"He'll come around. Where's Gray?"

"Over there talking to Pamela Rene's parents. Her mother doesn't want her to go to Ol' Miss, and I guess her father isn't too thrilled either."

"Good for her." Marty liked a kid with spunk. "The farther she gets from Momma's talons, the better."

"Ain't that the truth."

Betty and Bobby joined them. "We miss you," both said.

"And I miss you guys." Marty, being from Indiana, did not use the southern plural, *you-all.*

"Wasn't Felicity's speech good?" Betty enthused.

"Yes. She's a very accomplished young lady," Marty replied. A pause followed. "I haven't spoken to anyone for such a long time. All the construction on the farm is time-consuming, and then we took a trip to Vienna, which I adore, but when I came back and heard about Hope Rogers, I couldn't believe it."

"Terrible thing." Bobby started to change the subject, feeling it best on this special occasion to focus on positive things.

Before the old friends could continue, Tootie came over with her parents, Jordon and Rebecca Harris.

Everyone said their hellos, and Jordon, impeccably dressed in clothes obviously made for him, beamed. "Thank you for taking such good care of our girl, Master. She speaks of you and the club constantly." He fished for a moment; then the name came. "Mrs. Franklin, Tootie says you're a wonderful . . . uh—"

"Whipper-in." Tootie finished the sentence for him.

"That's very flattering." Betty loved the praise.

"See, she doesn't talk about me at all." Bobby teased. "Never glances back at second flight."

"Mr. Franklin, you have the hardest job of all." Tootie liked having her parents with the other adults she admired.

"Why is that?" Rebecca, diminutive like her daughter and ravishingly beautiful, asked.

"He gets green horses, green riders, and sometimes both to-gether. It's not a pretty picture, Mom." Tootie laughed. "But he straightens them out, and pretty soon they're fine."

Val bounced up. "Princeton, here we come!"

Tootie smiled but clearly viewed this prospect with less en-thusiasm than the class president and salutatorian. "Black and orange."

"You'll look so-o-o good in those colors," Val teased.

Tootie's parents laughed. They knew Val. She'd visited on holidays and Tootie had gone to Val's home. Since their danger-ous adventure at Mill Ruins back in March when a mentally un-stable hunt club member had threatened their lives, the two had drawn even closer.

Felicity joined them, Howie in tow, which always irritated Val although she tried to cover it. "The kitty has come to a grand total of $1,022. One dollar even came from Sister."

"No shit!" Val exclaimed.

"Make that $1023," Felicity said.

Everyone laughed, but Val did reach up under her robe to pull a dollar from her shorts pocket. She'd worn shorts just for the hell of it, but Pamela, to everyone's surprise, had outdone Val by wearing a bathing suit under hers.

"Where are you girls going to have your thousand-dollar party?" Bobby asked. The Jefferson Hunt people all knew about the kitty, a dollar bigger each time one of the girls swore.

Val surprised everyone. "Let's not have a party."

"What?" Tootie put her hands on her hips.

"Felicity's the business brain. I vote for letting her invest the money. Ten years from now let's see what we've got."

"Will you do it?" Tootie asked Felicity.

"Yes."

"How simple is that?" Val smiled.

All three shook hands.

After the group dispersed, Gray escorted Sister back to his car, a big Toyota Land Cruiser and his pride and joy.

"Memories." He held her hand as they walked along the path lined with Victorian streetlamps.

The Custis Hall buildings were a mix of Federal and Victorian architecture. To the credit of those headmistresses who held the reins after World War II, none of the buildings looked overly modern. Every new structure conformed either to the Federal or to the Victorian style, so the campus seemed timeless, warm and very inviting.

Also to the credit of those headmistresses, including Charlotte Norton, the emphasis still remained on a strict education, not fads. A girl had to take a minimum of two years of Latin plus a modern language to graduate from Custis Hall. She had to study math all the way through solid geometry and trigonometry; a calculus course was available for those with further interest. The strongest emphasis was on character. A Custis Hall girl was expected to take responsibility for her actions, to help others, and to participate in her community. A bronze plaque on the wall of Old Main listed the names of those girls who had died in the various wars, usually as nurses but one as a transport pilot in World War II, two who died in Desert Storm, and three in Iraq, second war. Those girls had been killed in combat.

Although she had missed the wars, too young for World War II and Korea, too old for Iraq, the values of Custis Hall remained Sister's values. In the back of her mind she always wished she had gone to war: an odd wish, perhaps, but in keeping with her spirit and her curiosity to know if she would withstand it.

"Memories," Gray whispered again.

"So many." Her eyes glistened. "Field hockey. The show-jumping team. Hunting with Jefferson Hunt as a teenager. The huntsman was Garland Valentine; God how we flew. Garland looked like Cary Grant. I was a little too young to appreciate what an advantage that bestowed upon him with the ladies, single and married." She laughed.

"I bet. Most of your classmates are still around. The ceremonial dinner you-all had last night, class by class at tables, was damned impressive."

"The old girls look good, and some of their husbands don't look bad either." She watched a milk butterfly dance in the air. "My teachers here pounded on us. I'm grateful. We were taught to think for ourselves."

Suddenly Tootie, robe flapping behind her, raced up to Sister, flung her arms around her, and burst into tears.

"Honey, what's the matter?"

"I don't want to go to Princeton. I want to stay here. Oh, Sister, I want to learn to be a huntsman!"

Neither Gray nor Sister made light of this. Some people are born to be with animals regardless of other gifts. Remove them from their deepest love and they never blossom fully, although they might be very successful in the outside world.

Gray put his hands on Tootie's heaving shoulders. "Tootie, maybe there's a compromise."

She released Sister, who prudently fished in her handbag for a handkerchief.

"Really?"

"Have you mentioned this to your parents?" Gray, ever practical, asked.

"No. My father would kill me. He's set on me going to Princeton. Val would kill me, too."

"What about your mother?" Sister inquired.

"I've kind of mentioned it, but only a little. She's more flexible, but I know she'd be disappointed. I'll be the first one in our family to go to an Ivy League school."

Gray wrapped his arm around her waist. "How about this: Go to Princeton for one year, even if you hate it like milk of magnesia. Give it one full year. But this summer, work for the hunt club." He glanced at Sister. "The budget can handle it, don't you think?"

"I'll see that it does, if I have to sit on Ronnie."

Ronnie Haslip, the treasurer, guarded the hunt club money the way Cerberus is said to guard the passage to the Underworld.

"I'll have to ask Mom and Dad."

"Tell you what. We'll go with you." Sister sounded encouraging, so Tootie wiped her eyes.

They found Mr. and Mrs. Harris chatting with other parents at the tent housing the bar, which was becoming a bigger draw as the day went on.

Gray quietly suggested that they slip away for a moment. Then he presented Tootie's case as Sister watched in admiration.

Jordon listened intently. "Tootie, pardon my French, but what would you learn cleaning up dog shit? And I'm nervous about what's been happening at the hound shows. I want you safe."

Tootie fought her emotions. Her father respected logic; he was uncomfortable with emotion. "Dad, we aren't going to any more hound shows. I'd be right here. I'm safer here than in the city."

"She can learn quite a bit with us, Mr. Harris." Sister's deep alto already had a soothing effect. "First she would learn responsibility. You two have drummed that in her head but she'd learn even more. She would learn how animals communicate; they do have languages. She'd learn some accounting, because she'd have to keep track of expenses. She'd ride the green horses. And she'd fall in bed each night exhausted, so there'd be no danger of partying."

Rebecca was tuned in to her daughter in ways that her husband, good man that he was, was not. "Is it possible for her to keep up with her German?"

"Of course," Sister replied. "One of our whippers-in, Sybil Fawkes, is fluent in German. And if she needs lessons, Sybil will find the right person."

Jordon's mind was moving along. "Isn't she the daughter of the philanthropist Edward Bancroft?"

"She is."

"Hmm."

"Where would she live?" Rebecca asked.

"I'd be happy to have her live with me, as long as she doesn't play loud music in the house." Sister laughed.

"And what would her board cost?" Jordon's mind rarely strayed far from money.

"Mr. Harris, not a penny. And the club would pay her minimum wage so she would be learning to manage her own money."

Jordon stalled. "It's dangerous, riding green horses."

"Well, what about seven dollars an hour?" Gray had Jordon's measure. "That's quite good for a young person just starting out."

"Dad, please."

"Sweetheart, what do you think?" The father had the great good sense to ask his wife before announcing his decision.

"She loves it, Jordy. And Tootie's not one to vegetate intellectually. She'll keep studying." A meaningful pause followed. "She's her father's daughter. That mind never stops."

This had the desired effect. Jordon was caught between three beautiful women, one of whom was his wife. He did what any smart man would do; he agreed.

"Oh, Daddy, I love you!" Tootie threw her arms around her father and then hugged her mother.

"We'll take good care of her," Gray said in a low aside to Jordon. "You can be sure of that."

As Gray and Sister once again walked toward his car, about a half mile away in the large soccer parking lot, Sister mused, "Val will pitch a fit."

"Honey, she'll wind up on the farm, too."

"She has a very good summer job."

"My money is she won't last a month."

"We'll see." They walked along, both of them pleased to have made Tootie so happy.

"Damned shame about Felicity's parents," said Sister.

"That kid's learning hard lessons early. She'll be stronger for this. If nothing else, she knows who loves her for herself."

"Before Tootie came up I was thinking."

"Yes?" He smiled slightly.

"Mo Schneider, Hope Rogers, and Grant Fuller—I'm assuming he's dead, too. Despite all the searching by police, there's not a trace of him, and it's been a week."

"He could have amnesia," said Gray.

"Possibly. Let's set Grant aside; maybe he'll show up in Aruba. But Mo and Hope each had connections to the hunt world and to the Thoroughbred world. So did Grant."

"Thousand and thousands of people fall into one of those categories. Fewer into both, I'll give you that."

"I think these terrible events are connected."

Gray shrugged. "Janie, people do commit suicide. As for Mo—well, he got what he had coming. But Grant missing? That's bizarre."

"He must have known something."

"The question is, What did he know?"

CHAPTER 13

The Bryn Mawr Hound Show fell on the same weekend as the Custis Hall graduation. Missing it disappointed Sister, for if the Virginia show was all trumpets and cymbals, Bryn Mawr was mellow woodwinds. But she couldn't be in two places at the same time, and after the events at the last two hound shows, she was almost relieved to stay home.

On the Monday after graduation, Tootie, with help from Val, moved into RayRay's bedroom at the end of the long upstairs hall. How wonderful it felt to have life back in that room!

Tootie didn't want to unpack, she wanted to get right to work, but Sister told her to get her things in order first; they'd have plenty to do tomorrow. Val would be driving back home, and she thought the two friends would like time together.

Usually, chore day was Thursday but Sister had odds and

ends that wouldn't wait, so she hopped in the car, hit up Southern States and Whole Foods, stopped by Keller & George to drop off an old watch for repair, and lingered over new watches.

Arriving at the little café early, Sister drank an ice cold Co-Cola and read yesterday's *Times* of London, her favorite newspaper despite its steep subscription rate (close to two thousand dollars a year) but worth every penny for the pleasure.

"Ah." She looked over the top of the paper, removing her reading glasses.

"Sorry, I'm late." Ben Sidell sat opposite her.

"You're not. I was early. Chaos at home. I'm enjoying the peace and quiet." She filled him in on Tootie's moving in and Val's help. Felicity and Howie were also moving into the vacant Demetrios farm, closer to Sister, that Crawford Howard had purchased because it abutted his land.

"Sounds like everyone's settling in." He smiled.

"And there will be a marriage ceremony the last weekend of June."

"Good." His brown eyes were merry. "Better to be married than not, I think."

"In Felicity's case, certainly." She smiled.

"In general." Ben leaned back. "Studies show that men who marry live longer and are happier than men who do not."

"And women?" She arched a silver eyebrow.

"As it happens, the statistics are not the same. Single women appear to get along just fine."

"Sure, because they don't have to do double the housework."

"Don't more men do housework now?" Ben rubbed his

chin. Judging by the light brown stubble there, he had left home this morning without shaving. "They must. Women are making more money, so they don't have to put up with deadbeats anymore."

"Well, I hope so. Ray wouldn't do laundry if he had to go naked." She laughed. "He did do the dishes, though."

Ben noticed the sports page sticking out from under the Sunday paper. "May I?"

"Sure." She slipped it to him.

After they ordered he commented wryly, "A lot of cricket photos. I don't know as I will ever understand that game. It takes forever to finish a match."

"Can you imagine living when people had enough time for games to last three days? Remember, cricket started out as a kind of farm sport, or perhaps I should say *a sport of the lower orders.* I actually quite like it."

He pushed the paper back. "You never cease to amaze me. Speaking of which, here's the background on Grant Fuller." He handed her a sheet of paper.

Their sandwiches came, and a refill of Sister's Co-Cola.

"Tennessee, Indiana, North Carolina, West Virginia." She tapped the side of her plate once with her knife and then put it down quickly, realizing what she'd done. "He was expanding the business."

"How well did you know him?"

"Just socially, and even then I saw him infrequently. The dog food he gave me to test was quite good."

"After you called me last night I got to thinking about all this. The three people seem to have nothing in common—mind you, I believe that Hope did kill herself—but then I thought, 'Well, the Silver Fox' "—he used one of Sister's nicknames— " 'told me to put my nose down.' What I did find is that both men had been charged with cruelty to animals."

"Grant?" This surprised her.

"That's why he sold his slaughterhouses. The newspaper report quotes him as saying he didn't know any easy way to kill large animals, and they performed this act as humanely as possible. Of course, the poor animals can smell the blood, the panic. They die in dreadful fear; we all know that. Much as I hate it, I'm not going to stop eating beef, pork, or lamb chops. Still, there ought to be a better way."

"I'm sure there is, if we'd apply ourselves to finding it. And I expect in future there will be less meat-eating because it's cheaper to get the calories from grain. This assumes that humans continue to breed like flies, outpacing the food supply."

"Um—well, Sister, as you know there's nothing I can do about *that*. My job takes effect after the act, not before."

She studied the states and dates again. "West Virginia. The date is the same as that terrible storm. Charleston, West Virginia. The same as the night Hope died."

"And?"

"Oh, nothing. Coincidence." She opened the small jar of mustard served with her sandwich. "Were there any other charges of cruelty against Grant?"

"No, the animal rights activists stuck to the slaughterhouse issue."

"If Grant Fuller is ever found, maybe we'll be closer to the truth. He certainly never struck me as a brutal man—unlike Mo."

"No break in that case yet."

"Too many people are still cheering." She smiled. "Thank you for going to the trouble of getting this information on Grant from the sheriff in his county."

"Turns out Grant is a meticulous record keeper. Once Grant's wife filed a missing person's report, his secretary handed the sheriff his desk daybook. It listed all his purchases. The sheriff said Grant must have had a hollow leg."

"Really?" Sister's voice rose. "I saw him exceedingly happy a few times but never bombed."

"Cases of Jack Daniel's Black and some Kentucky bourbons, too. Also cases of vodka."

"He lived in Tennessee; he would drink Jack. Also, Ben, much of his work involved socializing. I'll bet he had a traveling bar in his car. He was a student of bourbon. I know that and he got Hope into distilleries to meet the real artists, the actual distillers. Then his wife put an end to that."

"Too bad his wife was suspicious but maybe she had just cause. About his traveling bar, well, lubricate the customer." Ben polished off the last of his sandwich. "Feeding them first doesn't hurt either."

"Is that a hint for more?"

"I'm not a customer."

"You're right. You're a valuable member of the Jefferson Hunt Club who is learning the subtleties of hunting God's most intelligent creature. You truly have come a long way."

The praise made him blush. "Thank you. I had no idea how complicated it is."

"There are people who hunt for forty years and don't know

what's going on. Don't know when a whipper-in has blundered into the covert; don't know when hounds have overrun the line; never take into account the angle of the sun, the wind, or the time of the month."

"Time of the month?"

"Can't get foxes to run the day after a full moon. If they're out they'll pop right back into their den."

"Why?"

"Full as ticks. Hunting is fabulous during a full moon. Every creature is moving about. A predator doesn't have to work as hard to flush game."

"See? I learn something every time I'm with you."

"You flatter me. Dessert?"

"I want the bomb." The bomb was a huge round dome of chocolate-chip ice cream on a thin shortbread wafer. Over this was poured either chocolate syrup or crème de menthe.

"That sounds good."

He ordered one with chocolate syrup; she ordered the crème de menthe. They ate themselves silly.

After lunch, he walked her back to her car. "Now that the hound shows are over, maybe things will settle down. No murders, no disappearances."

"I was straining for a connection," said Sister. "Probably didn't have a thing to do with hound shows."

She was as right about that as Ben was wrong about future events.

CHAPTER 14

"All we want right now is for them to come happily when called," said Shaker. He was wearing a white light canvas tool bag filled with cookies.

Sister walked on the left side of the puppies while Tootie walked on the right.

The sweltering summer heat would kick in soon enough, but at seven in the morning the air still felt as fresh in mid-July as it ever did.

Puppy minds, like those of very young children, can concentrate for one minute, perhaps two. It's a good huntsman who knows to keep everything fun and not to push beyond that point. This way the puppies, like children, don't know they're learning their ABCs.

"Hold up," Shaker said softly. He hunkered down and held

out his arms and the *V* puppies ran to him, as did Momma Violet, whose presence ensured cooperation.

Fat and wiggly, the thrilled little seven-week-old foxhounds ran up, some tripping in excitement. Shaker patted their heads and solemnly gave each one a cookie. The puppies daintily took the treat, aware that they must have done something right, given his tone. However, just why they were being rewarded was not yet clear. It would take a week or so for the lesson to sink in. Violet also took a cookie. Shaker ran his hands over her crown, telling her she was the world's best mother.

Then they walked back from the front of the kennels, where the puppies were put in the puppy run, with more cookies liberally distributed.

The rumble of Betty's ancient Volvo station wagon, followed by Sybil's new truck, told the humans that the two whippers-in had arrived for hound walk—something the hounds had known from the time the vehicles turned off the state road, a mile and a half away.

Betty burst through the door. "Battery died, just as I pulled into the kennel."

"I'll give you a charge after hound walk," Shaker volunteered.

"Time to buy a new station wagon. Volvo has a six-cylinder one now." Sister enjoyed keeping up with current automotive models.

Sybil, picking a stone out of the heavy tread of her work boots, glanced up. "Why don't you call Dan? Hope's Volvo is probably for sale. It's only a year old, I think."

Betty considered this, her blonde hair shining as a shaft of morning light came through the window. "You don't think that's ghoulish? And how come Dan controls the estate, not Paul?"

"It's not ghoulish, Betty. Her estate has to be settled," said Sybil. "Remember when Hope bought the station wagon? She was already considering divorce, so she registered it in the clinic's name. What good is the station wagon to Dan Clement? He'll refer you to the lawyer, of course, but you'd be doing him a favor. Hope didn't have much by way of family after her aunt died. You know, I hadn't thought about it before, but I wonder what kind of will she left?"

"Maybe she didn't have one." Shaker lifted the lid off the big garbage can where treats were kept and refilled the two sides of the tool bag on his waist.

"She left a will. Hope was far too organized not to do so. She told me she was cutting Paul out of it," Sister said.

"Some people don't like to think about death." Sybil shrugged.

"Does that mean you don't have a will?" Sister picked up her crop and nudged her in the ribs.

"I have one. Daddy would kill me."

"Darn straight." Betty smiled. "I think I *will* call Dan after hound walk."

"What will you do with the blue bomb?" Sybil asked.

"Sell it, I guess. I mean, it runs. I've kept it up. Put four new tires on last year and a new alternator. Car's getting old; I'm getting old. I don't feel like fooling with it. It's an 'eighty-six, after all. The paint is so faded it looks as though it's powdered with blue chalk dust."

"Hey, I'm tired of waiting!" Dragon complained from the draw pen.

"Let's get this show on the road." Shaker smiled.

"Literally." Sister laughed.

Tootie walked with Shaker. He'd taken a shine to her because she loved hounds and had the gift. Also, she hung on his every word.

"Can't draw two strike hounds. You can for a walk but not for a hunt."

"Why?"

"Split the pack."

"That's why you don't take Cora and Dragon together?"

He smiled. "You noticed."

"Not until the middle of last season, but I wondered."

"You know, there are people who hunt for years and don't know one hound from another."

"But they're quiet in the field, and that's what counts," Betty chipped in.

"And they pay their dues," Sister added.

Bitsy, tiring of motherhood and feeling the nest was too small for four owlets, flew low overhead.

Tillie, the lemon-and-white draft from Mo Schneider's pack, had become less shy. *"Why does that screech owl hang around?"*

Thimble, coming on her second year, felt important enough to answer. *"Oh, that's Bitsy. She lives in fear that she'll miss something."*

"Ha." Bitsy clicked her bill, careful not to emit her signature call. *"Groundling. I see and know more than you could ever dream of. Dumb hounds."*

With that she pooped on Thimble's head before flying over near Inky's den.

The other hounds laughed at Thimble, who, good-natured, laughed, too.

Mist rose up from the wildflower field, long white streaks obscuring vision and then magically thinning into a pearly haze until they vanished altogether in a startlingly blue sky.

After an hour's walk, with everyone back in their respective runs, Betty called Dan on her cell. Hope's 2007 CV70 all-wheel-drive turbo retailed for $28,750. Dan had just put an ad in the paper.

"Dan, what about twenty-six thousand, and I'll bring you a check today?"

He thought about it. "Done. Make it out to the clinic."

Betty hung up. "I'm the new owner of a station wagon with only thirty-four thousand miles. I really love the color, that light mist-green metallic."

"I do, too," Sister agreed.

"What will you do with the blue bomb?" Tootie quietly inquired.

"Get whatever I can for it."

"I'd like to buy it."

"I'll jump it and take it to Tommy Harvey's. He can check it out for you and sell you a new battery. His prices are always fair." Shaker liked doing business with people who did what they said they were going to do.

"Actually, that's a perfect place to take the wagon. Tommy's got all the records," Betty said. "He can tell you what it's worth. Then maybe your dad will give you the money."

"I'm not asking Dad for anything. I've saved up." Tootie's

voice rose a bit. "Dad's paying for college. That's enough." She paused. "I wish I could stay here."

"You just go on to Princeton." Betty was firm. "Those four years will fly by. Then you can think about coming back to live."

"Mary Baldwin is just over the mountain." Tootie sounded plaintive. "I'd be happy there."

"Princeton is a fabulous school. You'll like it once you get used to it. New Jersey is so crowded. Not much real country left." Betty truly was delighted with the deal she'd just made and was feeling expansive. "And the blue bomb knows the way home. So whatever price Tommy gives you, that will be it."

"Okay."

The four women walked out into the warming air, feeling the rise in humidity. Shaker jump-started the Volvo.

"Tootie, just in case this takes more time than we think, I'll follow you there," he offered.

"Thank you." Tootie smiled, her teeth so white that they almost seemed fake.

"Lot of wheeling and dealing going on. Too much for me. I'm going to attack the Japanese beetles." Sister headed toward her garden shed.

"Don't say that," Sybil said in mock terror. "I haven't seen one beetle yet."

"That's because they're all here with me."

That night, Tootie pored over her savings account, a total of one thousand five hundred dollars to withdraw. Betty was selling the blue bomb to her for less than Tommy's evaluation.

At home, Betty was feeling a tremor of attachment. She'd had that Volvo when it was new, the Copen-blue paint shining, the interior without a spot of wear. Still, one must move on.

She opened all the cubbyholes and storage places in Hope's 2007 Volvo, pulling out little notebooks and odd pieces of paper.

"Bobby, look at these numbers." She handed him bits of paper.

"Huh?" He'd been reading the newspaper and reached absentmindedly for the papers.

"See?" Betty said.

"See what?" A flicker of irritation crept into his voice, for the day at the print shop had been a long one.

"Look at these order numbers." She bent over him, pointing over his shoulder. "That's the number for pure red ink. These are paper numbers, Strathmore mostly."

He sat up a bit straighter, put the newspaper in his lap with his left hand, and brought the small paper slips up to his eyes with the right. "I'll be damned. So it is."

"What was Hope Rogers doing with all that paper and ink?"

"Well, honey, maybe she was planning some kind of an invitation for a party."

"She would have come to us. We give our hunt club members and vets a discount—a very attractive discount, I might add. Your idea." She sweetly gave him the credit, even though the idea had been a mutual one thirty years ago, when they were young and just starting their printing business.

"Betty, she died first."

"I don't think so. For one thing, these little scraps are old.

See?" She pointed out the grease spots from Hope's fingers, yellowing at the edges on some papers. "She's had these for at least a year."

Bobby was as good a judge of aging paper as his wife. "That doesn't mean anything, honey. She could have had an idea about stationery or some announcement for the clinic and set it by."

"I still think it's odd."

"Well, maybe, but why do you care?" He looked at her quizzically.

"Maybe this will help us understand what really happened to her."

While Betty retreated to the kitchen to call Sister, Bobby wondered how his wife thought ink colors and paper types could shed light on Hope's demise. However, he'd been married to her long enough not to voice this question.

"I can't make head or tail of it," Sister said, after hearing Betty's report.

"If there were just a few numbers, I'd go with Bobby's thought that Hope had planned some form of announcement or whatever for the clinic. But there are a lot of numbers here, for ink and specific paper types. And it's not like she was comparing two reds or two blues. She'd obviously made up her mind."

"If only we knew about what." Sister, in the last seven weeks, had come up with nothing but frustration regarding Hope.

"I'm hanging on to these numbers."

"Do you ever feel her spirit is calling to us?" Sister asked, voice low.

"Like the spirits on Hangman's Ridge?" Betty paused. "You bet I do."

Later that same day, Sister wondered if spirits were at work or at least Hope's spirit.

The next day, Sister saw Paul Rogers in one of the aisles at the pharmacy. There'd been no service for Hope, a not uncommon practice regarding suicides. Depending on the denomination, some suicides are not buried in consecrated grounds.

As she and Paul had no activities in common, once Hope left him, Sister rarely caught a glimpse of him.

She stepped down the aisle. "Paul."

Startled slightly, he looked up at her. "Sister Jane."

"I know we aren't close, Paul, and divorce divides more people than just the formerly married couples, but I hope you're all right."

Grateful for the overture, he relaxed his shoulders. "Doing okay."

"Most separations are acrimonious. Perhaps in time you both would have remembered each other's good qualities."

"Hope cheated on me." His voice was flat. "I snooped. I'm pretty good with the computer so I got into her e-mails."

"I'm sure you were upset." Sister did not enlighten him with her views on monogamy.

"Grant Fuller." He nearly bit the words. "I think it started when he showed her around the distilleries." He tossed an orange box of Motrin into his cart. "Ended at the Mid-America Hound Show. Guess it was unpleasant. You know, she called me up to tell me it was over. How does that figure?" He sounded both bitter and still in love.

"Well, I don't know. Did you tell the sheriff?"

"Yes."

Back out on the road, she knew that she did the right thing in not revealing her personal information regarding Hope.

Today was Saint Vladimir's feast day, July 15. He lived from 955 to 1015. Originally a pagan with a penchant for violence, when he converted to Christianity in 989 he put aside violence as much as a prince could do in the tenth century. He also put away his many mistresses to marry Anne.

Sister thought neither she nor Hope capable of emulating Vladimir. But carrying on with Grant Fuller? That surprised her.

CHAPTER 15

On Thursday, August 7, the heat was shimmering off the hay fields and the dirt roads by seven-thirty.

"Too hot to have been born," Sister grumbled, as they walked twenty couple of hounds, including three couple of the second *T* litter: Thimble, Twist, Tootsie, Trooper, Taz, and Tattoo.

The youngsters had behaved so well that Sister and Shaker thought they could all go out together. They'd been walking in couple straps since late spring; then, by early June, they had gone out uncoupled but only four at a time. On a sweltering morning, young hounds would be less inclined to shoot off—or so the humans reasoned.

Sybil, on vacation with her sons at Prince Edward Island, would be home the end of the month. So this morning Tootie took the right side, Betty was on the left, Sister brought up the rear, and Shaker, as usual, walked in front.

"I can never figure out why I want the hounds behind me when I'm on foot but in front of me when I'm on a horse." Shaker had tied a bandanna around his forehead to keep the sweat out of his eyes.

"That *is* a puzzle," Sister agreed.

The hounds walked toward the foot of Hangman's Ridge. They were taken a little farther every day to prepare them for cubbing, which would begin after Labor Day. The youngsters had proved so obedient that the humans now thought they could relax.

Then, too, the heat created a lassitude. Even if one was bucking hay, there was a languor to the work.

"Aren't you surprised that Val stuck to her desk job?" Betty asked Tootie.

"Kinda. She likes the money, though."

"There is that," Betty agreed. "Saw Felicity yesterday. She's really feeling pregnant. Two months to go. I didn't have the heart to tell her that by the last month you have to walk leaning backward."

"Carrying to term through summer's heat." Sister shook her head.

"Remember all this, Tootie." Betty laughed. "If you get pregnant try to do it in summer. Then you'll deliver in spring. It's much easier."

"I'll bear it in mind." Tootie smiled. "You know, what did surprise me was Val coming back for Felicity's wedding. If it weren't for you-all and Val, I don't think anyone would have been there. Val still thinks Felicity is throwing her life away, but she doesn't say that to Felicity anymore."

"Both sets of parents will live to regret being so narrow-minded. At least, I hope they will." Sister still couldn't believe those people.

"Hell, some people never grow up. Look at Crawford." Shaker's loathing of Crawford had not dimmed with time.

Twist, tail up over her back just as incorrect as it could be, whispered to Taz, *"Let's run!"*

"Where?" Taz was the literal type.

"Up the ridge. We've never been there. The others say it's haunted." Twist's ears pricked up slightly.

"Ha." Taz dismissed it.

"Don't break from the pack," Diane, overhearing, advised the two girls. *"There are all kind of ghosts in the world—humans, hounds, horses—as you'll see in good time."*

But the thrill of rebellion was rising in Twist's chest. She nudged Taz and then charged toward the ridge. Taz followed.

Tootie started to run after the two bad girls but remembered what Sister had drilled into her: Keep the bulk of the pack together. She dropped her lash and stood still on her side, as did Betty.

Shaker, voice soothing because the other youngsters wanted to follow, crooned, "Relax. Relax. Come on now. Come along." He turned and the pack followed.

Tattoo and Tootsie hesitated a moment, but Sister pointed the knob end of her whip toward the two young entry—"Don't even think about it"—and they ducked their heads, trying to look inconspicuous.

When the pack returned to the kennel in good order in a half hour, Diane said sternly to the second litter of *T*s who remained, *"When those girls come back I will tear them a new one."*

"Can't do it," Cora remarked. *"They're in the wimpy girls' run."*

"I can think about it. And we can all give them a piece of our minds when they come back."

Shaker, on his way out of the kennels, called over his shoulder, "I'm going out on Soldier Road, just in case."

"All right then, we'll go up the ridge," Sister agreed.

"Shaker, I'll go with you, just in case. Might be easier, what with two of them to cajole or catch," Betty said.

"Good idea." He sprinted toward the old 454 Chevy half-ton.

"Tootie, let's go." Sister swept out the door as Tootie opened it for her.

Raleigh and Rooster were waiting patiently outside the kennels, ready to go.

"Boys, you stay here."

"But we'll know where the hounds are before you do," Raleigh protested, to no avail.

"Ass kissers," called Golly, lounging on a large tree limb in one of the huge pin oaks by the kennels.

"Regurgitator," Rooster called up, his lovely harrier voice resonating.

"My, my, what a big word for a dumb dog." Golly lorded it over both of them.

"You have to come down out of that tree sometime, Golly, and

when you do I'll get you." Rooster raised the fur on his neck for effect.

"You'll have forgotten by then," Golly sassed.

"I will not," Rooster called up.

"Ignore her. All she wants is attention," Raleigh counseled.

"He'll forget. Rooster's older than dirt. His mind is going." The calico thoroughly enjoyed the torment.

"I will not." Rooster was sixteen and there was a smidgen of truth to Golly's accusation.

"Doggy Alzheimer's."

Raleigh, hoping to make light of the situation, replied, *"Halfheimer's. He's not that old."*

"Oh, yes he is."

"You're nine yourself." Raleigh could count as well as anyone else.

"The prime of life!" She dropped her luxurious tail over the branch, allowing it to hang for effect, much as a lady might trail one end of a feather boa.

As the house pets indulged in their war of the words, Sister marveled at the clouds of dust. "Thank the Lord for air-conditioning. No more open windows."

"The Weather Channel said our water level is twelve inches down for this time of year."

"Tootie, I really believe Al Gore is right. I've seen too much change in the weather in too short a time. Damn those puppies."

"I guess it's better they run off now, rather than when we start cubbing."

"Wise words. No wonder you're going to Princeton." She smiled.

"I'm pretending I'm excited. Dad keeps asking why I'm not declaring a major in business right away."

"He'll let up," Sister predicted, as the red GMC climbed the twisting road to the top of Hangman's Ridge.

The two women got out of the truck. Even in the morning heat, a chill pervaded the air.

Sure enough, the youngsters had seen ghosts at the tree, which had so scared the bejesus out of them they'd scampered down the side of the ridge toward the farm. However, the underbrush was so thick, Sister and Tootie couldn't see them.

"Hey, what's this?" Taz crawled over to a big fox den.

Originally, this had been Georgia's den when she left her mother, but she had relocated closer to the kennels. The new living quarters were more pleasant, plus she could visit the hounds

at night. There was never a shortage of treats lying about the barns either. And her mother, Inky, was usually there. Inky and Diana were special friends.

"Fox den." Twist knew that much.

"Wow." Taz inhaled the heady scent of eau de Vulpes, plus something else equally tantalizing.

"Is someone in there?" Twist called down.

"Yes, you silly ass, and I'll thank you to leave!" a voice boomed out, making both hounds step back.

"Who are you?" Taz worked up her nerve.

"Who are you?" came the saucy reply.

"I'm Taz and this is my sister Twist. We're foxhounds, and we live at Roughneck Farm."

"Good. I'll run you two until you drop from heat exhaustion. I'm Thales, and I'm the fastest fox in the whole world." Thales certainly did not suffer from an inferiority complex.

"What's that other smell?" Twist edged up to the mouth of the den.

"An old toy. You can have it." The fox chuckled to himself because he figured his toy would bring them trouble.

Thales, named for a Greek philosopher, was far more sly than the original Thales ever was, a man so entranced by higher thought that he fell right into a well as he contemplated the sky.

"I hear them." Tootie pointed toward the steep incline.

"So do I." Sister walked to the edge of the ridge; a light breeze swept over her, for there was always some wind up there. "Come on, Twist, come on, Taz. Let's go."

Twist, boot in mouth—that was Thales's toy—said nothing.

Taz, beginning to understand that she had seriously discomfited her master, said, *"We'd better go."*

"I'm taking the toy." Twist dropped it for a moment. *"We'll see ghosts again."*

"If Sister's there, I won't be scared." Taz had confidence in the master.

"Tootie's there, too." Twist lifted her head, inhaling deeply. *"All right."* She picked up the boot.

"Stupid pups." Thales laughed as they pushed up through the undergrowth.

"There you are. Come along." Sister knelt down.

Taz ran right up but Twist wanted to show off her trophy. She circled.

"Twist, come on." Tootie knelt down, too.

Although the humans lacked the superior olfactory equipment of the hounds, the work boot, tongue chewed off, emitted the unmistakable odor of old rot.

Twist walked right up and dropped the boot at Tootie's feet. Involuntarily, she took a step back.

Sister blinked. "Let's get these two in the truck first."

Happily the two leaped into the front seat, where they would ride. Sister closed the door and she and Tootie returned to the grisly toy.

"There's a foot in there." Tootie held her nose. "Mostly bones but still some flesh down in the toe."

"The worms have given up on it." Sister walked back to the truck and put on her gloves. Then she carefully picked the trophy up and placed it in the bed of the truck.

Tootie squeezed in next to the hounds, and Sister, worried, started down the ridge.

"Sister, there has to be more than a foot," Tootie said, a slight wave of nausea rising up.

"That's what worries me. Violence is coming closer and closer to home."

CHAPTER 16

The blue-gray smoke from a true Montecristo—Cuban, not Dominican—curled overhead. Ben Sidell, not much of a smoker, treated himself to a special cigar every time he came back from the morgue. Viewing bodies in various conditions of decay or freshly ripped apart by violence was part of his job, but not a part he relished. How the coroner and his assistants adjusted to the stench amazed him. Even the odor of old death that had lingered in the work boot offended him, made his eyes water. So once back outside he lit up, inhaled, closed his eyes, and considered the problem.

One problem, not immediately apparent, was smoking a contraband cigar. He slipped the paper cigar ring off the dark-golden-leaf wrapper, dropping it in his pocket. Ever since he was a kid he had saved cigar bands.

When Sister called him that morning, he'd immediately driven out, taking a rookie with him. Along with Sister, Shaker, and Tootie, they scoured Hangman's Ridge. The chiggers feasted on the poor rookie, a suburban boy who didn't know that one had to smear oneself with insect repellant to thwart the tiny little irritants. Once the chigger burrowed in your flesh, no amount of digging, applying alcohol to the tiny pinprick site, or cursing removed the insect. And the scars from scratching—for there was no way to stop scratching—stayed for months.

After fighting through undergrowth and sweating like pigs, they found nothing—apart from the chiggers dropping off cedars—not even an eyelet from the chewed-off part of the boot.

After that exercise in futility, Ben returned to his desk at headquarters, blissfully air-conditioned, to pore over the file of missing persons reports from the last six months that his staff had assembled while he was on Hangman's Ridge. Most of those gone missing had been found, including a few older people who had wandered off from home, minds gone and families not able to afford full-time care; Ben studied these reports to see if, of those who had perished, the bodies were all intact. Yes.

After two hours of examining every detail, he slapped the folder shut. The coroner had estimated the age of the remains at three months. Decay accelerated in heat and humidity; even though pieces of foot remained in the toe box of the boot, the death and apparent dismemberment weren't recent.

That ruled out Grant Fuller. Although the businessman disappeared in Loudoun County, at Sister's request, Ben bore that in mind. Both knew the foot was older than Grant's disappearance but this was Sister's way of saying, "One thing can lead to another."

When the coroner called him he was happy to leave his desk. Now sitting in the squad car, air conditioner humming along with the motor, his curiosity grew stronger. Sure, it was possible that an animal dug up a shallow grave, breaking up the body. But how far would a marauder carry the gains?

He punched in the familiar number.

"Hello?" Sister Jane replied.

"Sister, dogs eat carrion. Do foxes, raccoons, or possums?"

"I don't think foxes prefer carrion, but if times are hard they'll eat it. They're omnivorous, as we are. Raccoons and possums aren't much interested. Any of the flesh-eating birds will gobble carrion. It's like candy to them."

"Such as."

"Crows are the most obvious. A cardinal wants seeds."

"Bigger game."

"Bobcat and bear?"

"Right. I'm wondering how far this foot walked, so to speak. Obviously an animal drug it."

"Not necessarily."

"What do you mean?"

"A human could have dropped it." She couldn't help herself. "Sheer carelessness."

He laughed. "Maybe he was putting his best foot forward."

"That's really bad."

"Hey, you need gallows humor in this job."

"You sure need it on Hangman's Ridge." She stopped and

thought. "Bears prefer sweets and berries. A bear tearing a human apart and carrying it around is pretty far-fetched. A mountain lion would hide meat in a cache. You've seen the caches foxes build? Well, the mountain lion's is bigger."

"Would a mountain lion eat carrion?"

"Cats don't like it."

"But you said that mountain lions, foxes, and bobcats build caches. The meat rots."

"Yes, it does decay, but it's different because it's covered. Kind of like a primitive crock pot. These animals return to their caches only if they can't get a fresh kill. It's not their preferred food, like it is for vultures, say."

"You don't think any of those animals would carry a foot a long distance from the rest of the body?"

"No. I don't think a coyote would either, and we know we've got them in this area. If a fox, coyote, bobcat, or mountain lion had torn apart a body, the farthest from Hangman's Ridge it could happen would be two miles."

"Lot of territory to cover."

"Yes, but I live here. I'd have seen the spiral of buzzards. And if I didn't, Cindy Chandler would, because Foxglove Farm is on the other side of Soldier Road." Sister took a breath. "Wait a minute. There *is* an animal with a huge foraging range that will gladly eat carrion and anything else."

"What?"

"A feral pig. Their usual hunting territory is ten square miles, but fifty is not uncommon if times are hard, and this is a drought summer."

"If anyone would know about feral pigs, it's you."

Sister had nearly been killed by a boar during a hunt. "That boar, the sow, and her piglets are probably still around over by Paradise. It's remote, much of it wild, so they're undisturbed. That doesn't mean there's a body over there. It only means that's where we encountered the boar. Could a boar or a sow have traveled here? Sure, but if the animal came by the kennels, we'd know it."

"Doesn't mean it didn't come through After All." Ben named the Bancroft farm. "There are three other ways up Hangman's Ridge apart from your farm."

"Then I think the thing to do is to call the Bancrofts and Cindy. As for the fourth way up Hangman's Ridge, the south face, it's mostly sheer rock with a narrow deer path. I'll check for tracks. That's all anyone can do at this point; given the drought and the dust, we'll be damned lucky to get one print. There weren't any on the ridge, because I looked."

He stubbed out his cigar. "Just for the hell of it, after I call around I'm going out to Paradise."

"Wait until dawn."

"Why?"

"Two reasons. First, dawn is feeding time for the day animals, and the night animals are coming home; they can tell you a great deal. The second reason is dew on the grass. If there's any hint of a depression, on a track or dirt road, we might see it then. Also, on the meadows, you'll see the slick spots where animals have walked. It's not as good as a clear track, but it gives you a sense of the size of the animal and the direction it's traveling. That's something."

"Do you have a shotgun?" Ben asked.

"I do." She anticipated his next remark. "Better to bring a long-barreled forty-five, though. I don't have one but if you do, wear it. We'll be traveling through heavy brush in some spots and a shotgun, which is heavy anyway, will just slow us down. I'll bring my thirty-eight. Do you mind if Tootie comes?"

"No."

"She's got sharp eyes."

"I'll meet you at the gate of Paradise at five in the morning."

"I look forward to greeting the dawn with you."

"God knows what else we'll greet."

CHAPTER 17

"What do you suppose they're doing? You think they'd have the sense to stay home," the large father of an otter brood said to his mate.

"Checking trails, I suppose. Now that Sister hunts Franklin Foster's land, she keeps up with it," his mate replied. "They'll be hunting in a month."

"Ah, well, none of my business. Let's play." He raced to the creek bank, flopped on his belly, and slid into the deep creek with a splash.

"What's that?" Tootie asked, her hands light on the reins, for which Aztec was grateful.

"Otters. Very jolly creatures." Sister smiled.

The creek crossing, ragged and rocky, allowed them to feel the cool air from the water. Ben, accustomed to riding Nonni, a sensible older horse, felt a little trepidation riding Lafayette, Sister's elegant Thoroughbred.

Lafayette could feel Ben's thigh muscles tightening constantly, but he bore it with good grace.

Sister rode Matador, glad she'd persuaded Ben to get on Lafayette. If they had driven ATVs back into the huge expanse of Paradise and Franklin Foster's adjoining property, they'd have scared game. This way they would see more, which could be helpful. Walking was out of the question, for it would take them days to cover what amounted to almost ten thousand acres, some of which touched on federal lands.

Sister's territory, granted to her by the Master of Foxhounds Association of America, stopped on top of the Blue Ridge Mountains. Skyline Drive was roughly the dividing line. Glenmore Hunt had the west side of the Blue Ridge for Augusta County, with Rockbridge Hunt enjoying the west slopes farther south. The MFHA had settled many territory disputes since its founding in 1907. Fortunately, none of these clubs had fussed at one another in over a century.

"A lot of water here." Ben noted the depth of the creek.

"Runoff from the mountains. Always water back here, and it's crystal clear," Sister replied.

Overhead, a red-shouldered hawk sounded its cry, high-pitched, doubled but not offensive.

Tootie leaned over, once they were on the other side of the creek. "Deer tracks."

"The great thing about all these streams and creeks is you know the animals will come to drink. It's a fast way to find out what's in your territory, assuming the ground's not loamy sand or baked as hard as clay." Sister loved tracking, loved anything to do with being outside.

They followed the creek bed, its sides becoming steeper. There was no indication of wild boar, although signs of everything else were in abundance, especially wild turkeys.

The trail picked up five hundred yards north of the crossing. They threaded their way through trails already overgrown in just one season. Virginia, drought or no drought, could sprout pricker bushes with ease.

"We'll have our work cut out for us here." Sister sighed.

The work of keeping present territory open, as well opening new territory, never ended, taking many hands. Sister had a knack for finding willing volunteers, but coordinating schedules was a full-time job. How much easier it would have been to hire laborers, as the very wealthy clubs did. But Jefferson Hunt members watched the pennies, especially Ronnie Haslip, who hovered over the account books. Ronnie was just what a club wanted in a treasurer, although Sister might fret at times over his tight-fistedness.

They walked under a cliff overhang, cool from the huge rock outcroppings.

"Heading toward the scene of the crime." Sister laughed.

Tootie, who'd ridden on the day the field came upon Arthur DuCharme's illegal still, smiled. "At least it won't explode."

"I took care of that." Ben, also on the hunt that day, had given Arthur a deal. He'd destroy the still and Arthur, recovering from cancer, had to promise not to reopen for business.

"He's a sharp one," Sister commented dryly.

"You mean because he made liquor all those years and

didn't get caught?" Tootie asked, a sweat bee suddenly finding her quite interesting.

"That, too, but with Arthur you have to listen to every single word. He won't lie to you, but you have to read between the lines," Sister replied.

"Glad Margaret's not like that." Ben was dating Arthur's niece.

"Did Arthur put the still back here because it's hard to reach?" Tootie thought making moonshine a touch romantic, rebellious.

"Partly, but you need a place where the water is good. It's sweet here," Sister answered. They rounded the last great hunk of rock, which hung out like a dislocated monster's jaw.

"Jesus H. Christ on a raft!" Sister exclaimed.

Ben, trotting up behind her, was speechless.

Tootie simply said, "Looks like Arthur broke his promise."

The three quickly rode down to the still, which was far larger and grander than the original.

Ben dismounted while Sister held the reins. He tried the door, found it unlocked, and went inside.

Tootie said, "Isn't it kind of stupid to build a still where we hunt?"

"Not necessarily." A trickle of sweat was sliding down Sister's back. The mercury had already climbed to the low eighties. "The time we rode up on Arthur's Glenlivet factory"—she winked—"he had no idea we'd gotten permission from Franklin Foster. He'd been undergoing cancer treatment and wasn't up to speed. He knew we'd be hunting Old Paradise, but the chances of us winding up all the way here were pretty slim."

"But why build here now?"

"Tootie, Arthur's a countryman and he's smart. On days we might hunt Foster's land, all he needs to do is drag a trail of fresh blood in a huge circle around the still, say at a quarter-mile radius. The hounds will be baffled by the fresh blood. A fox can run through to foil scent, too. It's an easy ruse. My money's always on Arthur. I've known him all his life." She paused. "He's not worthless, he's just—um, disinclined to pay taxes."

Ben emerged, walking quickly up to Lafayette. He led the Thoroughbred to a slight depression in the ground to mount up, for Lafayette was taller than Nonni.

Once up he said tersely, "I'll kill that son of a bitch. He lied to me."

"Arthur wouldn't lie, Ben, though he might talk sideways."

"Well, he damn well lied this time. You should see that setup. Huge copper kettles! It's a real distillery, not a couple of glass beakers and coils. He spent big money on this."

"Ben, don't jump the gun."

"I'm not." The sheriff was fuming. "I'm going to arrest him and throw his lying butt in jail!"

Sister decided to let him cool off a bit on the ride back to the trailers. She continued to look for boar tracks, any tracks really.

When all three had squeezed into the cab of the dually, Sister, cranking the motor, said calmly, "I called Binky before we came out here." This was Arthur's brother. The two did not speak to each other. "I also called Arthur and Margaret. Granted, I asked permission to ride over Old Paradise only to flag any work we might need to do to prepare for cubbing. If Arthur thought we were heading to Franklin Foster's land, he gave no indication."

"Of course not." Ben, window down, reached up and held the top of the window frame, feeling the air on his hand.

"But if he was worried, he would have given some hint or tried to head us off."

"That setup is too big to hide."

"True." She pondered this. "He could throw us off when we were hunting, but he couldn't really throw us off now. Still, I think I'd sense it if he was concerned. I *know* Arthur."

Not to be dissuaded, Ben allowed Tootie to clean up Lafayette for him, jumped in his personal vehicle, not a squad car, tore back to Old Paradise next to the Foster land, and strode into Arthur's workshop.

Arthur gave him a big hello. He'd been making a chest of drawers.

Ben wasted no time. "You lied to me."

"I did not." Arthur, full head of hair still mostly brown, big walrus mustache, stood to his full six feet.

"I rode back to the old still site, and Arthur, what you've got there is four times as big as before, plus it's full of damned expensive equipment. You're stepping up in the world."

"I did not rebuild my old still." Arthur's voice was level, his demeanor calm.

"Oh, come on. Who else knew about that location?"

"Sit down, Sheriff." Arthur pointed to a stool by the workbench.

"I'll stand."

"All right, then. For one thing, when you set fire to my still, everyone out Chapel Cross way saw the flames and heard the explosion."

"Sure they did. That's why I called the fire department and told them not to worry, I was on the scene. I kept everyone away."

"You think they didn't know?"

"What, that I blew up your still? When I threw in that torch, hell, the whole damn place sounded like a V-Two rocket hitting London. But they didn't know it was a still."

"They did. You haven't considered, Sheriff "—Arthur paused for effect—"that most of these folks were customers of mine. When everything went to hell, they knew, all right. Didn't have to tell them."

This was sinking in. "Had anyone been back to the still while you operated it?" Ben asked.

"I'm not going to incriminate my neighbors."

"All right, all right. You got an ATV?"

"I do."

"Then we're going back in."

It took them twenty-five minutes—the two men had to get out and walk around the massive rock outcroppings—but Arthur's eyes about popped when he saw the still.

"Holy shit!"

"Don't play me, Arthur."

"I'm not."

They hurried down. Ben threw open the door, and Arthur walked in like a kid in a candy shop. "This is beautiful. Beautiful." He touched the copper kettles and sniffed the charred barrels. The fragrance of alcohol in the cradle excited him.

"Sheriff, you've got folks here who really know what they're doing!" Arthur walked over to a full cask, pulled out the stopper, grabbed a small bottle and allowed some liquid to fill it, then quickly jammed the stopper back in. He held it to his nose.

"Well?"

"Trying to fake age, by the depth of the char in the barrel." He took a sip and held the bottle toward Ben. "Try it."

Reluctantly, Ben sipped. "Burns a little."

"Yeah. High alcohol content, but that will come on down. They'll cut it, obviously, or they'd kill their customers." Arthur laughed. "They'll cut it down to eighty proof. That's what I think."

"But I thought one of the attractions of moonshine was the potency."

"Not moonshine, *country waters,*" Arthur corrected him. "For the uninitiated, sure, they want that full mule kick in the pants. For the connoisseur, it's the smoothness, the flavor, the lingering taste on the tongue. Good country waters are as good as anything you'll get from a major distillery and a damn sight more individual."

"I almost believe you didn't know about this."

"I didn't, but I can tell you a few things." He looked around. "Whoever is making this hasn't been back here for maybe two months, give or take."

"How do you know?"

"Dust. Someone who cared would keep the place spotless and still probably have some grain fermenting. Here the process has stopped. The barrels are full, except for one." He pointed to a deeply charred white-oak barrel. "Maybe they got scared off."

"With this much money invested? I doubt it."

"Well, whoever is making this knows a good bit about the process. He's done this before, with other country people. Maybe he even once worked at a distillery."

"Kind of stupid to come back here."

"No. There's a ready market here and many ways to lead you-all off when you're hunting. All anyone has to do is let a fox go."

"Never thought of that."

"Sheriff, you're not country. Furthermore, you're from Ohio. No offense intended." He closed his eyes and lifted the bottle to his nose again. "Another thing. Coloring agents."

"For what?"

"You've got someone making cheap bourbon here and passing it off as high grade, I reckon."

"Jesus H. Christ on a raft!" Ben echoed Sister's earlier exclamation.

Arthur stroked his fulsome mustache. "Boy, you got a little country in you after all."

CHAPTER 18

"A perfect match." Sister held the paper sample next to a Maker's Mark label. She found the samples in Hope's office. She asked Dan for them saying she liked paper. He didn't care if Sister cleaned out all of Hope's desk. He was on overload.

The big Webb press hummed in the printing room at Franklin Press.

Bobby Franklin, fighting weight gain, feeling bulky, held up both papers to the light. "The ink's a match, but you can see the paper isn't the same as the real Maker's Mark."

Betty said, "Corporations must find ways to distinguish their product just like the government does with money, ways that aren't obvious to a buyer. You know, like the silver thread they're using now."

"I confess when the new bills were issued I tore one open to pull out the thread." Sister took the sheet of black paper held out to her by Betty. "Okay, what's this?"

"Jack Daniels Number Seven. Black Label. In this case, the paper is just about right but it's tricky, because the information isn't printed, it's a color block on the label."

"What do you mean?" Sister rubbed the black paper between her fingers.

"The paper is white. It's set up on computers—it's all computers now—so the paper is printed and the lettering stands out in white. Think of it as a dye. Easier that way."

"Like waxing the part of an Easter egg you wish to paint a different color."

"Exactly."

One of Bobby's workmen approached. "Mr. Franklin, will you check the first runoff here?"

"The wedding job?"

"Right. That silver ink is a whistling bitch."

"Be right back. Why don't you girls go into the office?" Bobby always called Betty and Sister *girls,* and that was fine with them.

Once inside the main office, paneled in a lovely pecan that was hard to find this far away from Alabama's pecan groves, the two women pored over paper samples and ink colors on the large smooth table.

Bobby came back in and Betty glanced up. "Okay?"

"Yeah." He sat down next to Sister. "Silver ink, any metallic ink, is more difficult to work with. Clogs more often and may not give the crisp impression you want. Sometimes, depending on the job, we have to run the paper through twice, and that is dicey. Then people fuss because we charge more for metallic inks. If you look at the label of a George Dickel bourbon bottle, let me tell you, that is one damned expensive print job."

"Hope didn't have that one." Betty matched up colors with bourbon labels.

"She stuck to Kentucky bourbons, except for Jack Daniels. The Japanese know about Jack Daniels." Sister rested her chin in the cup of her hand, elbow on desk. "I'm surprised and appalled."

"I'm pretty surprised, too." Betty sighed.

"Larceny." Bobby shrugged. "The lure of Mammon just grabs hold of some folks. Obviously she wasn't worried about getting caught. Betty found the ink numbers written on scraps of paper in the glove compartment of Hope's Volvo."

"But Hope Rogers? Who would have thought?" Betty shook her head. "She made a good living. What more did she need?"

"Ask that of all the people living in McMansions," Sister chimed in. "Bet there never was an aunt who died and left her money at all. She was raking it in on this."

"I underestimated Ben." Bobby was breathing heavily; he really did have to lose the fat. "He had everything in that still checked for fingerprints, and he did it fast. Hope's prints were all over the place."

"Here it is just three days from when we rode back in there, and the pieces of the puzzle are falling together." Sister lifted her chin from her hand. "Okay. She was making illegal bourbon or fake bourbon or whatever you call the stuff, and she obviously sold it overseas where palates aren't as sophisticated as ours regarding bourbon. I still don't think she killed herself." She paused. "She had a partner. She had to."

"Why? She did her research. She had the ink colors exactly. Paper is harder to duplicate, but she came up with close substitutes if she couldn't match it exactly. You know, specialty papers demand a lot of chemistry and a bit of art." Bobby appreciated high-quality work.

"If Hope had a partner, why didn't he or she go back to the still? Ben and Arthur said no one had been there in maybe two months." Betty drummed her fingers on the table, her habit when working out a problem.

"Isn't it obvious?" Bobby replied. "If she did have a partner— and I'm not sold on that idea—he or she needed Hope. She was the distiller. She was the one who had organic chemistry in college. You can't be a vet or a doctor without it."

"And she was the one who did all the research in Kentucky. Fascinating, really—her account, I mean. I think you're right, Bobby. Hope was the distiller. Her partner would be a marketing person."

"She could have done it by herself," Betty said, "although it's hard to imagine Hope hauling those large copper kettles back in there. So even if she didn't have a true business partner, someone else knew."

"Arthur." Bobby folded his hands over his stomach. "Bet you bottom dollar."

"He's sly. He could have helped her out and taken something for it," Sister agreed, "I'll give you that. But on the other hand, he did make a deal with Ben to give up the business when Ben caught him the last time."

"That's not the same as saying you'll never help anyone else." Bobby laughed. "Arthur can find the slightest hole and slip through."

"Ben will work him over." Betty, like Sister, felt something was missing.

"No, he won't. Because of Margaret," Bobby stated simply.

"Well, there is that." Sister nodded. "But Margaret will find out from her uncle herself. I'd bet my bottom dollar on that."

The three close friends sat there looking at the papers, the ink, and one another for a time.

Bobby finally said, "Blackmail."

"What?" Betty's voice rose.

"That's why she killed herself. Someone found out. She couldn't take the shame."

"Wouldn't she just pay him off?" Sister thought paying was the reasonable course until one could figure out how to get rid of the blackmailer.

"How much for how long?" Bobby shrugged.

"Bobby, Hope Rogers wouldn't kill herself over blackmail. She'd kill the blackmailer first." Betty's voice had the ring of a wife speaking to a dense husband.

"Mo Schneider?" Sister wondered, then checked herself. "But she was already on her way home."

"You don't know that," Betty said.

"Hell of a way to kill the jerk. Be a lot easier to pull the trigger," Bobby said.

"Yeah, it would." Sister reached over and touched Betty's hand. "I truly believe Hope was murdered. Whether it was because of this illegal operation, I don't know, but I do know whoever killed her is walking around free, probably right in this community. Think about it."

"Doesn't add up. The whistle was going to be blown and she panicked." Bobby's voice sounded authoritative.

"Honey, I disagree but I don't want to be disagreeable." Betty smiled sweetly, already feeling a trifle guilty for her manner toward him a few moments ago. "Like Sister, I believe she was murdered. And I agree with you: Things don't add up. We're still only seeing part of the picture."

"Right." Sister backed up Betty. "But the more I think about all this, the worse I feel."

CHAPTER 19

"That heat beats down like a hammer." Mitchell Fisher rested his pole saw against the big poplar tree and wiped his brow.

"The anvil outlasts the hammer." Sister, one handkerchief tied around her forehead and another around her neck, each filled with ice cubes, was managing the heat better than Mitch. She withheld her advice about ice in a neckerchief, however, because Mitch, like many doctors, betrayed an arrogance that left him unable to learn from others.

He was smart but not that smart. Then, too, physicians and academicians confuse intellect with wisdom. The two are poles apart, something Sister learned from her days teaching at Mary Baldwin. Some of the biggest idiots she knew paraded their expertise about one thing. Oddly, many people were awed by someone's knowing more and more about less and less.

This Saturday, August 16, thirty members of Jefferson Hunt had come, armed with chain saws, axes, hammers, nails, ATVs, and Gators, to clear trails and build jumps at Skidby. Their first work party at the end of June had accomplished a lot. This second work party would open the large estate for its first year of hunting.

Many a master is tempted to throw up jumps everywhere and cut many trails: impressive but unwise. Best to open new territory like a wheel. Get round the perimeter and make spokes into the center. Not that these trails would be straight lines, given the topography, but the wheel pattern made for best access. However, one doesn't know how the foxes will run. So save money and energy at first by only putting up jumps where absolutely needed. The second year, jumps can be added by taking into account the foxes' running routes.

Mitch rode first flight when he could. Like too many foxhunters he cared little for the hound work, but other than that Sister liked him well enough. His enthusiasm in opening Skidby rubbed off on everyone despite the heat.

Sister, Mitch, Barry Baker, and Gray Lorillard made up one work party, their job being to clear the trails. Bobby Franklin headed a group coming behind them, to build any jumps that might be necessary and double-check the trails. Work parties of four, each headed by an experienced foxhunter, fanned out in all four directions. They'd meet back at the barns at two for a late lunch. Given the hot weather, they'd started at seven-thirty.

Betty and Tedi drove a Gator filled with ice chests. People carried their own water but, knowing the heat, Betty arranged to visit each party with sodas, water, tonic water, Gatorade, and sandwiches. That way she could also assess how each party was progressing and see if they needed special help.

Barry, seventy-four, Sister, seventy-three, and Gray, sixty-nine, all outworked Mitch, who was only forty-five. Although relatively fit, Mitch wasn't really an outdoor guy. He usually paid others to do what he found himself doing today.

"How far are we from Dinwiddie Creek?" Barry asked, his red T-shirt soaked through as well as his neckerchief.

"Half a mile," Mitch answered.

"We've made good progress." Sister smiled. "Well, let's press on. Ought to be cooler at the creek."

As they worked, Mitch pointed out old meadows that the forest had reclaimed. "Second growth. I'll turn it back into pasture eventually."

"Hard work, that," Gray said laconically, as he cut a low-hanging branch from a fiddle oak.

"I'll let the loggers do it. Make a bit of money, too."

"Still have to get the stumps up, Mitch—burn 'em or bury 'em—and then you've got to smooth out the land and scratch it up real good, so when you put that first dressing of fertilizer on, it can work way down into the soil." Gray was simply transmitting what he'd observed.

Mitch took it that Gray thought he was stupid. "I know all that."

Sister prudently said, "Then you know what's ahead of you."

Barry stepped in. "Ever go into the caves where the officers hid after April 9, 1865? The date of our surrender at Appomattox Courthouse?"

Mitch brightened. "I did. Found a broken pipe, a piece of spur. Didn't go deep, but one day I'll really explore those caves. Who knows what else I'll find?"

"Perhaps you'll show me sometime." Barry whacked at dead vines.

"Be glad to," Mitch replied.

The whine of the green Gator's little engine announced Betty and Tedi. A minute later they appeared.

"Ice-cold drinks, food; get your ice-cold drinks!" Betty called.

"Looks like you-all could use them." Tedi hopped out to stretch her legs.

"How's it going with the other teams?" Sister asked.

"Good. Xavier's made the most progress. I never realized how organized he is." Betty had known Xavier, also called X, since he was a boyhood friend of RayRay's. "He lashes them on."

"Walter's struggling with the pond and the swamp, which he's now calling the Little Dismal." Tedi laughed. "I never heard our joint master cuss before, but today the air is blue."

"Beavers." Mitch smiled. "That pond will be twice as big next year, after they dam up the water."

"Amazing creatures. People used to shoot them." Barry grabbed a Gatorade. "That's frowned upon these days so they trap them and remove them, but soon enough another crew comes to wherever the first one lived. A good site is a good site, and beavers know what they want."

"I'll bet anyone here fifty dollars that whatever fox lives in that area will head straight for the swamps when we pick up scent." Sister turned to Barry. "Remember the time we were all out with Deep Run? Must have been 'seventy-two. The fox headed into a swampy area, swam out, and sat on top of the beaver lodge."

Barry smiled. "Never forget it."

"If our fox does that, I'll not only meet your bet, I'll give you an extra fifty." Gray winked at Sister.

"I can feel that money sliding right across my palm." Sister opened her neckerchief to put in more ice and grabbed an egg salad sandwich made by Bill Johnson. The Johnson family had joined recently.

Gray and Barry followed suit with the ice, but it didn't occur to Mitch to do the same.

"We're off. Next stop Shaker," Betty said.

"He picked that northwest corner. He'll be up and down ravines." Mitch smiled, glad they had the southeastern corner of Skidby, with its generous rolling hills and flat pastures.

"Yeah, but it will be cool when he gets to the bottom." Gray finished off his drink. "You know, we could institute a new tradition, a Gator to meet the hunt at checks."

"Ha. You won't be looking for Gatorade," Betty teased. "Something stronger."

"Fortifies the resolve." Barry slapped Gray on the back.

After the ladies left, the team picked up some energy. The brief rest and drinks helped.

Barry, veteran of many a work party with Deep Run, knew people fell into a rhythm. Chatting can help the rhythm and so can singing, but the younger generations had not grown up singing as they worked. Tempted as he was to start the rounds he loved in the fields, songs he heard as a child and sang as a man, he figured it would make Mitch uncomfortable. Mitch wouldn't know the words and would mistake the songs for slave ditties. Like many Americans, Mitch didn't really know his country's history. Field hands all sang. Color might determine the song, but it didn't determine the singing.

Gray, who'd also grown up singing, whistled. That was his solution to the problem. After all, Mitch was the landowner, and no one wished to make him ill at ease.

All hunting depends on the generosity of landowners. A hunt cannot pay to hunt; the Master of Foxhounds Association forbids it. It's a good rule that prevents rich hunts from driving out poor ones. Also, since farmers have to agree to allow their lands to be hunted, the contact brings a community closer together. Over time, landowners and foxhunters not only become friends but realize their political interests are identical. There is strength in numbers.

Barry was working alongside Mitch. "Never asked you. Why did you choose research instead of a practice?"

"Residency taught me I'm not good with people. I was fascinated by their symptoms but I lacked a good bedside manner. Hell, even Lutrell chides me about it." He laughed at himself.

"Bedside manner to a woman means you worship her as a goddess." Barry laughed. "Sure worked with Noddy."

"What was her real name?" Mitch asked.

"Gertrude. She hated it. Didn't even like Trudy, which I like. Her mother called her Noddy because she'd nod off to sleep in church."

"Lutrell was named for her mother's family. She never says much about it one way or the other, but have you ever met a

Lutrell who was ashamed of being a Lutrell?" Mitch, not being old blood, thought it silly.

"No. That's the southern way. If your mother's maiden name can be used as a first name for one child, do it. Then use other family names, if they're grand enough, for middle names. Or you can take the maternal names as the middle name. You know, Mitch, if you pay attention to someone's name, you already know a lot about that person here."

"What do you make of Mitchell Charles Fisher?"

Barry threw a tree limb off to the side of the trail. "Couple of ways to look at it. Fisher could be an Anglicization of Fisk or Fisker, Old Norse for fish or fisherman. Or it could be straight Anglo-Saxon. But it's a name attached to a task, just as Wright or Carter is. The list is endless. Mitchell is a strong name, so your parents wanted you to be a strong man. Oh, the other thing about Fisher is it could be a Jewish name. Often the names from central Europe puzzled the men at Ellis Island so they gave the Jews more English-sounding names or the folks did it themselves once they lived here for a while. Diamond, for instance, is usually a Jewish last name."

"Don't think anyone was Jewish. It would be a help in my profession." Mitch smiled. "You must have learned a lot, sitting on the bench. About people, I mean."

"Sure did. I'd study the witnesses, study the defendant, the accuser, the lawyers. Even if the proceedings became tedious, my mind kept busy."

"Miss it?"

"*No.*" The reply was forceful, and Mitch's raised eyebrows

elicited further response. "By the end my disgust level was so high I felt like retching."

"Lawyers will do that to you."

"That's the rub, Mitch. Most lawyers are decent enough and a few are truly brilliant. Hearing their arguments, watching them shape a trial—and the great ones do—could be thrilling. It's the flotsam and jetsam who come before the judge. Scum in a three-piece suit. People who commit evil and then want to wriggle out of it describes ninety-eight percent of the people I saw. My retirement day was one of the happiest days of my life." He shook his head. "Enough of that. You picked research. Do you like it?"

"I do. I can help people, but I don't have to deal with them."

"What about the dogs?"

"What?" Mitch stood up straight.

"I'm a judge. I can find out anything. I know exactly what you do."

"They're not mistreated. And the work we do saves human lives."

"Starving a dog seems like mistreatment to me." Barry's voice carried an edge.

"You can't make an omelet without cracking eggs."

"Human life trumps all other forms of life?"

Without a second's hesitation, Mitch boomed, "Of course it does."

"Those two sure have a lot to talk about," Gray said to Sister. They had moved ahead of the others.

"Can only catch pieces of it." Sister grunted, intent on leveling a stub in the ground with an ax. "I hate these damned things."

"Yeah. Have to keep at them every year."

"Mitch and Lutrell want to have a big breakfast the first time we hunt his fixture. Given that September can be bloody hot, what do you think about mid-October?"

"Perfect. The leaves will be turning, the pastures will still be green, and with any luck the air will be a bit crisp."

"Luck is right. Sometimes you'll get a seventy-degree day followed by a forty-eight-degree day. Changing temps make me feel like a shuttlecock."

"Janie, I can't imagine you as a shuttlecock." He laughed.

They heard Barry's cell ring but didn't pay much attention until they heard a loud, "What?"

Mitch stopped too, for the expression on Barry's face was one of intense attention.

Barry said, "How could they not know? That's crazy."

They all had paused in their work. Might be rude to eavesdrop but they couldn't help it.

At last Barry flipped the phone shut. Sister moved toward him with Gray.

"Barry, are you all right?"

"Grant Fuller was found hanging in the freezer of one of his former slaughterhouses. Fonz called. He heard it on the local radio station. He's in Arkansas, as you might remember. And how could they not see a man hanging from a meat hook?" He scanned the faces of the other three. "Fonz said Grant was found at the back of the freezer, which must be huge, and he'd been put in a large garment bag."

"Good God!" Mitch exclaimed. "That really is crazy, hanging a man on a meat hook."

"So he was preserved?" Gray inquired.

"Fresh as a daisy—according to what Fonz heard," Barry added.

A pileated woodpecker, a huge bird sometimes close to two feet, sang its primitive song. Sister listened to the woodpecker, then ventured an opinion. "Maybe he wasn't in the freezer all this time. I don't care how big the freezer is at the slaughter-house, someone would have noticed. He could have been on ice somewhere else and then moved. Why?" She shrugged. "Who knows, but these weird murders—and I swear to you-all that Hope was murdered also—are too much a part of the equine community, if you will."

Barry stared at Sister. "Your mind amazes me."

"Just thinking out loud." She brushed off what she hoped was a compliment.

"Honey, why would someone freeze Grant Fuller, then hang him up now?"

"I don't know, Gray. And I find it peculiar that he was in a bag. If the killer wanted to scare the bejabbers out of people, you'd think he'd just hoist the body up there." She stopped. " 'Course, if he was already frozen and then moved, how would the killer get the meat hook through his back? Guess I answered my own question."

Barry leaned against a tree, then wished he hadn't, for ants marched up and down the trunk. "Bet you're right about the meat hook."

"Revenge. Grant's death and Mo's death are revenge kill-ings," Sister said.

"Could be." Barry nodded.

"You knew Grant about as well as I did. Any thoughts?" Sister asked Gray.

"Affable. Glib, even." Gray considered the person they'd met socially on occasion. "He didn't strike me as a man to arouse passions one way or the other."

Barry, listening, added, "He was getting a little roly-poly." He smiled. "A surefire passion killer. Although there are other forms of passion. The only thing I heard—gossip, really—is that Grant showed such an interest in introducing Hope to the distillers that his wife nipped their association in the bud."

"It was Grant who introduced her to bourbon." Sister could picture it.

"Her fascination with distillers took over," Barry continued. "She was a scientist—vets are—and distilling is a science. I could see why she'd become obsessed with it. A lot easier than subduing a thrashing horse to operate. The trick is getting close enough without getting kicked to stick the tranquilizer in."

"You got that right." Sister knew animals in pain could hurt you unwittingly. "Perhaps someone gave Grant a tranquilizer before doing whatever. Awful thing to be hoisted on a meat hook."

"It's grotesque." Mitch wiped his brow and then his arms with an oversized handkerchief.

"If the point of the killing is revenge, why tranquilize the man? Letting him suffer would seem to me to be what the killer wanted." Barry had hit the nail on the head.

"The things you do in this life catch up with you sooner or later." Sister was aghast at the news but wanted to get back to work. She could be single-minded, especially when it involved hunting.

"Karma?" Barry smiled at her.

"More like bad luck, I'd say." Mitch paid little heed to anything that couldn't be quantified scientifically.

"Remember your Dante? The lowest circle in Hell has the Devil encased in ice." Gray thought that was a haunting image of the paralysis of evil.

"Karma." Sister repeated Barry's judgment.

CHAPTER 20

"I'll be glad when cubbing starts." Sitting on the patio facing west, Gray leaned back against the big pillows in his comfortable wooden chair. Sister's old house afforded a gorgeous view of the Blue Ridge Mountains.

Large bug lamps glowed as the sun set behind the mountains, the clouds above reflecting an undergirding of gold. It was Friday, August 22.

"Me, too." Tootie agreed. Then suddenly her face registered dismay. "I forgot. I'll be at Princeton."

"Once you settle in up there, Sister will write you letters of introduction to the neighboring hunts. Most people don't know it, but New Jersey has some good clubs. Always has." Gray sipped a refreshing Tom Collins.

Not a heavy drinker, he did enjoy an end-of-the-day drink: gin or vodka mixes in summer and a scotch on the rocks in winter.

Sister carried out a large tray of fresh vegetables cut in thin strips, crackers, and some cheese—Raleigh, Rooster, and Golly following closely, in case she dropped something edible—and set the tray on the outdoor coffee table. She picked up her glass of tonic water with its big wedge of lime and dropped in a chair to the left of Gray.

He reached out his hand and she held it. "I was just telling Tootie that I'll be glad when cubbing starts."

Sister beamed, for she loved that he shared her passion for hunting, although perhaps not to her degree. "Sugar, I'm thrilled to hear that."

He touched his military mustache with his right forefinger, smoothing it first right and then left, a slight grin twitching the carefully groomed mustache upward. "Always like seeing the young entry, and—well, once you're hunting perhaps all this worry about the summer's ugly events will fade away."

"Been that bad, have I?" She squeezed his hand.

"I didn't say that," he replied diplomatically.

"Didn't have to." She turned to Tootie. "How bad have I been?"

Tootie stalled a minute, then said lightly, "Mildly obsessed."

Sister leaned back, stretching her long legs onto the wooden footrest that matched the chair. "I know."

"Here's a rare moment." Golly immediately jumped onto Sister's lap.

"She admits things—sometimes." Raleigh always defended his beloved human.

"I can count them on the claws of one paw." Golly held out one razor-sharp claw to make her point, as well as to remind the lowly dogs that she could do serious damage.

"My master used to say, 'Give Janie enough time and she'll come round. Push her and you lose her, maybe forever. She doesn't cotton to force.'" Rooster quoted his deceased master, Peter Wheeler, a former lover of Sister's whom she still loved, really.

"Force? I'd like to see someone push her around. She might be old, but she's quick as a cat. Well, almost." Golly, in a revealing moment, praised Sister. It wouldn't do for a cat to admit too much love for a human.

"I think Peter meant pressure more than physical force," Raleigh commented soberly.

"You should be a lawyer." With that Golly flopped on her side, closed her eyes, and pretended not to care a fig for the continuing conversation.

The three people had gone over Hope's labels yet again—which Sister saw in the print shop—as well as the fact that Mo Schneider's killer and Grant Fuller's killer had never been found. They had moved on to the decayed foot that young Twist had retrieved.

"There are a lot of people up there"—Gray held his glass toward the Blue Ridge Mountains, color deepening to flaming scarlet in the clouds as the ridgeline itself turned cobalt blue—"who don't come down. They live apart from what we euphemistically call civilization. They die in their cabins or out walking.

They aren't found except by vultures, feral dogs, and the like. I expect the foot comes from such a source."

"I thought the people who lived up there had been run off." Tootie couldn't believe how vivid the sunset was, the colors changing every minute.

"You mean during the Depression when the federal government bought up land and built the Skyline Drive?" The stirring of twilight breezes started up, and the first bat darted overhead as Sister spoke.

"Right. Wasn't it a terrible thing? Whole families torn off the land?" The beautiful girl liked reading history.

"Was." Gray had heard about it from his parents, aunts and uncles who thankfully lived at the old Lorillard home place and suffered no ill effects from the upheaval. "And some folks died shooting, too. Not all the stories made the history books. In fact, most of them didn't. We digest a pabulum version of our history. By design, of course."

"Cynical but true." Sister nodded.

"However, some people who were forced off their land crept to some other place below the federal lands and made do. In the sixties, people came from other parts and vanished into the ravines and hollows. It's one of the odd things about our country: We don't study the thousands—maybe millions—of people who choose not to participate in the Great American Way." Gray heard a high-pitched bat squeak.

"Which is?" Sister squeezed his hand again, then let go to pet Golly, still pretending to be asleep.

"Grabbing and getting. Been that way since 1607. You think

those folks from England sailed over here to be poor?" Gray laughed genially.

"Some came to escape persecution," Tootie answered.

"Not in 1607. But you're right, many did who came later. 'Course some of them, once established, relished the joys of persecuting others." He leaned over to look directly at Tootie. "If I can teach you anything, Tootie, allow me to teach you this: The human animal stays the same. All systems of government and religion try to effect change, and all fail. The best you can do is manage the animal."

"And some manage better than others," Sister pointed out. "I think we've done pretty well, even with our outstanding flaws."

"Slavery." Tootie named what she perceived as some flaws. "Killing off the Indians."

"Are we back to calling them Indians now?" Sister meant this with genuine curiosity. "It became Native Americans, then it was First Americans. I hope we're back to Indians, because the word conjures up pictures of bravery, glamour even. *First American* sounds like an insurance company."

"You're not PC." Gray laughed at her.

"No. And while I'm on this tear, what is that drivel about someone being *hearing impaired*? If you can't hear, you're deaf. If you can't see, you're blind. Use the true word, the word that has power, not some watered-down treacle. I hate euphemisms. Those words are for people who can't face life."

"Maybe." Gray liked engaging in ideas, observations. "Most people don't live authentic lives, honey. There are so many layers between them and the truth, whether it's the truth of nature or the truth of power, that even their language is anemic. They aren't temporizing. At least, I don't think they are."

"My dad's like that." Tootie loved her father but didn't always like him.

"Your father?" Sister was surprised.

"What Dad knows is banking. He's incredible. He's always getting put in charge of things like the Heart Fund. But he thinks that's the world. I mean he thinks everything will conform to what he knows. That's why I disappoint him."

"Honey." A rush of emotion flushed Sister's face. "Your father loves you. He's not disappointed. Granted, he doesn't understand your love of hunting and the outdoors; he sees it as a pastime. But he's proud of you."

"Then why does he want me to be like him?"

Gray knocked back the rest of his drink. "Because he loves you. That sounds like a contradiction, but *he's* happy in his world and wants *you* to be happy, hence the desire to see you doing what he has done. It will be difficult for him to accept another path for you, should you take it. But he will. Sister is right; your father loves you. He hasn't abandoned you like Felicity's parents have done. I don't think he would, even if you take a different path from what he thinks is best. I know he's hard on you. I was hard on my kids, especially my son. When he wanted to be a veterinarian specializing in cattle, I didn't get it. I thought, Here goes my son, every damned advantage I could give him and he wants to spend his life in blood and manure. Actually, I thought of a different word than manure."

"Then over time you saw he had to be his own man," Sister added.

"I did, and I'm glad he held out for what he wanted. I have a real man for a son, not a pale imitation of me."

"You really think in time my father will be glad I became my own woman?" Tootie had assumed she'd spend the rest of her life either avoiding discussions with her father or endlessly explaining herself.

"He will, but don't expect an overnight conversion." Gray chuckled. "Men can be hardheaded."

"God, I think I need a drink!" Sister exclaimed in false shock. "Write the date down: August twenty-second: Gray Lorillard admits men can be hardheaded."

"Oh, come on, I'm not that bad." Gray stood up. "I'm going to refresh my drink. What would you like?"

"How about another tonic water with a splash of that gin in the blue bottle?"

He took her upheld glass.

"Isn't anyone going to eat the vegetables?" Rooster thought food on a plate should be consumed.

"I'm not eating tiny cauliflowers." Raleigh watched the sunset, too.

Golly opened one eye. *"Good. They make you fart."*

"I do not!" Raleigh loathed her sometimes.

"Oh, la!" Golly sassed, rolling on her back so Sister could rub her tummy.

Gray returned. "Have you ever seen anything like that sky? Scarlet, flamingo pink, lavender, purple, and the mountains cobalt blue all the way to the bottom. Look over there, a streak of pure gold. Paradise."

"Which reminds me." Sister took a taste: quite nice. "Didn't see one boar track when Ben and I were out there two weeks ago. Plenty of otters, deer, everything else. Well, it was a long shot going over there to see if the boar were around, but they hunt a huge territory and they like carrion. And I killed two birds with one stone."

"Which is?" Gray sat down and plucked a tiny sweet carrot off the tray while Rooster watched.

"Checked how much work we need to do in the fixtures."

"You never stop," he said, with admiration.

"No master does." Sister noted Tootie's empty glass. "Another Coke?"

"No, ma'am. Keeps me awake if I drink too much."

"Promise me you will learn everything you can at Princeton. Soak it up. Then come back to me and I'll teach you how to be a master."

"Promise." Tootie reached out her hand and Sister took it, a left hand shaking a right.

"You'd better teach her how to make some money," Gray added dryly.

"Spoken like my dad." Tootie laughed at him and he laughed at himself.

"How do you like your drink?" Gray asked Sister.

"Very very nice. The hint of gin on the tongue on a languid summer's night feels lavish."

"Seize every pleasure." Gray smiled.

Sister wanted to say she had but didn't.

"I haven't harped too much on Hope, the foot, and the rest of it." She looked up as a giant blue heron flew home for the night. "But I'm not giving up."

"When you find the body, there won't be anything left," Gray joked.

"I'm more concerned with finding the murderer than finding the body." She paused to listen to the heron's croak, for high as he was she could hear that distinctive sound. "Tootie, I am going to miss you so much, but in a way I'm glad you'll be safe at Princeton because who knows what all this is about. You'll be out of harm's way."

"You won't—" Tootie started to say more, already sorry she'd said that.

"Maybe. But I'm old. If I go, it's no great loss. If you do, it is."

"If you go, darling, we're all lost," Gray said softly.

CHAPTER 21

On September 6, the first Saturday after Labor Day, hounds bounded out of the kennels. Traditionally, Jefferson Hunt began cubbing from home. The draw-pen door opened and out dashed fifteen couple of hounds, including two couple of young entry. Two of Mo Schneider's hounds packed in, too.

"*Whoopee!*" shouted Giorgio.

"*Shut up, young fool,*" Asa grumbled, a touch of melancholy in his voice. He knew he was slowing down, which would be obvious to staff.

"*Aren't you excited?*" Tinsel, wide-eyed, danced around the older tricolor.

"*Yes, but no one likes a babbler. Respect tradition.*" Asa liked Tinsel, whereas he wasn't so sure about the gorgeous Giorgio.

"Hear, hear." Cora seconded the stalwart Asa.

Staff surrounded the pack, no thongs down, just quietly waiting.

By seven-thirty in the morning, forty riders had turned out, seemingly as excited as the hounds. Given September's heat— and often it was a dry month, too—it was best to start early: dew still on the meadows, temperature in the high fifties to low sixties. Hounds might pick up a fox but the run wouldn't last long, for as the sun rose higher, the mercury rose with it and scent vanished.

Sister, knowing the riders to be the hard core of the hunt, simply said, "Good morning. Let's go."

Tootie and Val, down from Princeton even though it was a big football weekend, grinned. Judge Baker rode next to Daphne Wigg of Deep Run. Daphne, a strikingly good-looking woman, especially on a horse, kept him smiling; they were old friends. Everyone was smiling, especially Gray.

Much as Gray enjoyed hunting, it wasn't the center of his life. Knowing it was life itself to Sister, and knowing how hard she and Shaker worked during the grueling summer days, he loved seeing her in her glory.

"Hounds, please." Sister nodded to Shaker, who headed down the farm lane toward the old apple orchard, moving past the deep ruts in the track.

"Did you notice how the hounds waited?" Tootie whispered to Val.

"They always wait." Val hunted to ride whereas Tootie rode to hunt.

"It's a big step for young entry." Tootie was so glad to be back on the farm she was verging on tears.

Georgia lounged outside her den after a night of gorging on the sweet feed the horses had dropped from the buckets hanging on the fence. The black fox had also consumed far too many sour balls that Sister left in the barn by mistake, package open.

"*Bother.*" She sighed, making no effort to pop back into her den.

Shaker couldn't see Georgia. Leaves still festooned the trees, and her den sat smack in the middle of the orchard.

"Lieu in, there," Shaker commanded, sending hounds into the orchard.

Sister waited on the road as Betty rode at ten o'clock and Sybil at two; their salt-colored sack coats, light linen, made them easy to see against the deep green.

"Here." Tinsel found the line, and Cora checked it.

Within seconds, the entire pack roared and it was only seconds, too, before Georgia slipped into her den.

Hounds milled around the tidy opening.

Twist stuck her head into the den. *"I know you; you visit the kennels at night."*

"Of course you know me, you twit. I come with my mother, Inky."

"Come out and play." Twist, first year, lacked a concept of a true hunt; she'd only worked at fox pen, where young hounds can be trained on fox scent.

"You must be joking, Twist. Will you kindly remove your face from my foyer?"

Before the confused but happy hound could reply, she felt a strong hand on her stern.

"Come on, young'un." Shaker pulled her out. "Good work."

Although the run only lasted seconds, Shaker blew Gone to Ground, for they did den their fox. Laughing, he could barely get the notes out.

After the garbled sounds, he patted the glossy heads, put his foot in the left stirrup iron, and swung up on Showboat, the horse chuckling, too.

Sister turned to the field. "World's shortest run. Someone be sure to notify *Guinness Book of World Records.*"

Ben Sidell, in first flight for the first time, stuck close to Kasmir Barbhaiya, who promised to look out for him. Kasmir, generous in heart and pocketbook, was fast becoming a much-loved member. The Vajays, his friends from India originally, also rode first flight on lovely Thoroughbreds.

Riding behind Ben, Mitch Fisher wished he'd not worn his tattersall vest under his coat.

"Where to?" Diana looked up at Shaker.

Shaker stared down at his anchor hound and then looked up. No wind. Calm, mercury rising, not a cloud in the sky. These are not ideal hunting conditions. However, dew lay thick on the grass. If he punched down into the cool air currents that often follow creek beds, the pack would have a shot at another run and that would probably be it.

He jumped over the new coop in the fence line at the wildflower field. It was well sited, offering easy takeoff and landing. Some jumps can only be placed in difficult spots. A foxhunter must be able to ride off, his or her eye even turning sharply after a landing. Count strides and you're dead.

The new coop, freshly painted black, put off some horses. Horses grow accustomed to seeing the same things, just like a person driving to work. They do it by rote. Introduce a new element and a horse will usually look. Is this a strange-appearing predator? Many creatures like horse meat, the French being among them. In these circumstances, a rider has to boot over the horse. Many a grunt and groan filled the air, with the humans grunting and not the horses. Ahead of the field, Sister occasionally heard a hard rap on the coop's edge. Across the wildflower field they cantered, Shaker trying to get to the next cast before it was too hot. He soared over the hog's-back jump that divided Sister's land from the Bancrofts. Within a minute, Sister and Keep-sake popped over.

The hounds reached Broad Creek shortly thereafter, the temperature already cooler from the heavy woods. At this location, two miles from the main house, Shaker most often cast west toward the mountains. Since wind usually came from the west this made good sense. However, this day was still as a tomb so he cast down the creek, southeast. The distinctive odor of water filled his nostrils. If Shaker could smell the water, he hoped hounds could smell whatever scent might be tagging a ride on the cool current.

Deer crashed out of the woods.

"Big!" Tattoo let out a yelp.

"Don't even think about it," Peanut warned, feeling herself a veteran now.

If Shaker had possessed a better nose, he would have picked up a scent smelling like old wet wood as they traveled downstream.

Dasher noticed it first. *"What do I do?"*

"Legitimate game," Diana replied. She opened on the line and off they went.

Sister knew the hounds weren't on deer, but they didn't sound quite right, even factoring in the higher squeals of the young entry. Still, Shaker was blowing them on, so she squeezed her legs on Keepsake.

The path by the creek, wide and well worn, made for easy going. That, too, surprised her. A fox would have used the creek, picking those spots where the bed was deep and sharply cut, leaping off to swim to the other side, sometimes crisscrossing to foul scent before veering off into heavy covert, if it was available, or using the woods to slow pursuers.

None of this happened. Hounds roared down the creek path, noses down, intent. Betty, on the northeastern side of the water, for the creek bent sharply at that point, looked ahead and spurred Outlaw on.

Sybil, to the right, rode off the creek path in the thick woods, where she couldn't see much. When Shaker got round the sharp turn, he put his horn to his lips, blowing three sharp blasts, then calling, "Hold up!"

Ahead of him, moving quickly for such a bulky animal, a black bear hurried along.

Sybil, hearing the three notes, moved toward the creek

from the woods. Unfortunately, she came out in front of the bear, perhaps fifty yards away. Bombardier, a sensible Thoroughbred, nostrils wide open, caught one whiff of the big boy and started shaking all over.

"All right. All right." Sybil patted him, but she had to stay where she was in case some hounds flew past the bear.

Fortunately, all returned to the huntsman, even the young entry, who had never seen such game.

Without missing a beat, Sister appraised the situation and called out "Tally Yogi" and then "Reverse."

Following her command, the field turned around, without waiting for the field master to lead. Instead, it was up to the last person to lead them back out, until the field master could come up front.

Shaker followed the field while Sybil gratefully moved back into the woods.

The bear sat down for a breather.

The last person happened to be Lorraine Rasmussen, a novice, but she did her best to lead them out.

Once into the small clearing, with little fire stars dotting the area brilliant red, Shaker brought hounds through, followed by Sister.

The field waited as Shaker and Sister conferred.

"Tally Yogi?" He laughed.

"Better than 'Tally bear.'" She grinned, then added, "Let's lift. The temperature has already come up to the low seventies, I swear it."

"Okay, Boss." Shaker felt this was the right decision.

They turned toward the west. The Bancrofts had cut many paths through their farm over the decades, a godsend to the hunt staff.

They emerged from the woods, three-quarters of a mile up from the hog's back they'd jumped to get into After All farm. The jump in the fence line here, three large stacked and tied logs, looked formidable, but horses would rather take a solid obstacle than an airy one so over they went.

Walking through the wildflower field, Jerusalem artichokes not yet opened, black-eyed Susans thinking about blooming, Queen Anne's lace filling the field with white, the group was nearing the southernmost part of Hangman's Ridge. A last finger of the glacier that created the Blue Ridge Mountains also piled up Hangman's Ridge. The unusual top, smooth as glass, had slopes covered in creepers, thorns, and all manner of prickly bushes. The southern side looked as though it had been sheered off with a knife, but bushes grew out of the rocks and tiny little lichens gave a green-gray cast to the rocky terrain. A path from Soldier Road, which ran east of Hangman's Ridge a mile from the ride, was the closest one could get to the top from this side, although smaller animals could zigzag up the face, depending on their agility.

Tootie, scanning the southern rocks, had learned from Sister to read "everything." By that Sister meant to read the wind, the temperature, the soils, the kinds of rocks and animals, the angle of the sun, the plants, the birds, and the tracks. Never stop experiencing nature, for one feels as much as one sees and hears.

A faded blue baseball cap with an orange V in the center, hanging near the top, caught her eye. "How'd that get there?"

Val, amused, looked up; then she and Tootie noticed at the same time.

"Holy shit!" Val exclaimed, but there was no Felicity to collect a dollar this time. Felicity was only a week away from delivering her baby.

Since there was room for her to do so without jostling, Tootie rode past the other people to Sister, where she whispered something.

Sister, face suddenly ashen, turned to the field. "Gray, will you lead everyone back? I'll be with you shortly."

Gray counted hound heads. He knew whatever this was did not involve picking up a lost hound.

Then Sister quietly drew alongside Ben and they rode back to Val, whose exclamation had unfortunately drawn other eyes to the blue baseball cap with the V for Virginia on it.

Although it was above them and so high they had to squint, people who looked hard could see a skull and some hair, sticking out from under the cap, wedged between the base of a slender bush and the rock. An old frying pan was also wedged in a rock outcropping.

Sister told people to move along.

Ben stopped below the point and stared up. "If this belongs to the foot, we might get an ID from the teeth. From here all of them look to be there."

"And grinning at us," Sister added grimly.

CHAPTER 22

"How can these body parts show up when there's no missing person's report?" Back at Roughneck Farm, Val, ever logical, chatted as she cleaned tack.

Working on the tack hanging from the other hook, Tootie said, "The sheriff checked for central Virginia."

"Someone is missing somewhere." Val stated the obvious.

"Like the Jimmy Buffett song, 'It's Five O'Clock Somewhere'?" Sister came in the back entrance of the barn after throwing hay for the horses.

"Was kinda cool, wasn't it?" Val tossed her blonde ponytail.

"As long as you weren't the head." Sister entered the tack room as the girls stood in the aisle with the tack hooks, buckets in front of them full of water.

"Gray," Sister called out. Gray was walking across the pea-gravel walk from the kennels to the barn.

"Yes, master," he said teasingly.

"Will you call your brother and find out if he knows if any of the street drunks are missing? I have a hunch, thanks to the frying pan, that the man under the cap lived rough."

"Good idea." Gray checked his watch. "He's still at work." Flipping open his cell, Gray punched the speed dial button. "Sam."

On hearing the voice of his big brother, also his roommate, Sam replied, "What do you want me to pick up on the way home?"

"Nothing. Do me a favor. Ask around to see if any of the street people are missing."

"They go missing a lot and usually turn up later after a colossal bender. But yeah, I'll ask." Sam knew his brother would give him details later, no need to talk overlong at work because Crawford might notice.

That man noticed the smallest thing.

"Crawford hunt his hounds today?" Gray's voice carried a note of sarcasm.

"Don't ask."

"All right, tell me later, but if you hear anything before I get home call my cell."

"Must be important."

"Could be." Gray flipped his cell shut. "He'll get on it."

"Good." Sister sank down in a worn chair.

"Don't you think the sheriff has asked the street people?" Val called from the center aisle.

"Sure, but they'll be more inclined to speak to one of their own—one of their former own, I should say—rather than to a badge. Dammit, I hate this," Sister replied. "Sometimes street people get tired of being moved along by the cops, tired of being helped by the Salvation Army, so they head out into the country. Like I told Gray, it's just a hunch."

The two young women looked at each other. They'd never heard Sister speak quite like that.

"You hate not knowing." Gray humored her.

"That's a fact. But have you considered that Hangman's Ridge is *my* land? First a foot, now a skull and a frying pan. I want to get to the bottom of this."

"Me, too." Gray put his arm around her.

"Creepy," Tootie said, as she cleaned the bit with fresh water. "The foot was bad enough, but the head—that really creeped me out."

"Way gross, but still we'll be telling our grandchildren about the skull hunt." Val did enjoy drama.

Tootie giggled. "I can't imagine you as a grandmother."

"I can't either," Val agreed. "Hey, let's call Felicity when we're done and tell her. Better: Let's go over."

"If you go, I made a big casserole, since I figured we'd be eating together. You can take some to her. Will you be back for supper?"

The two conferred. "I'll take it to her, but we want to eat it with you," Val said.

"All right."

Two hours later, Sister was pulling weeds in her garden. The ability of weeds to thrive when perfectly beautiful flowers die never

ceased to amaze and irritate her. Golly supervised. Raleigh and
Rooster slept under the Japanese maple. The kids had driven
over to see Felicity. Gray was in the den, cheering on Syracuse,
his alma mater. There could never be enough football for Gray
but especially Syracuse football. Sam had graduated from Har-
vard and spent a year at Michigan law before transferring to the
Darden School at UVA. He was a rabid Michigan fan. The air at
the old home place sometimes thickened with sulfur as the two
brothers discussed their teams.

Gray's phone rang. "Better be good," Gray said. "Third
quarter, Syracuse up by six."

"It is," said Sam. "Jake Ingram hasn't been seen since the
end of March. Got to the point where he'd drink anything, even
Sterno. Everyone figured he wandered off or died."

"No one reported it."

"Of course not. Sometimes people go back home or get
smart and go into rehab. They don't want to see any of the old
gang. Makes sense, if you think about it."

"Did anyone go to wherever Jake lived?"

"He lived on the street. Used to live down by the train station, but you can't do that anymore, now they've built those
apartments across the tracks. The guys hang around the parks or
the Greyhound station or they move farther out. These days they
move a lot."

Gray called Ben Sidell, who thanked him. Then he tore
himself away from the game because he knew Sister would kill
him if he didn't tell her straightaway.

After hearing the news, she looked up from under the straw
cowboy hat. "Jake Ingram. Never heard of him. Well, Ben can

track down his dental records. Might make for a fast matchup, but the name doesn't ring a bell."

"If you don't need me, I'll go back to the game."

She waved him off—for Gray, football took precedence over everything else—and said to Golly, "I hope I never have a heart attack during a Syracuse game. He'd wait until after the game to call the ambulance."

"I'll revive you." Golly felt she had great powers.

"Right." Rooster opened one eye. *"She'll smell that tuna breath and gag."*

Golly puffed up, shot out of the garden, raced to the Japanese maple, and hit Rooster with all four paws as she shouted, *"Death to dogs!"*

Then she prudently climbed the graceful tree as Rooster threatened from below.

Sister wiped her brow. "What in God's name gets into her?"

CHAPTER 23

The name Jake Ingram rang a bell so loud for Mitch Fisher that he nearly went deaf.

Ben Sidell sat across from the doctor in the living room at seven-thirty in the evening. Thanks to Sam Lorillard's tip, Ben asked Larry Hund, one of the area's leading dentists, if Ingram was a patient. He was not, but Larry remembered that Dr. Sandra Yarbrough often performed work on the indigent and victims of violence as a community service. Both she and her husband, Nelson, also a dentist, took care of the unfortunates with no fanfare. Sandra, home when Ben called, dropped everything, drove back to the office, and met him at the morgue within an hour of the call. The records matched up. Also, there was evidence of periodontal disease, not uncommon among alcoholics and especially among people hooked on crank.

Lutrell, Mitch's wife, looked in on them. Noticing Mitch's ashen face, she left right after ascertaining no libations were needed.

"How did he die?" Mitch had liked Jake as best as one can like a person in the grips of addiction.

"We don't know."

"If his head was severed from the body, it must have been horrible."

"No clean cut of the neck vertebra. His head was torn off by an animal. We haven't found the rest of his body. Probably won't, since he was somebody's lunch.

"When did you fire Jake?" Ben asked.

"A year ago. Came in late and smelled of liquor—you know, sweating it out of his system." Mitch folded and unfolded his hands, a nervous gesture. "I knew for years that he went on benders on the weekends, but until it affected his work it was none of my business."

"How many years did you work together?"

"Four. He had good skills, and he was responsible. Lab techs, good ones, are hard to find."

"I can imagine. Was there an outstanding incident that forced you to fire him?" Ben asked.

"Not so much that as an accumulation of late mornings, especially in the last six months that he worked for me. If I was operating, he was still good."

"Was he angry when you fired him?"

"No. Defeated."

"I see." Ben folded his hands together and leaned back in the cavernous club chair. "Did you ever see or hear of his having major problems with anyone?"

"Hope Rogers."

"What happened?"

"Sheriff, I only got this from Jake, so the story is highly colored, but he said she accosted him in the Food Lion parking lot and accused him of animal torture: stealing dogs and horses. According to Jake, she was one hysterical bitch."

"Doesn't sound like Hope, does it?"

Mitch shook his head. "No, but people get very emotional about animals. Children and animals. Possible. Not likely, though."

Ben looked Mitch directly in the eye. "How much did you pay for dogs?"

Mitch hesitated, then replied. "Used to be five bucks a dog, but now it's twenty-five. Or I should say that was what I last paid. Research using dogs shut down in this area four months ago, thanks to all the bad press. Public outrage built, and this year it finally hit the red zone." He paused and removed his tortoiseshell glasses. "I understand the outrage, but many advances have come at the cost of the suffering of animals, to put it bluntly."

"I'll take your word for it." Ben remained noncommittal. "Were you shocked when you heard Hope Rogers shot herself?"

"I was."

"Was she your equine vet?"

"No. She wouldn't work for me because she was so adamantly opposed to research using animals, even rats. Again, I understood her position and it was not discussed between us."

"Certainly seems to have been discussed between her and Jake."

"Again, I took his version with a grain of salt. Jake wasn't a confrontational guy but, as his deterioration accelerated, let's just say there were copious misunderstandings."

"Did you think, after you'd fired him, that he might seek revenge in some way?"

"No. He wasn't unreasonable. When his mind was clear he knew he was a liability."

"But that's it, isn't it? His mind wasn't clear. Did he ever threaten you?"

"No."

Ben unclasped his hands, thinking, then said quietly, "Did you ever see him after you'd fired him?"

"Once at the shopping center. That was—oh, Christmas. I remember it was snowing a bit. I was shocked at his appearance."

"Did you talk to him?"

"Yes. He was embarrassed to see me. I gave him fifty dollars. I guess that was stupid. He probably went right into the ABC store and loaded up on good liquor. I can't imagine what he'd been drinking without money."

"Let's just say folks can be imaginative in trying to extract liquor—even from Listerine."

Mitch grimaced. "He couldn't beat it. Maybe he's better off dead. That's a terrible thing to say, I guess, but it's what I think."

"Back to Hope Rogers for a moment. Did you get a feeling, even if fleeting, that Jake would get even with her?"

"No."

"Well, you've been helpful and I'm sorry to break the news

to you. Even though you'd let him go, I can tell that you harbored some good feelings for the man." Ben stood up to leave. "If you think of anything, anything at all, please call me."

"I will." Mitch walked Ben to the front door, the hallway lined with nineteenth-century colored plates of military men from the English publication *Vanity Fair.*

Ben walked slowly, admiring the prints. "Guess appearing in *Vanity Fair* in those days was like *People* today."

"Higher class of reader," Mitch commented dryly.

"Yes, I suppose." As Mitch opened the door, Ben stepped out, turned, and said, "One more thing. Has anyone ever threatened you about your research?"

"Occasionally."

"What is the research?"

Mitch, hand still on the door latch, thought how to put this in simple English. "My work involves the amount of fat surrounding major organs. One of the causes of death at the end of certain kinds of cancers, and a contributing factor to death in famine-cursed countries, is the lack of fat around organs. It's fascinating, really. On the one hand, we have an obesity epidemic, and on the other, people can't keep warm because they don't have sufficient body fat."

"So you starved them, killed them, and then operated to study the organs."

Stunned at how quick Ben's mind was, Mitch swallowed. "Yes."

"Again, thank you." Ben left.

As Ben drove out, he passed a tidy two-story dependency, taupe clapboard with maroon shutters. Stepping out into the cooling evening air was Barry Baker, all spiffed up. Barry waved.

Ben stopped the car. "Going to be a long weekend here for you?"

"Love it here. Just love it. Quite a hunt today."

"Yes, it was. No one will ever forget it."

"You and I have both seen the worst of human behavior," said Barry. "I was in Korea, and I'll tell you, Ben, individual crime is worse. War isn't personal, if you know what I mean."

"I do. We found out who that skull used to be. It was a lab tech Mitch fired. Alcoholic."

"That's a sad end. Ever see Hogarth's drawing *Gin Lane?*"

"Have."

"Accurate then. Accurate now."

"Sure is. Say, you look ready for action."

"You never know. It's the vest, isn't it?"

Judge Baker wore a handsome tweed herringbone jacket, a red vest, and a white shirt with a forest green tie embroidered with foxes. Pinwale tan cords and expensive handmade calf shoes completed his attire. Of course, he wore his platinum watch.

"I'd be chicken to wear a red vest. I've got to hand it to you."

"Take a lesson from an old man: Women notice clothes. In fact, women notice everything; they can recall a pinstripe shirt you wore three years ago at a cocktail party. Money spent on good clothing is never wasted. Of course"—he smiled rakishly— "time spent with women is never wasted either."

"I'll remember that." Ben waved and drove off.

Two hours later, Judge Baker and his red vest were relaxing in the perfectly proportioned living room at Roughneck Farm.

Sister had had the entire interior of the house repainted two years ago. The living room walls had been freshened with a creamy eggshell; the trim was sparkling white. Now she was glad she'd endured the upheaval because the room looked spectacular.

Val, Tootie, Gray, Barry, and Sister glowed as people tend to do after a wonderful meal. The men sipped at brandy; the girls drank iced tea, as did Sister.

Val, as usual, proved entertaining. "Felicity waddles!"

"She's due next week," Sister informed the men, although Gray already knew. "In my last weeks of pregnancy I felt a strange kinship with hippos."

"You. Never?" Judge Baker roared with laughter. "I remember when you were pregnant, and you carried it off with your usual aplomb."

"That's base flattery." Sister smiled.

Val devilishly taunted the men. "Didn't you feel guilty when your wives were pregnant?"

Gray, holding his brandy snifter, sighed. "I did. I confess I did. She had a hard time of it. Sick from the beginning."

"We didn't have that problem." Barry said *we,* which spoke volumes about his relationship with his deceased wife. "I wondered how I was going to pay for it all. Then I thought about college and, if it was a girl, the wedding. I allowed myself an overactive imagination. Well, the first one was a girl and the second, too. We managed."

"I still think Felicity is throwing her life away." Val lapsed into her old complaint, one she'd been harping on since Felicity had first revealed her pregnancy.

"Val, she's happy." Tootie had been disagreeing with Val since then, too.

"Happy? How can she be happy when she's a blimp? She can't bend over. If she sits down, she can't get up without help. How can she be happy?"

"She is." Tootie turned her attention to the others. "She really is. She wants to get it over with, but she's so excited."

"It *is* exciting." Sister smiled. "Val, I don't know if you will ever become pregnant, but if you do and if it's what you desire, you truly will forget the pain and remember the joy. And what is more exciting than giving life? I get giddy every time I whelp puppies."

The corners of Gray's mouth turned up. "You like whelping pups better than giving birth yourself. I'd bet on that."

"I would, too. Janie loves her hounds better than people." Barry lifted his glass to her.

"Oh," Sister mused, "half and half. Or how about even-steven. I like them both, but there is something to be said for not having to produce the child yourself."

"Men have been saying that for years." Barry laughed again. "Say, to change the subject—or to expand on it—is a puppy's life as valuable as a human's?"

"Is this a trick question?" Val's response was swift.

"You're going into politics, aren't you?" Barry began to feel his vest was too warm.

"Maybe." Val proved his point right there.

Tootie looked to Sister, since she felt the master should answer first.

Sister, sensitive to Tootie as to few others, said, "Go on. I'll go last, how's that?"

Tootie stated her belief concisely. "I think all life is sacred."

"Sacred, yes. But are those lives *equal*?" Barry pressed.

"Yes." Tootie didn't hesitate.

Gray, relaxed, his sleeves rolled up, replied. "Much as I love the hounds, the horses, and, of course, Golly,"—he had to say that when she jumped on his lap—"I believe human life is more valuable."

"Even someone like Mo Schneider?" Barry prodded.

"I suppose if you take it on a case-by-case basis, some animal lives are more worthy than some human lives, but on the whole I value human life more," Gray responded.

"Me, too. That doesn't mean there aren't people I wouldn't like to kill," Val chimed in.

"Really?" Barry's eyebrows shot upward.

"Sure. Haven't you ever been mad enough to kill?" Val boldly questioned him.

"Many times."

"Sister, haven't you been mad enough to kill?" Val turned to her master.

"I have, and it was usually my late husband who provoked that combustible emotion."

Gray and Barry laughed.

"Back to life." Val directed this to Sister. "You didn't tell us what you think."

"I think my hounds' lives are as important as human lives. My horses. Raleigh. Rooster. Golly. I can't distinguish because my love for them is so great." She pursed her lips to say something; then her eyes lit up. "Funny, must be a year ago now, Hope Rogers and I were talking about this very thing. I know you-all are bored with my not accepting that Hope killed herself, but this discussion just reminded me that Hope must have stumbled upon some kind of cruelty. She wouldn't say what it was, exactly. But we did talk about the slaughterhouses closing and people who were letting unwanted horses starve to death. She was on overload from overwork. She told me horror stories about people loading unwanted horses onto rickety vans and crossing the line into Mexico to go to those filthy slaughterhouses. The Thoroughbred Retirement Foundation was Hope's true passion. I think she lifted up a very big rock and the snake underneath bit her. If you think about it—Mo, Grant, even that homeless man, Jake—all of them were considered cruel to animals in some fashion, except Hope. Maybe that's what these deaths have in common."

A silence followed.

Barry, finally unbuttoning his vest, answered softly. "You think like a fox. You feel things—or sense things—the rest of us can't. It's not circumventing logic as much as surmounting logic. Your mind works in ways ours do not." There was a pause, followed by a long draft. "I wouldn't be at all surprised to find you're right.

CHAPTER 24

September 9, Tuesday, hounds met at Mudfence Farm. Try as they might, they couldn't get a thing. No master or huntsman likes a blank day, but it's foolish to keep hounds out, especially young hounds, when scent is so poor. They worked hard for an hour and a half. Then, when heat came up fast, Shaker wisely lifted the hounds.

Back in the kennels, glad for the high fans in the ceiling, hounds slept on their benches.

With Shaker's help, Sister had finished washing the feed room down and cleaning the runs. She'd taken care of Aztec and HoJo. She already missed Tootie and Val, who had driven back to Princeton late Sunday.

"Boss, think I'll ride Kilowatt Saturday."

"You forget Thursday?" She was teasing him: The club always hunted Tuesdays, Thursdays, and Saturdays.

"No, just thinking about Skidby."

"We accomplished a lot with that work party. Enthusiasm for the new fixture is so high we're hunting Skidby on Saturday instead of an old fixture. Means, of course, we can't take young entry."

"Figured as much." Shaker, while not a political person, had been in hunt service long enough to appreciate some of his master's decisions.

"Much as we need to get the young entry out, we also need to keep the Fishers and the members happy. And it's only once, maybe twice, during the cubbing season."

"Ever wish we could just hunt?"

She winked at him. "Can. Staff hunt."

This type of hunt involved only staff members, no field. Often it was to work the young hounds, but just as often it served to tune up staff work. No matter how many decades staff hunted as individuals, everyone could stand to scrub off the rust spots during cubbing.

"I say we hunt from the Demetrios farm and head toward Crawford's." He let out a guffaw, since Crawford had closed his land to the Jefferson Hunt.

"We could sell tickets to that hunt." She could just imagine Crawford's eruption. Better yet, imagine the eruption in his kennels.

"Pay attention to me!" yapped little Valentine, born May 28 during the storm.

Victor, her littermate, did just that. *"Tag, you're it."*

Within seconds, the five puppies were chasing one another, giving what they considered tongue while Violet looked on, rapidly tiring of motherhood.

Sister and Shaker, walking in from an adjoining run, laughed.

"That reminds me." Sister strode toward the kennels and walked into the office.

After years of association, Shaker knew she'd tell him whatever it was that she remembered after she wrote it down or performed the act. He hummed to himself as he followed her into the office.

She picked up the old phone and dialed. "How you doing?"

Felicity, on the other end, replied, "I'm doing."

"Any minute now?"

"I hope so, Sister. I can't stand much more of this. I wish Howie were here, but he's at work. Matt Robb said he'd give him the day off when the baby's born."

"That's very thoughtful for someone to do for a new worker. Howie's only been at the construction company since graduation."

"I know. The whole Robb family has been so good to us. How's hunting?"

"Today was a blank. But it will get better. The first day of cubbing was pretty good."

"That's what Tootie and Val said." Her voice rose up. "And the skull."

"No one will forget that." She changed the subject. "Do you need anything?"

"No."

"I'm closer than Howie. Aren't they working up in Orange County on a house?"

"A two-million-dollar house! I can't imagine that." Felicity, watchful of money, thought unnecessary expenditure ghoulish. "How much do people need?"

"Quite a lot—some, anyway. Before you rush to judgment on whoever is paying for this house, remember inflation. These days I couldn't afford to buy the house where I live. Impossible."

"You're right. I hadn't thought about that."

"That's the interesting thing about age. The value of money is set when you're young. So I think a dollar should have the buying power it did in the fifties and sixties."

"It should." Felicity, despite her discomfort, enjoyed the conversation.

"Well, honey, what I was saying is that if your water breaks, call me. You have my cell. You have Shaker's cell. We can get to you in ten minutes if we break the speed limit. Don't worry."

"I won't."

They chatted a bit more, and then Sister hung up.

Shaker remarked, on hearing her end of the conversation, "We could deliver the baby. We've delivered enough puppies and foals."

Sister laughed. "I expect we could, and we'd be a hell of a lot cheaper." She grabbed an iced tea out of the small refrigerator, passed it to Shaker, and took one for herself.

"Tight with the buck, that kid." Shaker popped the top of the can.

"In the main, that's a good thing, but if you're too tight, you can miss some of life's pleasures." She sat on the edge of the desk. "It's all a balancing act, isn't it?" She took a long swig of the commercial sweet tea, which wasn't half bad.

"I keep trying to find the middle ground."

"Me, too. Sometimes I hold it for months, and then sooner or later I go a little too much one way or the other. Balance." She repeated her theme.

"Heard Athena last night. Haven't heard her much this summer." He referred to the great horned owl who lived on the farm.

Athena and Bitsy would get together for chats, and Bitsy's voice allowed Sister and Shaker to pinpoint the two owls, so very different in size, call, and temperament. Bitsy was always thrilled to gossip, whereas Athena preferred to observe.

"It's a beautiful song, the great horned. Liquid, low, and a touch of melancholy." She finished the can of tea. "I was thirsty. I keep meaning to ask you: Did you go into the caves at Skidby?"

"Not into them, but we made a trail around them and marked the entrances." He grimaced. "I don't like going underground. I could never live in New York City and ride the subway."

I'm not overfond of it either." She felt herself revive a bit; she'd been up since four in the morning, and it was now eleven. "Had a thought when I woke up this morning."

"Just one?"

"Yep, I'm slowing down." She laughed at herself. "But it's an interesting one. You remember when we cleared trails at Skidby that Barry received a call from Fonz?"

"Yeah, Grant Fuller was hanging on a meat hook in a slaughterhouse."

"That's just it, Shaker. It was a slaughterhouse Grant used to

own, and my thought was maybe he still owned it. Either he sold it to a shill or kept an interest."

"Possible."

"Of course, Tennessee is a long way from Virginia—well, it seems a long way—so this isn't Ben's case. Anyway, I called and left a message for him—no reason to wake him up—to see if he could find out if Grant still owned all or part of the packing company and the slaughterhouse."

"And if he did?"

"If he did it might mean nothing. Then again, it certainly would give him a conduit for fresh horse meat. I know it's illegal, but he was making dog food. If he paid off his employees, who would know? Right. Humans can't smell the difference between beef byproducts and equine."

Shaker thought a long time about this. "And Hope Rogers found out?"

"Could be. Her fury at Grant would have been boiling hot. You know, I'm so disappointed that she was running that bourbon scam." She stood up. "Disappointed—but I liked her. She loved animals and she was a good vet. I won't let it go."

"I know."

Once her chores had been knocked out, Sister, with Hope very much on her mind, drove over to Paradise.

Arthur DuCharme was in the big shed, working on a 1973 John Deere.

"Sister, what are you doing out here, feeding foxes?"

"Not today. What are you doing?"

"Cleaning the fuel line. I don't know how I did it but I

clogged it up. I've been running this tractor since the day I bought it in 1967, and this is the first time I've had a problem. Can't complain."

"Pretty much anyone who owns a John Deere can't complain. It's an expensive tractor, but you get what you pay for."

"Said a mouthful." He wiped his hands on an old red rag.

"I'm here, Arthur, hoping you will talk to me. I vow whatever you tell me stays with me."

"The still?" He'd known Sister all his life.

"Yes."

"I didn't set it up. Hope talked to me. I told her what I knew and, yes, I told her the water was some of the best I'd tasted, coming straight down the mountain. And I told her I thought the water on the east side of the Blue Ridge is better than the water coming down on the west side."

Being a geologist, Sister knew that the Blue Ridge, an ancient chain, did have variation on the different sides, different counties; it was part of what made this area and these mountains so fascinating.

"Did you show her your old site?"

"I did."

"Did she pay you?"

He wiped his hands again, carefully studied the red rag, and then draped it over his left shoulder. "Not in money. She sent me a new refrigerator and a big new water heater. She asked if I wanted a percent of her profits and I said I didn't because the still was on Foster land, not DuCharme." He stopped and folded his arms across his chest. "She was a good girl, Sister. She was carrying the Japanese a little fast but they deserve it. Make 'em pay

through the nose for the next two hundred years, I say. I'm not ever going to forget Pearl Harbor."

Sister didn't feel that way, but she did understand the animosity in others. "Funny, isn't it, how both Germany and Japan underestimated us. Thought we were soft. Dictatorships, whether by individuals or an elite, can't grasp democracy. That's what I figure. And you know, brilliant as the attack on Pearl Harbor was, they had a tiger by the tail. Should have left us alone."

"So what do we do?" His voice rose. "We rebuild them after the war, and then we make them rich by buying Toyotas. The money should stay here." He patted the John Deere as if it were a horse.

Of course, John Deere is manufactured in Illinois.

"War's over."

"People say that about the War Between the States."

Her eyes lit up. "That's different."

Then they both laughed.

"Like I said, Hope was a good girl. She helped a lot of people; she helped animals. So she was making a little potent drinking water. Washes your troubles away."

"Think she killed herself?"

"I don't like to think she would." He paused, pulling the rag on his left shoulder down with his right hand. "No. No, I don't. And Paul didn't kill her either, though some people want to think he did. He's the type to bring you down with words, you know? Not a killer."

"Was there anything you saw in that still that you didn't tell Ben?"

"Sure didn't give him the secret for making good stuff." He

laughed. "I was surprised when I saw the still. I knew it was there but I hadn't been back to see it. It's none of my business, plus whoever is running a still wouldn't want people back there. What surprised me wasn't the still but the size of the operation—and the equipment. Good stuff. Really good stuff."

"Think she was killed over it?"

He shook his head emphatically. "No. That would be really stupid. The woman was good. Now mind you, I was pretty shocked when she brought me a sample. Can't say as I ever knew any woman to run a still before, but that one sure knew what she was doing. Women are full of surprises." He winked.

"Think she could have been shot by a rival distiller?"

He moved a wad of chewing tobacco from one side of his mouth to the other. "No. I sit on the porch at sunset. Like to watch the sun go down. And I think, *Suicide. The sheriff says suicide.* Would someone in my old line of work know how to make a murder look like suicide? I don't think so. Hope's death had nothing to do with cheap bourbon."

"Any other thoughts?"

A long silence followed, "Maybe horses. She found something bad. Some of those people are so rich they could have hired a professional to take her out, know what I mean?"

"Yes. Arthur, thank you for this."

"Thank you for being a modifying influence on Ben Sidell. It's possible to interpret the law too harshly." He tipped back his head and roared.

She laughed with him. "Arthur, truer words were never spoken."

CHAPTER 25

All the mornings of the world seemed reflected in the morning of September 13. The sweet air carried a hint of coolness. The rim of the sun peeked over the horizon in the east. Night hunters returned to their lairs, nests, and dens. Day hunters awakened, along with every rooster in central Virginia.

Sister, walking along on Rickyroo, thought her heart would burst through her body. She never felt more alive than when fox-hunting. The cares of the man-made world vanished as once again she touched the fingertips of the gods.

Behind her rode sixty-seven people. They'd arisen at four or five in the morning, depending on how far they lived from Skidby. They'd fed, groomed horses, if lucky, perhaps grabbed something for themselves.

Jefferson Hunt members prided themselves on their turn-out. Cubbing allowed more individual expression. Kasmir wore a splendid bespoke tweed, a tan herringbone. A creamy silk stock tie with tiny dots of red was immaculately folded, and a red silk handkerchief peeked out from his breast pocket. But everyone had the wisdom to select colors that showed them to good advantage while staying within the bounds of hunting fashion.

Sister turned to look behind her as she trotted over a pasture shimmering with dew. Glints of silver and gold appeared as the light touched the grass. Perfect, she thought. This moving tableau had been enjoyed by countless Virginians over the last three centuries. When those departed souls rode out on mornings such as this, they surely felt that life was meant to be lived full gallop. Sister had the sense to be thankful.

Hounds, sterns up, fed off the emotions of their huntsman, but they, too, could sense the mounting anticipation from the field. A new fixture added to their high spirits.

As Shaker and Sister discussed, they'd brought experienced hounds, although Giorgio had slipped into the draw pen somehow, managing to get by the head count, too. Occasionally this happens. Shaker couldn't allow the youngster to sit in the trailer howling his head off. Giorgio packed in during morning walks and had shown promise at the fox pens, so he might as well hunt.

Rickyroo, opening his nostrils wide, called out, *"I can beat any horse out here today."*

Kilowatt, Shaker's mount, whinnied back, *"Dream on."*

Barry, riding next to Gray, commented, "Makes a man feel twenty again."

Kasmir, directly behind them, remarked, "I'll settle for thirty."

People usually didn't talk in the field, for Sister just wouldn't have it, but a bit of chat on the way to the first cast wasn't the greatest of sins.

Mitch Fisher rode behind Tedi and Edward Bancroft. They asked him if he wanted to move ahead of them but he declined. The Bancrofts most always were right behind Sister. Beautifully mounted, they had been riding together for over fifty years, and few people could ride harder or better. As this was the first time at Skidby, Mitch's desire to be in the forefront was understandable. He, too, had labored over his turnout, surprising everyone by wearing a bow tie with his tweed. Nothing against it, and the regimental colors looked good on him—which, of course, he knew.

A half mile from the house, away from the paddocks where Mitch and Lutrell's yearlings were frolicking, Shaker cast hounds into a light moist west wind.

Sister felt the slight change in the air. Clouds would be rolling in within the hour. Her bones proved far more reliable than the Weather Channel.

A crease in the land hid a small creek surrounded by dense brush with wild roses entwined throughout and a few large hickories and oaks on either side. Good covert to start.

"Lieu in there," Shaker called out, then blew the notes to reinforce the message.

In dashed the pack of twenty-four couple hounds, including Giorgio, who hopped up and down like a kangaroo.

"Will you keep your paws on the ground?" Trudy admonished the handsome young dog hound.

As Trudy was a third-year hound, Giorgio put his nose down, trying to do right.

Betty on the left and Sybil on the right noticed, along with Shaker, that sterns began to wave just a wee bit. Soon the sterns moved like a rudder in current.

"Red!" Dreamboat called out.

As this hound was only in his second year, Cora checked it.

Asa came over, put his nose down, then lifted his head along with Cora and the curtain was raised.

Rickyroo's ears swept forward, for he spied the healthy, glistening, red dog fox scoot out from the point of the covert.

Sister, knowing to trust a true hunting horse, followed Rickyroo's gaze and let out a deep "Tally ho!"

Shaker, down near the fold of the land, couldn't see the point, but if the master gave a holler, he knew it was good. On the other hand, field members in their excitement had been known to tally-ho cats, squirrels, and the occasional groundhog.

As hounds, at the moment of viewing, were not behind their fox, Sister was correct in calling out. If they'd had their noses down, on the line, she would have kept quiet. Never bring up a hound's head.

Diana, on hearing her master's voice, knew they'd burst their fox clean out of the covert. *"Come on. Step on it."*

The whole pack sang as one, the ancient sound bouncing back off the ridges toward the west.

In the field, shoulders snapped back, heels dropped down,

and reins were picked up a bit if slack. Chins up, eyes forward, and they were off.

The red, although not accustomed to being hunted by a pack, was mature. He'd eluded larger animals before. This time he had to outwit a number of them but, confident in his abilities, he scorched straight up from the point of the covert, across the pasture, and then turned eastward, winds blowing his scent away from hound noses.

This ruse bought him only a few seconds' time, for the dew held what scent there was on his pads. As the pack whirled five hundred yards behind him, catching his line again, he realized he'd better get out of the open, so he turned on the afterburners and, like a Formula One Ferrari, he zoomed for the woods.

A new zigzag jump in the wire tensile fence line was the only way into the woods. The gate was a half mile away, so Bobby Franklin and his posse of Hilltoppers burnt the wind getting there. There were times when Bobby and second flight ran harder and faster than first.

Betty had already cleared the zigzag as she pushed up to her ten-o'clock position. Sybil had negotiated a coop down in the corner of the fence, so she was also out front. Shaker cleared the fence next, and Sister was cleanly over one minute later.

The red ran a tight circle in a patch of running cedar. That fouled his scent briefly but the older hounds knew this trick, so they cast themselves on all sides of the large patch to find out where he'd come out.

"Here," Ardent called.

"Devil take them!" the fox said, as he ran straight for the

deeper creek, a thirty-foot expanse. He launched off a fifteen-foot bank, hit the water, and swam to the other side. Then he ran alongside the creek, turned, and swam back across, blowing through heavy covert thanks to the fact that he was smaller than the hounds. He was heading back to his den, and if they closed again he knew where he could drop them—or hoped so, anyway.

Hounds barreled to the spot where the fox jumped into the creek and everyone except Giorgio flew over that bank without a second's hesitation. They went under, came back up, and swam for the opposite bank.

"That's scary," the young entry wailed.

"Come on, you weenie. Either you're a foxhound or you're a cur!" taunted Pickens, second year and feeling full of himself.

Shaker came up to the spot first. He trotted along the bank to find a better place to jump in, dropping only six feet instead of fifteen. The water splashed up but his boots didn't fill. Kilowatt, water halfway up his legs, surged forward, and Shaker clambered out on the other side. That, too, was a bit steep but a huntsman always tries to stay with his forward hounds. Of course, in Jefferson Hunt territory, there were times when Jesus Christ himself couldn't have ridden with the forward hounds.

The pack picked up the red's line, right to where he'd jumped back into the creek. As hounds hit the water again, Sister came up to the creek.

She reined in Rickyroo, sat, and watched hounds swim back. Giorgio came up to her. *"I don't like the water."*

"Young'un, go to them." She spoke to him with warmth.

The sound of her voice instantly made him feel better, and

since the pack was now swimming back across he could meet them on this side. So he rushed down to the place where they'd emerge. The most tantalizing odor curled into his lovely black nose.

"He came out here!" Giorgio said and damned if he didn't run the line through the heavy underbrush, pushing forward, heedless of the thorns.

Diddy and Delight, right out of the water and immediately behind Diana, said to each other, *"Shit, there'll be no living with him now."*

The three girls hurried to the place where Giorgio opened. They opened too, and as hounds came out of the water, some not even bothering to shake, they ran up to Giorgio. Tillie, the slight yellow spotted hound Mo Schneider bred, was right in there doing yeoman's work.

Shaker, riding back out of the creek, figured out there was no way through the covert.

"Huntsmen!" he bellowed.

The riders on the trail backed into the woods, not easy in some places, so Shaker could pass through with their horses' heads facing him, not their hindquarters. One lash from those hind hooves could break a huntsman's leg if it found its target. It could also hurt the huntsman's horse, and good huntsmen's horses aren't easily found and made. It takes special boldness to negotiate all the obstacles first and to hear the horn blowing over those sensitive equine ears.

Shaker flew through and then Sister came behind. Each field member fell into line as the rider before came back out onto the trail. This maneuver, so important to foxhunting, is rarely well executed, today being no exception. A hapless rider, not able to hold his horse, shot out right in front of the master.

"Go forward," ordered Sister, having been in this situation before.

The person at least had the sense to obey and not try to wedge his horse back into the woods. So he galloped in front of the master until they came back to the zigzag jump. He turned to the side, Sister sailed over, and he waited until his turn into the line, thinking he'd done the right thing. Given the tight quarters, he should have taken the jump before the master and then gotten out of the way. As it was, some horses balked at seeing another horse standing there and then had to go to the end of the line. This rankled the rider. Finally Ronnie Haslip called up to the new member, "Come back with me. You're spooking horses." So both men slid along the line, with Ronnie trying in few words to explain what the fellow should have done.

It was already out of Sister's mind as she and Rickyroo charged over the pasture, affording them another view of their quarry with the pack closing and together.

"Come on, boy, get into the covert," Sister whispered to herself.

Rickyroo answered, *"He will."*

Sure enough, the red hit the covert and popped into his den, where he had to consider this new event. Over time he would give it a lot of thought.

All the hounds crowded the den. Shaker dismounted, threw Kilowatt's reins over his head, and fought his way into the covert. The sight of all the hounds surrounding an impressive piece of fox habitation, a big pile of bones and feathers off to the side of the entrance, was worth the scratches and thorns which always managed to embed themselves in his face.

He blew the wavy notes of Gone to Ground, patted each head, and walked out, again fighting what he hadn't pulled down on the way in.

Sister, next to Kilowatt, held the horse's reins.

Shaker looked up, took the reins, and said, "Not much of a housekeeper."

They laughed, then turned northwest as the cloud cover was coming down, a blanket of deep rich gray with streaks of cream.

They stayed out for another hour, picked up a gray fox, enjoyed another good run, a big figure-eight, then turned back to the house and the sumptuous breakfast awaiting them.

The only fly in this ointment was that Giorgio wouldn't give up a line he had found, and off he ran.

The breakfast, a triumph, capped a perfect morning. Sister, crowded with people, couldn't tell who was coming and who was going. After forty-five minutes she did see Barry come in for the breakfast, wearing another tweed. This, too, if one is being strict, is proper. You don't wear your hunting coat to the breakfast since it may be muddy and plastered with thorns, importing the smell of horse sweat as well as your own.

Sister wore a light green tweed, not the jacket she hunted in. She noticed that most people had changed.

"Good on them." She smiled inwardly.

"What a way to christen Skidby!" Barry came over just as Gray reached Sister and handed her a tonic water with lime.

Sister often never made it to the table. Occasionally she was so famished she had to ask people to give her a moment to eat. Then they could talk.

"What a morning!" Barry held up his drink.

All three clinked glasses.

A cheer went up when Shaker, Betty, and Sybil finally walked in, having gotten up all the hounds but Giorgio. In American hunts, servants eat with members. Very often in the British Isles, the distinction between servants and members keeps them apart socially. Shaker didn't care about all that. He usually missed breakfasts because he wanted to get the hounds back. Sister brought back the horses.

But today was special and he knew Sister would want him to say a few words to Mitch and Lutrell personally.

He found Lutrell and thanked her. He didn't see Mitch, so he grabbed a ham sandwich, a whole fat sandwich, not a ham biscuit, wrapped it in a napkin, and pushed his way through to Sister.

"Shaker, well done." Sister kissed him on the cheek.

Barry shook his hand. "Don't worry. I won't kiss you."

Shaker laughed and Gray clapped him on the back. "Me neither, but if I had to kiss a man, I'd kiss you. You did a great job today."

"Thank you." Shaker smiled, truly happy with the morning. "Boss, I can't find Mitch to make my manners. I need to take hounds home. I'll come back for Giorgio. But would you blow for him a few times before you leave?"

"I'll do better than that; I'll stay and hitch a ride home with someone. Betty can drive the rig back and Lorraine can help her in the barn; I don't think she'll mind."

The breakfast kept going, turning into a party. But an hour and a half later, no Mitch was in sight yet.

Lutrell began to worry; Sister reassured her.

"I'm going out to look for a hound. With all these people, he's probably been in and out of the house and we haven't noticed. But I'll look for him, too."

Sister walked outside, waving her goodbyes, and blew the horn. In the distance, northwest, she heard Giorgio. Light drizzle started.

Skidby had good farm roads. She went back in the house and asked Lutrell if she could borrow the farm jeep.

A minute later she cranked up the iconic vehicle, which had been giving service since World War II, and drove northwest. Weather often came in from that direction, and soon the drizzle had become a light rain.

She stopped, rolled down the window—no fancy buttons on this machine—and blew the horn. Giorgio answered, but he was young and confused. The answer carried worry.

She put the jeep in second and drove on. As the road smoothed out, she popped into third. As she gained attitude she downshifted again. Ahead of her, now visible through the silver veil of rain, were the Skidby caves.

She stopped and blew again. Giorgio was up somewhere behind the caves.

Putting the jeep in creep gear, she climbed higher, the road now rockier. She noticed Mitch's handsome stag-handled crop

on the front seat, so he must have been driving the jeep on coming in or at least tossed his crop inside.

At the foot of the caves, a small smooth place marked the
end of the road. She turned around, the jeep having a pretty
good turning radius, to park nose out. She got out, blew the
horn.

Giorgio was coming closer. She opened the door, yanked
out the huge nine-volt flashlight on the floor of the passenger
seat. Mitch, like most all country people, kept a flashlight in each
vehicle as well as a Red Cross kit.

As Giorgio was coming down toward her she kept calling him. He'd be a couple of minutes so she thought she'd stick her head into one of the caves. She'd never been in them before. The wind kicked up. She thought she heard a clanking sound but dismissed it.

Walking into the one closest to her, she flashed the light around. Old campfires, dug in the ground, remained. Initials, with names and occasional military ranks, had been carved on the walls. She walked out, calling again.

"Don't leave me. Don't leave me." Giorgio was coming closer.

She thought she heard a far-off motor as she walked into the second cave.

"Good God!" She came up behind Mitch Fisher, stripped naked, chained to a post by an iron band around his neck, a handkerchief stuffed into his mouth. His wrists were cuffed and chained by two feet of heavy links.

She yanked the handkerchief out. "Are you all right?"

He nodded. It was clammy in the cave, especially with the rain, so she took off her coat and threw it over Mitch's shoulders. She had no way to unlock the chain, but she thought she might be able to wriggle the stake free. She worked on it and he tried to help, having limited use of his hands. He pulled with her. Wouldn't budge. Also, the coat kept falling off.

"Who did this?"

Before he could answer a familiar voice replied, "I did."

She whirled. With their grunting and with the rain she hadn't heard Barry Baker come in. Dumbfounded, she could only stare at him.

"Unlock me. I swear I won't bring charges," Mitch pleaded.

Barry walked over and backhanded him so hard his head snapped back. "I'd rather see you starve, just like you starved hundreds of dogs in your research."

"Barry, please don't." Sister had no weapon but the nine-volt flashlight.

Giorgio called again. *"Where are you?"*

"Come to me," she called.

"That will be a good hound." Barry smiled.

"Please let Mitch go," she asked, unsure if he had a gun or a knife and not knowing what to do.

"No."

"Did you kill Mo and Grant?"

"I did. With help from Fonz."

"Hope?"

"No. I didn't kill Hope. She had uncovered the illegal use of Grant's slaughterhouses—horses still being slipped in—but I didn't kill her. Grant must have done it when their affair blew up. I can't prove it but I think under Grant's genial exterior there beat a selfish heart. He deserved just what he got."

"I think I know why you killed them." Sister, voice calm, noticed blood running from Mitch's mouth, a tooth on the floor.

"If anyone would understand, you would." Barry seemed relieved. "The brutality these people have shown toward animals offends me far worse than brutality to people. At least people know why they're hurt whether they deserve it or not. I'm not long for this life, Janie. I want to leave having performed some justice. God knows, I couldn't do that from the bench."

Mitch trembled but had the good sense to shut up.

Barry removed Sister's jacket from his shoulders.

"Let him have it."

"No. Let him suffer." Barry noticed Mitch's genitals. "No balls. People who hurt animals have no balls."

Sister, hoping to divert him, smiled. "Parts shrink in the cold. I'm curious. Why was Mo barefoot?"

"Made him run barefoot until he was near dead. It's what he did to horses and hounds." A triumphant note crept into Barry's voice.

Just then Giorgio burst into the cave. *"Mother!"*

She knelt down to hug the youngster. "Good boy."

Barry patted Giorgio's head. "How could anyone hurt a hound, a cat, a horse? They're more useful than most of the humans that muck up the earth."

"Barry," Sister said gently, "they ask that we love them, not kill for them."

He looked into her eyes. "Do you hate me?"

"No. But let him go."

"There's no way I can do that. He'll squeal to Ben Sidell the minute he pulls his pants on."

"How do you know I won't?"

"I don't think you will. You know Mo and Grant deserved to die. So does Mitch."

"What Mo and Grant did was wanton cruelty," said Sister. "Mitch's animal research eventually would have helped others. I don't like it. I think it was wrong—believe me, I do—but the circumstances were different."

"The results were the same for the dogs." Barry's jaw set hard, then loosened. "Here." He handed her the keys. "I want you to know that every minute I've spent with you has been a delight. You and Ray were old friends." He pulled out a .38 from the inside of his jacket. Sister froze. Was he going to shoot her? Shoot Mitch?

"Are you going to kill me?" Her voice was calm.

"I hope not." He grinned. "Would you shoot someone you'd slept with?"

Forcing herself to remain relaxed, she smiled. "Barry, that's the *only* man I'd shoot."

He laughed. "Janie, you're one of a kind."

A gust of wind sent rain into the cave. Giorgio jumped up, startled by the sound of the wind in the cave, and knocked Sister into Barry.

Barry kept his hand on the gun but stumbled backward, just far enough that Mitch could swing the chain between his hands over Barry's head.

"Mitch, no!" Sister yelled.

But Mitch, eyes glazed, his powers of reason having fled, gave one final terrible twist and Barry was dead.

Relaxing his grip, Mitch watched Barry's body slump. He started shaking again.

Strangely, Barry never dropped the gun. It seemed frozen in his right hand.

Giorgio, shocked, pressed his whole body next to Sister. The reverberations in the cave from the wind and the men's struggle made him tremble harder.

She placed her hand on the beautiful crown. "It's all right."

Mitch began to think again. He looked at the fresh corpse, looked at his hands, looked at Sister.

Sister took a deep shuddering breath.

Giorgio started for Barry.

"Leave him," Sister said quietly, and the youngster, terribly upset, did.

She unlocked Mitch and held him, for he shook violently. "You did what you had to do."

He could only mumble through his smashed mouth—it surely must have hurt when the air touched those broken teeth— "Thank you."

CHAPTER 26

Later that day, when Ben and his crew scoured the caves, they found a tiny little tombstone with painted letters, faded but protected from the elements so the words were legible:

MICHAEL ALDRIDGE
FEBRUARY 12, 1973

Last winter, two women had died at Wheeler's Mill, Cabel Harper and her fanatically dutiful friend, Ilona Merriman. Aldridge had been Ilona's maiden name. She would have been in college in 1973.

Funny how mysteries are finally solved but the profound emotions they generate have a way of living on for generations. The foxhunters at Wheeler's Mill would never forget the dramatic events that had transpired there, just as those who hunted Skidby would not forget what had happened today.

Ben added Jake Ingram to Barry's list of victims and put out a call for Fonz, back in Arkansas, to be brought in for questioning.

Sister, home with Gray, was deeply shaken by Barry's disintegration. Now that it was out in the open, it made sense. She knew the murders had had something to do with the abuse of animals, but she certainly didn't think her old friend capable of such violence. While he had considered an animal's life to be as valuable as that of a human—she believed it herself—she hadn't thought these feelings would lead him to murder.

Betty, on being called by Sister, turned around. She'd just finished the barn chores and was driving home in the Volvo. She walked into the kitchen to find Sister and Gray sitting at the table. Shaker came up, too.

No sooner had they begun talking than the phone rang.

Sister answered. "Hello?"

"Sister"—Felicity's voice was loud—"the baby's coming!"

The two women jumped into Sister's Forester, arriving at the old Demetrios place just as the ambulance came. Sister had had the presence of mind to call for it—and to call Howie. Then, at the hospital, with Sister and Betty by her side, Felicity delivered a healthy seven-pound-two-ounce baby boy in record time, as his daddy was driving as fast as he could from Orange County.

Betty, euphoric as many people are in these circumstances, laughed. "Felicity, you're fast. I was so long delivering my second child I thought I'd be the only woman to give birth and go into menopause at the same time!"

Holding her little guy in her arms, Felicity, plain worn out, couldn't stop smiling and crying.

Sister sat by the bed. "What a glorious day!"

"We'll stay until Howard gets here. Gives us more time to admire the best-looking little boy in the world." Betty loved babies. "What are you going to name him?"

Felicity reached for Sister's hand and put it under those tiny red fingers. "We're naming him Raymond, in honor of Sister."

It wasn't until she left the hospital with Betty that Sister let the tears roll. Betty held her.

"Looks like you're a grandmother." Betty held her tightly and patted her shoulder.

"What a miracle life is." Sister hugged Betty back.

Betty agreed, then added, "If the ambulance hadn't come in time, we'd have had to deliver that miracle."

"Piece of cake." Sister snapped her fingers. "Just a bigger puppy, that's all."

The two dear friends laughed.

Not only is life a miracle, it can be sweet.

RITA MAE BROWN is the bestselling author of
(among others) *Rubyfruit Jungle, Six of One, Southern
Discomfort, Outfoxed,* and a memoir, *Rita Will.* She also
collaborates with her tiger cat, Sneaky Pie, on the *New
York Times* bestselling Mrs. Murphy mystery series. An
Emmy-nominated screenwriter and poet, she lives in
Afton, Virginia. She is master and huntsman of the
Oak Ridge Foxhunt Club and is one of the directors
of Virginia Hunt Week. She founded the first all-
women's polo club, Blue Ridge Polo, in 1988. She was
also Visiting Faculty at the University of Nebraska in
Lincoln. Visit her website at www.ritamaebrown.com.

ABOUT THE TYPE

This book was set in New Baskerville, a typeface based
on the design by John Baskerville. The original was
cut by John Handy in 1750. Noted for its high con-
trast and sparkly look, it saw a renewed popularity
when the Lanston Monotype Corporation of London
revived the classic Roman face in 1923. The Mergen-
thaler Linotype Company in England and the United
States cut a version of Baskerville in 1931, making it
one of the most widely used typefaces today.